# Research Can Be Murder

by

Caryl Janis

The Wild Rose Press, Inc.
PO Box 708
Adams Basin, NY 14410-0708
Visit us at www.thewildrosepress.com

Publishing History
First Edition, 2024
Trade Paperback ISBN 978-1-5092-5447-7
Digital ISBN 978-1-5092-5448-4


Published in the United States of America

# Dedication

For everyone of any age who welcomes new
adventures.

## Acknowledgements

With sincere appreciation to Joanne Dobson for her valuable Page-Turning Fiction class at the Hudson Valley Writers Center where this book began. Heartfelt thanks to wonderful fellow writer Katie Ferriello for her insightful and encouraging comments and to my fabulous beta readers, Anne Petekiewicz and Ann Marie Frissell. Deepest gratitude to my superb editor, Dianne Rich and to everyone at The Wild Rose Press. And as always, a world of thanks to my husband Richard and daughter Daria for always cheering me on.

Prologue

*A Few Days Before Halloween*

*Boredom takes many forms, but standing in the archive's museum room and facing a loaded gun is not one of them.*

*This all began in an effort to combat boredom and when the boxes and trunk arrived, a new and exciting world opened up. Most of it was good, but I just couldn't let the other part go. Finally, I got in over my head.*

*Now—trapped between dusty display cases crammed with antique silver and decaying letters from bygone luminaries—a little boredom would be welcome.*

*This is no random threat. The owner of the gun is not a stranger.*

*You just never know with people.*

Chapter One

*Weeks Earlier*

"What *are* you going to do with those boxes, Emma? And why on earth did your brother dump them on you?"

I rolled my eyes. "He thinks I have nothing better to do, even if he didn't say it in so many words." I frowned at my reflection in the spotless windowpane, wisps of brown hair escaping from a hastily pinned-up twist. "Maybe I should be insulted."

But my brother Ralph came painfully close to the truth. Despite enrolling in weekly film appreciation classes, indulging in my beloved crossword puzzles, and walking two miles a day in my new orange running shoes, it wasn't enough. I was bored...until the boxes arrived.

The contents of those boxes now dominated the conversation as my best friend Della and I caught up over some ridiculously pricey caffeine at Reese's Café. I paused to sip my perfect marshmallow-crème latte. We've never regretted one penny spent at Reese's.

Pushing aside her green-streaked blonde bangs, Della looked up from my cell phone. She'd been scrolling through photos of my discoveries from box number one, and the last image was getting her particularly close attention—a pair of century-old women's button-up shoes.

"Any more funky shoes? I love these." Della's fashion was eclectic. With her hip clothes and multiple ear piercings, no one would guess she was a babysitting grandmother.

"Not yet. There's a lot of odd stuff in that first box. Like a dozen glittery stick masks, a weird looking cane, and a big hat with a ridiculously long hatpin."

Tackling the first of those three large, snugly taped boxes was an undeniable thrill. And my anticipation surged at the thought of plunging into the old-fashioned steamer trunk, its leather straps studded with spidery cracks. No one had probably so much as peeked an inch inside any of it since long before World War II.

Della paused for one last look. "Ralph doesn't know what he got rid of."

"And he doesn't care. He and Sheila have become—what do they call it—minimalists? They want to enjoy their new retirement condo free of *stuff*, as Ralph calls it."

"Em, you've got yourself a fascinating project. Who knows what you'll find? Later on, you could do a display of vintage collectibles for the women's club or sell them at auction or…"

I laughed so hard that two startled elderly ladies nearby looked up from their cappuccinos. "I doubt Sotheby's will be knocking at my door anytime soon. But it's fun and it came at the right time. Ralph said he felt bad about my being out of a job, just when the kids both moved away and Steve got swamped at work. He said I'll have more time to spend with the *stuff*." I grinned. "At least he didn't say I'm too old to look for a new job."

"Good old Ralph. Getting more sensitive in his mature years?" Della smiled.

"You never know."

The demise of JJM Consulting had been predictable. It was a pleasant job as part-time assistant to a project manager, but the steady drop in clients sounded a warning. Not much call anymore for commemorative local and corporate histories. Finally, the company closed its doors.

JJM left one of several holes in my life. Like Della, although minus the hipster look, I'm old enough to be babysitting grandchildren. But my two grown kids haven't settled down yet. They moved out around the time that JJM folded and my husband Steve and his business partner were suddenly crushed with more projects at their architectural firm.

Ralph and his wife moved to their new condo and unloaded their attic's stash as if on cue at just this particularly appropriate moment. Serendipity? I felt far less aggravated with my brother than I might usually have been. The boxes and trunk gave me a purpose. Tossing the contents would have been easy but, truthfully, I welcomed a chance to check out these items and their history.

Della leaned forward now, her long feathery earrings almost dipping into her latte. "I haven't seen you this excited in a long time."

"Shows, huh? You'll have to come and take a look."

Della's face lit up. "Tomorrow afternoon? I'm not babysitting the Butterflies then."

The Butterflies, her twin granddaughters, were so named because they seemed to fly instead of walk.

Della helped her daughter with them while they were still in this pre-school age.

"Perfect! And I really want your opinion on whether it's worth doing some real research into what I've found."

Now, I moved my orange shoes into full view—one of my few concessions to flashy attire. My gray sweatshirt emblazoned with a crossword puzzle didn't count. "I guess it's time to rack up a few more miles on these things before I go home."

"Are you actually running in those?" asked Della.

"I'm working my way up to a fast walk," I said with a grin.

"Well, happy trails."

****

I sprawled face down on the plush carpet, my nose grazing its geometric design. *Clumsy*! Despite my morning treat at Reese's, I'd still grabbed a chocolate marshmallow square from the kitchen, gobbling it hastily while rushing back to the box-and-trunk collection. Box number two capsized when I tripped and a variety of items flew out at random—a framed embroidery, some loose papers, and a cowbell that clanged as it rolled into a corner. Nothing was broken, but plenty of chocolate marshmallow was smashed into the carpet.

I sat up. The place was a mess. Somehow, though, the chaos gave me comfort. These objects had once belonged to real people, my ancestors mostly, I guessed. They might have been proud to know they weren't totally forgotten. Perhaps they needed me in some universal way. And people who needed me seemed few and far between these days.

Our family room was always a favorite place with its view of our little stone patio and green, inviting backyard. When our kids were little, we played board games here and munched on pretzels, pizza, and other treats. Our little terrier Scruffy would receive his share with all the dignity of his royal status in our household. And Steve made sure we had fun movies to watch, everything from animated classics to comedies. Our family nights were a big deal. Everyone looked forward to them, Scruffy included.

Now, Scruffy was gone. Josh was off leading adventure tours. Leeann was in graduate school in Montreal. And Steve worked ridiculous hours. The room was empty and silent. But as soon as I started delving into the boxes, it began to feel alive once again.

*Quack-quack.* My reverie was interrupted by my cell phone's startling ringtone. I chose this particular sound at super high volume to be doubly aware of incoming calls from our kids. But they preferred email and Della liked texts, so my brother Ralph was my most frequent caller.

As usual, he skipped the social niceties and plunged right in.

"So, what was it you wanted?" he began. "Couldn't get back to you yesterday because we went over to our new next-door neighbor's house for a drink and…" Ah, same old Ralph.

"Already in the social circle, are you?" I broke in. "And after only a few weeks, too."

"Good idea to keep in tune with the neighbors."

Ralph always thought ahead to the possibility of borrowing a hammer or hitching a ride somewhere. Being on friendly terms with the guy next door was a big part of his playbook.

"So, the boxes. Any idea who owned some of this stuff? There aren't many clues."

"You know I'm not into that whole genealogy thing, Em. It's mostly from Mom's side of the family. Otherwise, I have no idea. Why don't you call Mom's cousin Louise and ask her?"

I was taken aback. "Louise? We haven't seen her in ages. No more Christmas cards even."

"She's the only person left from that generation who might remember something… Oops! Sorry, gotta run. Good luck with Louise." A click signaled the end of our conversation.

I picked my way through the cluttered room, processing Ralph's suggestion and feeling bad we'd lost touch with Louise. A lot had changed, but maybe a phone call might be nice.

Now I gathered the papers that scattered when I fell. They appeared to have been ripped out of some sort of book and were filled with the elaborate penmanship of a bygone time.

Curiosity got the better of me. I grabbed a couple of the frayed pages and moved to the bright light by the windows to read the faded handwriting. Although difficult to decipher at first, I soon became absorbed. But the details on one page weren't related to those on the next.

*Mrs. Mallory kept a neat and respectable boarding house next door. My mother said it was a blessing that such law-abiding and polite people lived there. It was not like other places. These were honest and hard-working types with nice manners. They always said hello to us on their way to church on Sunday morning. I wanted to know more about them but my mother said I should mind my business and be grateful to have such God-fearing people as neighbors.*

Who was Mrs. Mallory? Her boarders? But, even more important, who had written this?

*The well-dressed man lingered under the streetlight. His coat was made of fine wool. It was obvious he was a gentleman. He appeared to be waiting for someone but then thought better of it. When he turned to walk away, and for just a brief moment, a shiny object glistened in his cravat under the flickering light.*

These pages must have come from some sort of diary. Clearly the diarist was quite observant. Did the man live in the boarding house? If so, did church-going gentlemen wear sparkly objects, maybe some sort of jewel, in their cravats? I thought they were supposed to be serious, plain people back in the old days. But what did I know?

But the next page really grabbed my attention.

*Abigail came to me that night. She was crying very hard and said she had done a terrible thing. "I'm so sorry. Please, you've got to help me. It was wrong. It was all wrong. I needed to do it for my sister. I did not want to steal this...not if I had to do something so bad to get it..."*

Who was Abigail? What had she done that was so wretched? And how did she fit in with Mrs. Mallory and her church-going boarders? And the gentleman with the shiny object in his cravat? Or did she?

Who was the diarist? An ancestor of mine? The handwriting, ornate and elegant, appeared consistent. But the information was random and a lot of it obviously missing. I needed to find other pages and put them in order. Make sense of it. But did any more pages exist or had the rest been lost to time?

Chapter Two

"This looks like a rummage sale." Della stepped through the chaotic piles in the family room, trying not to puncture anything with the heels of her fashionable mocha suede boots. She picked up several large, colorfully illustrated pieces of sheet music and began reading titles.

"Here's a good one—'Everybody Works But Father'... Wait, listen to this." She opened the oversized sheet and sang off-key:

*Everybody works at my house*
*But my old man.*

"They don't write 'em like this anymore," she concluded.

"Too bad. We could use some funny songs these days." I smiled at Della's enthusiasm for those old tunes. "There's more over there," I added. "They go back to 1904 and 1905."

"Hey, look at this one, Em." Della held up another sheet music cover. "It's called 'Under Southern Skies.' Check the hat on that lady in the cameo photo—Lottie Blair Parker. It says something about her making 'millions laugh and weep.' "

"Maybe she was an actress or a singer," I suggested.

Della moved on, squatting down to get a closer look at the items on the floor by the wall. "What a gorgeous bowl." She ran a finger along its scalloped golden edges.

"So, what's the big mysterious find?" she asked with an impish grin, grabbing a glittery stick mask from the nearby pile and holding it up to her face.

"That's *so* you!" I laughed.

I pointed to the pile of papers on the table. "C'mon over here. Have a look."

We slid into chairs at the table, and I handed her a page from another new pile I discovered last night. Their musty aroma was distinctive. "See what you think of this."

Della gingerly held the old paper. She squinted and started reading out loud, hesitating every few words. The antiquated handwriting wasn't easy for her either.

*Word spread quickly. There were stories of people screaming for help. Of the hideous fire that destroyed everything in minutes. Of little children being thrown overboard to safety. Of people drowning, being lost forever. Hundreds of them. My mother was shaking badly when she walked in the door. She barely made it to the chair when she collapsed. She began sobbing uncontrollably. "Greta was on that boat. Greta and her two babies."*

Della gasped. "Em, this sounds terrible! Who wrote this?"

"I wish I knew. I'm trying to gather all the pages together, but everything's unrelated." I handed her another new one I found during last night's foraging. "Read this."

*It was the most thrilling event that had ever happened. I purchased my ticket, clutching it close to me. I would be one of the first to go for a ride. It was hard to contain my excitement, to act like the lady I had been taught to be.*

"It doesn't make sense." Della looked up quizzically. "What does this have to do with Greta and her babies?"

"Nothing that I can figure. Here, check these out." I handed her the original pages about the boarding house, the man with the cravat, and Abigail. Della read carefully.

"They must be from an old diary, right?" I asked. "But it doesn't exactly read like the one I kept as a kid."

"You mean those little books with the tiny lock and key? I had one, and I kept crossing out things and changing whole pages." Della rolled her eyes as she spoke. "It was sort of a tirade about school and cliques and fantasies. And sometimes I didn't write in it for weeks."

"Yeah, me too," I agreed. "But maybe diaries were different back then. This one probably came apart from age. And whoever packed these boxes just threw in the loose pages with everything else, whether they thought they were worth saving or not. Maybe when I go through everything, there'll be more. Then I can put them in order and make more sense of it."

"So, what else is next?" asked Della.

"Ralph suggested calling Mom's cousin Louise to see if she knows something about it." I swept my hand across the room at the random piles of objects.

"Jeez! How old is she?"

"She was younger than a lot of the others. That would put her somewhere maybe in her late eighties. She might have plenty of stories to tell...or not... I guess it's worth a try, but I feel weird picking up the phone and calling her out of nowhere about this."

"Why don't you just do it, Emma? Even if she doesn't remember anything about family history, she'd probably be really happy to hear from you."

"Yeah, I guess you're right."

"So, what about Ralph? Doesn't he know anything? Or maybe I shouldn't bother to ask."

Della knew how Ralph operated.

"Ha! Aside from dumping the boxes on my doorstep, his only contribution has been telling me to call Louise. Otherwise, he's busy enjoying the retired life and chatting up his new neighbors, probably hoping to borrow their lawn chairs or beach umbrellas next summer."

"Some things never change."

We paused for a moment to contemplate Ralph.

Della broke the silence first. "It *is* intriguing. I could help you draft out some sort of summary that we could link to the diary pages. It might give you a talking point with Louise."

I couldn't help smiling. "*We* sure could. So, you're in on this adventure with me?"

She didn't even pause. "Yup. I'm way curious already."

I stopped. "Thanks, Dell. I really appreciate this."

"Not a problem," she replied in her usual breezy fashion, adding a dazzling smile. "You've helped me out with a lot of stuff, too. Besides, I love those funky boots. That high-buttoned look could become a new craze. Maybe I can borrow them once in a while."

"Of course, you can."

We brainstormed for a bit, agreeing that the few dates on the pages matched the copyright years on the sheet music. "And probably the hats and boots and china were from around then from the looks of things," added Della. "And we should look up when cravats were worn. Do people still say 'cravat?' "

After Della left, the family room was quiet. I sat there for a while, gazing at my newly discovered items. I felt compelled to learn their stories. But the diary pages were what really grabbed my attention.

The last box and the trunk remained untouched. Dinner would have to come first.

I spent a few minutes neatening up before heading to the kitchen. As I walked past the hat pile, I couldn't resist picking up the feathery blue one. Tentatively, I put it on, feeling foolish as I adjusted it at several different angles while checking myself in the mirror. It did emphasize my blue eyes and, yes, tilted to the right worked best. The hat seemed to erase some of the fatigue on my face, and my light brown hair— carelessly swept up to keep it out of the way—took on a softer look, even a bit old-fashioned like the hat itself. I smiled as I studied my reflection. *Silly*, I told myself seconds before the front door opened.

Steve. Maybe there was some chance of dinner together. My casserole just needed reheating, and a bottle of wine was in the refrigerator, the perfect companion to my garlicky chicken and rice. I carefully replaced the hat on the pile with just a fleeting backward glance.

"Steve?" I ran to the foyer in time to see my exhausted husband hanging his jacket on the coat rack. At first, he didn't seem to register my presence. Finally, he spoke.

"Hi, Emma," he said, a forlorn look etched on his

face. "Long day."

"You look tired. I'll put the casserole in to heat, and we can have a nice glass of that lovely wine Leeann sent...You won't believe what's in those boxes. I can't wait to tell you."

"I'm so sorry, Emma. I should've called you. Hank and I grabbed a sandwich." He tentatively reached for my hand. "Could we save the wine for a more relaxed night? I'm so tired. Maybe you can tell me about the boxes in the next couple of days. I just need some sleep now."

"Get some rest. You look like you need it. Is everything okay?"

"It's just busy." He paused. "I really need to fill you in...soon."

For a second, I thought he would begin now, but he pointed toward the stairs. "I just need to sack out for an 8:00 a.m. meeting tomorrow with a client. No rest for the weary," he joked.

I headed for the kitchen to reheat the casserole for myself. When I sat down to eat, though, it seemed tasteless, despite its pungent garlic. I was sad that Steve was so wrung out. Were this many new clients worth it? And was Hank working just as hard? Was he all right? The last I heard, Hank's wife was away helping her mother. We weren't close, although we did see each other on rare occasion. But it had been a long time now, so it wouldn't have been appropriate to get in touch.

After eating, I thought about doing a few crossword puzzles, but they were no match compared to the lure of that last box. So, I tackled it with a vengeance, scattering the jumbled contents. There was a strange mandolin-shaped instrument with no strings and several ornate hand mirrors. Old theater programs sent dust flying into the air. I picked up my pace.

Then my heart started to pound. Two familiar looking sheets of paper were lodged in a remote corner. The handwriting, with its elegant loops and neat script, was the same. I picked up the slightly crumpling pages and, trembling ever so slightly, began to read.

*"I need you to keep this for me, just for a while." Abigail pressed something hard into the palm of my hand. "And if anything happens to me," she continued, "you must find its rightful owner and return it." Something gleamed ever so slightly from under the edge of the cloth that covered it.*

Again, Abigail. Who was she?

I turned to the next page. Same paper. Same handwriting.

*Almost midnight.*

*These were the most brilliant lights I had ever seen. We were entering a new era. I could feel it, and I was a part of it. The excitement of the crowd was exhilarating. So many faces turned upward, almost as one. All of us part of such a historic moment.*

Midnight when? Where?

I eyed the trunk. It was all that was left. I was eager to open it, too, but a deep weariness was now beginning to set in. I sat down and leaned over, putting my head down on a dusty bundle of fancy pillows…just for a moment…

When I woke up, it was long after 1:00 a.m. The trunk needed to wait until tomorrow. I trudged upstairs, climbing into bed next to a snoring Steve.

Chapter Three

The next morning, I was vaguely aware of Steve heading for the shower. He was long gone by the time I dragged myself into the kitchen to make coffee. I sadly contemplated our missed dinner together. Maybe Steve and Hank needed to take on a junior partner.

After coffee, a blueberry muffin, and a long, hot shower, I felt better. I pulled on jeans, my old floppy sweatshirt, and my orange running shoes and headed to the family room, another mug of coffee in hand. There I faced my number one priority: the trunk.

Coffee was not enough to meet the challenge. The clasps were stuck, and I tried forcing them open with a pair of salad tongs and a metal bottle opener from the kitchen. The tongs broke in half and the bottle opener bent, but the clasps remained intact. I tried kicking in a side panel. It looked flimsy. Looks are deceiving. I turned back to the clasps. Better than breaking a foot.

Off to the basement for an assortment of hammers and wrenches. Twenty minutes later, after considerable pounding and twisting, one of the clasps, then another, broke free. Next was the lid. Steadying myself with one foot against the wall, I lunged with all my strength. Gradually, it moved and, with one squealing creak, it loosened, hitting the floor with a resounding thud.

Dust scattered in a million directions, floating lazily in the rays of sun that shimmered through the windowpanes and blended with the unmistakable stench of mold. But it had been worth it. The trunk was open, and its generous interior was crammed full.

Staring in awe at my newly opened treasure chest, I dove into some of the items near the top. First, theater programs, exuding their nostalgic charm. Some titles were familiar, Victor Herbert's *The Red Mill* among them. Others, like *A Woman's Struggle*, had been lost to time. Next came the old magazines—*Argosy, Munsey's, Ladies' Home Journal.* Random items filled another layer with decorative fans and a lovely doll with a glittery jewel in her soft cloth hat.

But then I stroked the outside of a dusty velvet sack, its pliable black surface soft in my fingers. I held my breath as I opened it. A striking bracelet, a gem-studded U-shaped pin, a fine cameo brooch, and a jewel-encrusted creature of some sort spilled out. Then, wrapped in soft cloths, was a large pocket watch, forever stopped at four minutes past nine.

I carefully replaced the jewelry and set it aside, as much afraid of breaking the spell of discovery as I was of damaging any of these items.

Suddenly, the loud *quack-quack* of my cell phone made me jump. It was my brother.

"What's up, Ralph?"

"Have you called Louise yet?"

"Actually, no. I was waiting until I opened everything so we'd have more to talk about. You wouldn't believe the stuff that's in here. Especially the trunk. I'm just clearing it out."

"Great, great. Glad you're having fun." As always, Ralph was eager to get to the point. "So, listen, we were just unpacking more things, and I found a large catalog envelope with a bunch of papers and scraps with notes on them. Remind me to give it to you when we see each other. We sure don't need more clutter. When I saw this stuff, I thought of you immediately."

"Thanks, Ralph." *I think.* "How's the new place shaping up?"

"We love it!" Ralph took a deep breath. "Downsizing is the way to go. And speaking of going, I have to run. Sheila and I are picking up some things for an Autumn Leaves potluck at our community's social center. It's a pre-Halloween thing. Getting to be that season, you know."

"I guess. Well, enjoy. And don't eat too many treats, if that's what they're feeding you."

He signed off with a wicked cackle.

Ralph's call was a good reminder to get in touch with Louise. At the moment, though, I needed to finish picking my way through to the bottom of the trunk.

I grasped at some red ribbon neatly tied around a pile of yellowed, fragile newspapers. My eye caught a headline circled in faded ink, "The Successful Thief Asked to Please Call."

Carefully untying the ribbon, I lifted the newspaper onto my lap and read the story of a man offering a reward to the thief who'd stolen his lion-head scarf pin. No questions asked. A treasured gift from his uncle, he just wanted it back. *Interesting twist to this tale.*

No harm in taking a look at one more newspaper before going back to the trunk. The next circled headline was tragic, "1,000 Lives May be Lost in Burning of the Excursion Boat *Gen. Slocum*." A boat, hired to take a large group of women and children to a special church picnic event, caught fire in New York's

East River and sank. It was a heart-wrenching scenario.

My gaze wandered to the diary pages piled neatly on the table across the room. I thought of the entry about the woman sobbing over Greta and her two babies. They'd been on a boat. Although painful to contemplate, could they have been on this awful excursion? Surely this was just a coincidence of some sort. *But then why had this headline been circled?*

I picked up the next newspapers, some folded to inside pages. A variety of circled headlines ranged from "Held as River Pirates" to "Attend This Grand Opening Sale." Issues from 1903 were interspersed with 1904 and 1906. I'd need to set aside some time to read through them. They were fascinating, and the circled articles made me even more curious—theft, social announcements, fires, elections…murder. It might be time to start some outside research to see what made those articles special.

Right now, though, I returned to the trunk's large interior to pull out the final items before getting further sidetracked. There, I discovered a misshapen shawl, a book of poems dripping brittle pressed flowers, and more newspapers bundled in beautiful ribbons.

But what was next made my heart give one wild pound. More of the diary.

I held my breath and carefully leaned back onto a sofa pillow, gingerly holding the pages in my fingers. Afraid. Afraid of tearing them. Afraid of what I might discover. Some pages only showed smudged dates and random words. But then there was a page with an entry. I began reading slowly.

*Abigail held out a lustrous black velvet bag. She grasped my hand and curled my fingers around the bag.*

*Once again, she pleaded with me, just as before. "Please keep this safe. I need to sell them but...not yet... For my sister." Without another word, she ran out the door.*

*The velvet pouch contained jewelry, as had the little piece of cloth she had already given me. First, a large gold pocket watch with initials engraved on its exterior. At the bottom was a pin in the shape of an animal's head. It was studded with diamonds, as the large horseshoe-shaped stick pin had been, the piece I had already hidden for her.*

*I felt faint. Abigail was a thief. Or worse? Why was I helping her by hiding these pieces? The police would surely come for me now.*

This time, the diarist was truly frightened for Abigail and, certainly, for herself.

I held my breath and re-read the page. When I finished, I stared at the table where I left the jewelry from the trunk. *Could these pieces be the ones from Abigail?*

Chapter Four

"This one's for Pink Butterfly…and this one's for Purple Butterfly."

I held out two sparkly tee shirts with Joy's and Julie's names spelled out in their favorite color glitter. Della's granddaughters squealed with delight and gave me big hugs. They put on their new shirts and danced around, twirling and jumping over some colorful toy blocks.

"You're spoiling them," Della said with an amused grin.

"Thank you, thank you, Aunt Emma," they sang in chorus, continuing their dance.

"Okay, ladies," Della called out. "It's time for *Animal Circus*."

"Yay!" The Butterflies jumped into their soft bean bag chairs near the television, ready for their favorite show. Then they grabbed the snacks Della set out for them. This would give us a half hour to sit nearby, sip our tea, and mull over new developments. It wasn't a lot of time.

I took a deep breath. "I think the jewelry I found in the trunk was stolen."

"What?"

I launched into a brief rundown of the jewelry and new diary pages I just discovered. Then I described the old newspapers with their circled headlines and articles.

"I'm worried that I'm holding onto stolen property. And that maybe something bad happened when it was stolen."

Della looked at me thoughtfully. "What would it matter now? I doubt the cops will come after you," she joked. "Those pieces must be more than a century old."

I took a gulp of my tea and continued with conviction. "I know, but I want to return it…the jewelry…to them. I mean to the descendants of the real owners. You know, it looks like that's what Abigail wanted. Well, at least that's what she said with the first piece of jewelry. And then some poor ancestor of mine got involved unwittingly." I was taking off like a runaway train now. "But I guess the problem is to figure out who Abigail was and exactly who each piece of jewelry belonged to. And what happened when it was stolen."

"*And if* it was stolen," Della added softly. "Em, the jewelry could have belonged to your family, fair and square. There might be more to the story. I mean it's an understandable thought with the diary, the jewelry, and the newspapers. But you really don't know anything for sure."

I contemplated my orange sneakers for a minute, unwilling to admit that my theory might have a few holes. "I know, but it's still pretty coincidental."

"Right. But don't you need something more to link it all together?" Della quickly glanced over at the girls. They clapped in time to a song about imaginary tigers. Joy was already out of her bean bag chair and dancing in a circle.

"Look." I pulled out my list of newspaper headlines with an opposite column of topics from the diary. I pointed to the newspaper side. "Here's one about ten burglaries in millionaires' homes. There's a lot about jewelry in that one."

"But what does that prove?" asked Della over her shoulder, already taking Joy's hand and bringing her back to the bean bag chair.

"I'm not sure," I answered as Della quickly returned to the table. "But someone circled that headline. And the article mentions a pocket watch that was taken."

She listened carefully. "Em, tons of men owned pocket watches back in those days." We both glanced at the twins who clapped even louder. "And there've always been thieves."

"Forget about thefts for a minute. What about the *General Slocum* disaster headline?"

"All right, please run that one by me again," said Della.

"Back in 1904, an excursion boat left Manhattan on a large church outing. It caught fire and sank in the East River. More than a thousand people died, mostly women and children." I paused. "So, remember the diary entry about Greta and her two children who were on a boat?"

"Sure," Della answered as she shook her head at Julie who pointed to her empty snack wrapper. "The person who wrote the diary said her mother was sobbing over them."

"I'm thinking this could be tied to the news article. Maybe Greta was on that boat."

Della frowned, no doubt remembering her startled reaction when she'd first read that diary page. "Yeah. Except for one thing. How do you know for sure that

Greta and her children were on that *particular* boat in 1904? Maybe they were on some other boat that sank the same year or even in 1900 or 1910 or something. Or maybe it could have been in another city."

"Maybe, but the headline was circled and then when I took a quick look at some of the other newspapers from 1904, more stories about the *Slocum* were circled. No names matched, but someone was sure interested in that disaster."

Della whistled. "Makes you wonder. But what does that have to do with the jewelry?"

"I don't know. But it's all got to be connected, right?"

"Maybe," said Della. "How? And," she added softly, "maybe it wasn't connected at all."

I paused for a moment. "I don't know," I admitted, unwilling to let go of my theory.

A cheer erupted from the twins as a giraffe tap danced across the screen.

"All right, but back to the jewelry." I couldn't stop now. "In the first Abigail entry, she gave something to the diarist to keep and return to the owner if need be. Something that gleamed under the piece of cloth. Remember the guy with the sparkling thing in his cravat? Could he have been followed? Maybe he was one of the millionaires who was robbed when he got home...and maybe hurt? Or maybe he was the guy whose diamond pin was stolen the day the New York subway opened."

"Theft was pretty common in those days, just like now," began Della. "And the cravat guy might have been a thief who was wearing stolen goods." She sighed. "Do you really think Abigail stole all the pieces

25

in your jewelry pouch? And they're connected to those headlines?"

"It's something to think about. Della, I have to start researching some of this at the library. There's more than just a coincidence here. I can feel it." *Or was I just getting carried away by a wild fantasy growing from too much extra time on my hands?*

The twins were laughing and clapping. We didn't have much more time before *Animal Circus* ended and the Butterflies would want to play games.

"Okay," said Della. "Let's just say there is a connection and maybe the jewelry was stolen. Finding the descendants of a robbery victim could be next to impossible."

"I know. It was a long time ago. But I have to try. I'm making a complete inventory list and taking cell phone photos of the diary pages, the jewelry, and some of the important articles. Then I'm putting the real things in a safe place. It's a start."

"Okay. I'll check online about some of those jewelry and clothes styles, too," offered Della. "At least I can help you get an idea of when they were popular and where. Couldn't hurt."

I smiled. "Thanks! Every detail will help. And I'm going to look for connections between the newspapers and the diary at the library."

A rousing theme song signaled the end of *Animal Circus* and interrupted our conversation. The girls cheered as the cartoon animals paraded across the screen and sang.

Della turned off the TV, just as a commercial for Halloween costumes launched into its catchy advertising jingle. The eager twins took special note.

"I want to be a lion for Halloween." Joy jumped up, with Julie right behind her.

"Tiger," shouted Julie.

I remembered when Josh and Leeann were little, and Steve and I had so much fun getting them ready for Halloween. But the twins' exuberant shouts brought me back to the present.

"Tiger!!!"

"Lion!!!"

I gasped.

"Wait!" My shout rang louder than the twins combined. "Lion! That's right! It's a lion!"

Della gazed up in surprise. Even the twins stopped to look at me, puzzled.

"There's a lion in my jewelry box. It's a pin. The diary said something about an animal head pin. That's what that creature looks like. A lion!"

My excitement spilled into the air. "One of the circled articles. It offered a reward to the thief. To return a lion-head scarf pin!"

Chapter Five

"Frankly, there hasn't been any interest in those books for at least ten years." The reference librarian looked up from her computer, a thin line of annoyance etched on her face.

I tore my eyes from the oversized brooch that commanded the lapel of her plain brown jacket—a metallic replica of a United States map. It reflected harsh rays from the light of her desk lamp with sufficient intensity to reach Mars.

"The books are no longer available onsite."

"What?" I responded, dumbfounded by this news. "But where are they?"

"Our space at the library is limited," she continued, returning her pen to the desktop with frosty emphasis. "Many of our reference books are no longer here. They are available online."

"But where did the books go?" It was difficult to comprehend that what had once been a generously stocked reference section seemed to have partially vanished.

"They were either given away or disposed of. We needed the space." She waved her hand in the direction of the missing bookshelves. As she moved, her brooch reflected additional beams from the desk lamp. Maybe it had vaporized the books. "It was necessary to make room for extra tables and chairs and to provide a café area for beverages and snacks during our prime hours. The library is a community-friendly place."

*Beverages? Snacks? When had the library started doubling as a catering service?*

With crisp authority, she handed me a piece of paper. "Here, Mrs. Streyt. You may use Computer #5 to access our online reference site and find books that will be helpful. Some are only available through our system. You may come back to the desk if you have questions."

Still in shock, I retreated to Computer #5. I had done some online research at home, but I was looking forward to holding one of those old reference books in my hands, leisurely paging through the history of turn-of-the-century New York City. Instead, my fingers rested on slightly greasy computer keys. Perhaps someone sampled the café snacks before tackling their research. Several prominent fingerprints also smudged the screen, fueling my growing annoyance as I pulled up each new search item. History had never seemed so remote and lifeless.

I was painfully aware of the conversations from the café nearby. Words and phrases wafted in my direction, ripping my attention from the search screen.

"You look great," gushed a middle-aged woman in worn gray jogging pants as she greeted an acquaintance.

"Did you hear the lady in that corner house passed away?" asked a voice at another table.

Comments from various tables now mingled together in a hushed, yet audible cacophony.

"That new sandwich shop is disgusting! Don't say anything, but I heard they have rodents in their parking lot."

"Not so loud. We don't want to bother the librarian."

"Sorry, sorry. But is it true that Budget Busters is closing?"

I finally abandoned Computer #5 in defeat.

It had been a while since I'd been to the library. I fondly remembered how we brought Josh and Leeann there when they were young. They loved the children's area, often telling stories to the stuffed animals kept there. Now, I was afraid to peek into the children's room. What if kids were telling stories to computers instead of the giant stuffed teddy bear who used to nap in his treasured corner? What if the place had been transformed into a food court?

When I worked at JJM, there hadn't been a lot of time to visit the local library. Instead, I enjoyed reading books I bought or borrowed from friends and co-workers. However, my company had a lovely library that I used for the research component of my job. It was one of the things I missed most about the place. Of course, the company had computers that we used for research, too, but the library was left intact—a nice balance of the old and the new.

"It's modern times, Em," counseled Della when I called her later. "I didn't even leave the house and I found some really great stuff about those hats. I showed the Butterflies the online photos. They sat still for five minutes and begged for hats like that on their next birthdays."

"I'd say you had a very productive research session."

"You bet. But first, what did you find out?"

"I have a batch of facts about events from 1904 and

1905, but I already knew a lot of this from my online surfing at home." I coughed uncomfortably before my next admission. "Okay, I did find some extra details at the library, but I just hate to admit they came from that greasy, smudgy computer. I guess I'm still feeling really bad about the books that are gone."

"Rebelling against technology, are we?"

"How could you guess? But what I really need now are more specifics. The things you can find, or maybe find, in really rare books or directories or other diaries. Like names, everyday events and places, and personal recollections." I sighed. "I'm going to go to the city to do some digging at New York Public Library in their local history collection."

"Hey, who knows?" joked Della. "They might even have real books there."

"Very funny."

****

After getting off the phone with Della, I took out the little pink, blue, and green index cards I was using to organize everything and spread them across the kitchen table. While I was busy sorting, I heard the rumble of Steve's car. Early for him, especially in the past few weeks.

"I'm organizing my research," I explained as he walked in, noting his curiosity and hoping to begin a conversation we could continue while eating the dinner I had yet to cook.

"Find anything good?" He sat down in the chair opposite me.

"Most of the interesting stuff is from the early 1900s—pages from a diary and a lot of old newspapers with some articles circled. And there's unusual jewelry, too."

I was glad he was able to sit down and talk. Up close, though, I could see the deep fatigue lines under his eyes. He nodded at my description of the items, the hint of a smile on his face.

"Ralph picked the right time to give you those boxes."

I began telling Steve about the changes at the library while promising to have a simple dinner ready soon. It seemed as if we might finally be able to have a relaxing evening together.

Then, abruptly, Steve's cell phone rang. He stood and answered it, running a hand through his thinning sandy hair as he listened to the caller. "Okay. I'll be there soon." Suddenly, the air was charged with tension. Our all-too-brief connection was gone.

"I have to go."

"But you just got home."

"I'm really sorry, Emma. I thought this might have been a chance to take a break. I wanted to hear about your research. And I wanted to tell you about work." He stopped to give me a long, weary look. "Look, Emma. I *need* to fill you in on everything."

"Then why *don't* you?" I was losing patience.

Stunned by my reaction, he paused for a moment. "I'm sorry, Emma. Soon." He grabbed his car keys. "That was the accountant. We need to talk through some complicated details. It's important. I really didn't expect him to get back to me so...so urgently. Certainly not tonight."

He was heading for the front door as he spoke. Where was Hank in all of this? They'd been business partners for decades. "Why can't you just talk on the phone tonight?"

Steve's extra tight, white-knuckle grip on the doorknob looked painful. "Long story for when we have time. I'm hoping this meeting tonight will explain everything." He sighed. "But now I'm not so sure I want to hear that explanation." Then, he was out the door. I felt guilty for snapping at him, but I was angry. I felt he owed *me* some sort of logical explanation.

"But what about dinner?" I shouted.

"I'll grab something on the way home," he called out in parting. "It could be a late night."

Shaking my head with a sigh, I went back to the kitchen and put away my index cards. Something was definitely wrong.

A few minutes later, the *quack-quack* of my own phone sounded. Ralph. For once, I was glad for the distraction.

"Let me guess," I began. "You're doing more party decorating for the community center and you need my advice."

"You're a riot, Em. But that's not why I called." Ralph always got to the point quickly.

"So, what's up?"

"Before I get to that, I found something else you might like. Actually, Sheila found it."

"Mmm."

"More stuff we just tossed into a box before we moved. Sheila found a candy tin filled with old handkerchiefs that Mom saved someplace. You know, those lacy things women used in the old days. Fancy monogrammed initials and all—Mom, Cousin Louise, Grandma, and a few others. There was H.M.W. Hortense Marie Waters. I mean, who would name their kid Hortense? And then Antonia Emmaline Waters. Who else could have been A.E.W.?"

"Mom's great-aunts, right? Or something like that?"

"Yeah, I guess. Made me remember hearing something when I was a kid. Mom was talking to one of her friends…"

"You mean you were eavesdropping," I interrupted.

"Whatever. They were talking about people's signatures, and I first thought it was about us needing to get our report cards signed. Remember when we had to do that? It made me think about the time one of your teachers thought you forged Dad's signature on your report card because he had such crazy handwriting. That was hilarious."

"Right." I grimaced at the embarrassing memory. "And what else do you remember?"

"Just that some relatives signed their names only with initials or something like that."

"You mean you lost interest in their conversation because it didn't have anything to do with report cards?"

"That's about the size of it. Anyway, you're getting these along with that catalog envelope of papers. Sheila can't wait to get rid of them. But that wasn't the main reason I called. We're having a combination Halloween-housewarming party the Sunday before Halloween. A few friends, family, and a couple of our new neighbors. You and Steve have got to come, and why don't you ask Della, too? And you *have* to be in costume."

"Okay. Thanks. I'll talk to Della. This'll really be

fun, especially for Steve. He's been working around the clock on projects these days."

"That's pretty dull. Do him good to get in costume and loosen up a bit. We're having really great six-foot subs."

"You're sure partying a lot these days. Didn't you just go to that decorating party?"

"Yeah. Got to get in the seasonal spirit." Ralph was always getting in the spirit of things.

"Thought I'd give you lots of notice about our party, though. Oh," he continued, "could you also make a few dozen of your special pumpkin cookies and bring them?"

Ah, finally, the true motive for Ralph's call.

"Yeah, yeah. And I'll even dress like a pumpkin, too. Good enough?"

"That would be excellent."

Chapter Six

"Just fill out this request and bring it back to me."
The pleasant young man smiled and handed me a form,
a welcome relief from the starchy woman at my local
library. New York Public's venerable rooms had real
books, too. Lots. Only one small problem. There were
also lots of real people waiting to access them,
promising a fair amount of time before some useful
volumes would be in my hands. When I needed
additional selections, the process would have to be
repeated. But it was worth it and uplifting to be among
others who also valued this world.

A vast sea of computers lined the tables. I told
myself that unlike my local library, their noble purpose
was for the recording of research findings, nothing
frivolous, and certainly not for wiping off the remains
of café snacks on the keyboards. I avoided glancing at
the screens as I walked by. It would have been a shame
to break the spell if I'd spied retail or dating sites
displayed instead of the high-minded texts of scholarly
narratives. At a remote table, some dedicated souls
furiously took notes, pencil and paper next to their open
volumes. They resembled scribes in an ancient
monastery, their presence comforting.

My books arrived, but after an hour of checking, I
realized they didn't contain what I needed, even though
I wasn't totally sure what that was yet. Did I really

think I'd open a book and "Abigail, The Jewel Thief" would be a chapter heading? Or *The Adventures of Mrs. Mallory's Neighbors* would occupy a special shelf in reference?

My next books came after a longer wait, but the story was the same. It was going to be an extended hit-or-miss process over many visits, and I was beginning to feel out of my depth. I was looking for information that might shed more light on the newspaper articles and diary pages in my possession. Were the names and lives of repeat thieves written about? Their victims? Could I locate personal stories about the *General Slocum* disaster? I was desperate to connect the dots, and I wasn't quite sure how to go about it. But this was a start anyway, I told myself.

By afternoon, the room was filled with researchers. Their requests piled up at a matching pace. I was overwhelmed. Suddenly, a cup of coffee felt like a good move. Maybe the crowd would thin out in the meantime and I could ask for a little help from the clerk in privacy.

There was a coffee area and gift shop tucked into a space near the lobby. I tried my best to ignore its existence, the scene at my own library fresh in my mind. Still, I concluded that real books hadn't been tossed in order to create this retreat that was far away from the actual library rooms, so no polyphonic conversations would distract those engaged in research. Part of me hated giving in to any culinary invasion of a library, and the other part felt a guilty sense of relief after finally sitting down to sip my coffee amidst the hum of activity nearby. Like the research room, though, it was becoming crowded with gift shop browsers as

Caryl Janis

well as library patrons craving a jolt of caffeine in the midst of what was supposed to be cerebral calm.

"May I join you?" A short, stocky woman I recognized from the research area stood by the unoccupied chair next to me. It was the only empty seat left in the room.

"Sure." I waved my hand toward the chair with a nod. She placed a giant coffee on the table along with a soft green sack stuffed with papers and notebooks. Sitting down with authority, the shiny black braid that hung long over the back of her forest green sweater swayed with matching force. Green was surely her color.

"I saw you at the desk inside. Busy, busy today. More waiting than usual," she began.

Evidently my time for quiet reflection and people-watching was transforming into a café chat. So much for the myth of unsociable urbanites. Perhaps this didn't extend to libraries.

"I don't mind waiting if I could just find what I need," I said in an attempt to be friendly.

"I know the feeling! I'm doing research on the social impact of the 1918 flu epidemic. I was digging into some of the local details this morning, and it's been slow going."

I was at a loss as to how to correctly respond to the woman's enthusiasm for this unfortunate historic event. "Umm, you sure have an…intriguing topic."

"Gruesome, right?" She grinned. "I was hired to research and write about it as part of an article series on historic medical events. Go figure. The subject's a bummer, but I told them I'm in. Helps pay the rent." She took a matter-of-fact sip of her coffee. "By the

38

way, I'm Geraldine."

"I'm Emma. Nice to meet you."

"Same here. So, what are you digging for in our marble halls of research?" Obviously, she was a frequent flyer at the library.

I shared a brief rundown of my project, including the possibility of returning some lost jewelry to the heirs of its rightful owners, even if it was more than a century later.

"Now *that*," began Geraldine without a moment's hesitation, "is an intriguing project. Sure beats tallying up symptoms and statistics."

"Yeah, but you're a professional and getting recognized for your work. My research is sort of a luxurious hobby, something I've been doing to fill my time since my kids moved out and the company I worked for closed." *Why was I telling all of this to a complete stranger?*

"Don't sell yourself short, Emma. I started researching because I loved it, *and* I loved working freelance. At first, I got paid pennies—and I *do* mean pennies—for some ridiculous projects. Then I started writing about my research, and people got to know me. One thing led to another. And here I am, an expert on historic disease." Her genial laugh bounced through the air nearby. Geraldine's breezy, irreverent patter was certainly entertaining.

"I used to do some light research for my job and enjoyed it, but that was different, and I'm really not trained," I admitted. "And everything seems more complicated now with new computer programs and all. One of the downsides of getting older, I guess."

Geraldine nodded in agreement. Maybe she wasn't

that much younger than me after all. Her energetic mannerisms and the candid expression in her green eyes exuded youth. Yet, up close, the fine lines of experience on her face could have equaled a few more years than were apparent at first glance.

"Lots of people aren't really trained in research. Me, either. It's a hybrid world out there, and a lot of us are making it up as we go. Join the club, Emma. You have a great project."

Although Geraldine was a bit eccentric, her can-do type comments had an easygoing charm and made me feel hopeful that I was on the right track, no matter how inept I felt.

She continued. "You could turn your research into something that really pays off. Maybe writing about your experiences digging into your family's past or giving talks about something special from that time period, like unusual collectibles, crime, penmanship styles, the diary craze. Who knows, Emma? This could lead to something big."

I smiled at her enthusiasm. "If I could just clear up a few details, I'd be happy."

"Can I make a suggestion?" Geraldine was going to do so anyway, with or without my permission. "You're concentrating on the early twentieth century and around then, right?"

I nodded. "Yeah, pretty much. Everything I've found points to it."

"Well, I came across this crazy little research archive when I was doing an article for one of those university magazines. You know, the glossy kind that wows the alums into giving money. Anyway, it was about little-known specialty archives and museums.

Now *that* was an education for me! I absolutely swear that this one place, if it still exists, is something you should check out. I mean there are others, but this one has your name written all over it. Its focus is right smack in the middle of your time period."

I leaned forward. "Tell me more."

"So, there was this woman whose social circle was enormous." Geraldine waved her hand in a wide arc, her silver bracelet adding eloquence to her words.

"This was back in the day, of course," she continued. "The woman was a hoarder and saved all kinds of things from her family. Valuable books, newspapers, relics…and some total crap, too. Oh, and did I mention she was filthy rich?"

Geraldine came up for air, took a generous gulp of coffee, adjusted a ripple in her beaded neckline, and marched on. "She endowed a small archive with an attached museum display room to save a lot of this stuff for posterity. Her friends and family were thrilled to dump their old *treasures* on her. Couldn't wait to get rid of it all."

*Just like Ralph. Maybe I could open an archive and museum display in our family room.*

"Anyway, most of it focuses on New York from the 1890s through World War I, an era the woman felt was a turning point. So, she set up this place, and it's like something out of another century. It's on the first couple of floors of her old home on a sort of forgotten street. Her nephew, who is old as dust, lives like a hermit on the top floors and spends time in the archive. When he dies, though, the whole thing will probably crash, so you better check it out soon."

"What would happen to it then? When he dies, I

mean."

"Rumor had it that the old guy has a son who'd probably sell the property for millions."

"But isn't it legally protected...a landmark or something?"

"Haven't a clue. I just investigated it as one of a few offbeat research places for my article. And you never do find out what's really going on behind the scenes."

"So, anyway, who can use this archive?" This was getting crazier by the minute.

"Anyone. It used to be that you would fill out a form with the reason for your research and then meet with them, just to prove you're not recently escaped from the slammer or that you don't claim to be an extraterrestrial or something."

It was my turn to sip coffee as I processed this bit of information, and not without skepticism. The whole thing seemed implausible at best, lunatic at worst. And Geraldine was a total stranger and certainly eccentric. She could be making it all up. If not, I had to question the wisdom of getting involved with such a weird place, and probably even weirder people, especially since I was now sitting in a leading research library. It might be better to stay here and keep on digging and summon the courage to ask for help from New York Public's busy staff.

"Here." Geraldine whipped out a business card from a side pouch of her green tote bag and jotted something on the back. "It's called the Bauwers Archive. My website is on the card, and a copy of my article is linked there. Just call them, or even walk in. You might find something right up your alley. If not, there's a few other places to try. Then you can come back here and figure out how to navigate the overwhelming millions of possibilities in this place."

She rose and handed me the card. "Gotta head out now. Let me know what happens."

Then Geraldine strode off, her long shiny braid swinging with confidence.

I returned to the reference room but Geraldine's comments echoed long after she blended into the afternoon crowd. Certainly she was eccentric with her quirky sociability and irreverent chatter, not to mention her bizarre epidemic project. Who knew if that Bauwers place was real? If it did exist, maybe it was filled with a batch of certifiable oddballs just like her—people who picked conversations with hapless strangers, all the while sticking their noses into books about sewer alligators or Gilded Age pickpockets. Wiser to ignore the whole thing.

But I couldn't.

For the next thirty minutes or so, I half-heartedly skimmed through material about turn-of-the-century local history. Nothing seemed relevant. I returned the books and left. I was lost in a sea of information but instead of seeking the help I needed here, my thoughts kept going back to that little archive. Damn Geraldine and her ridiculous story.

I turned her card over again. Geraldine's name appeared in bold, no-nonsense type followed by the title *Researcher/Writer*. On the back she'd hastily scribbled the archive's name. I grabbed a corner seat on one of the balcony's smooth marble benches and found an address for the archive on my cell phone—a street tucked in a remote corner of the city. I wasn't surprised.

It was getting late. I should have thought about going home but, instead, found myself heading toward the closest subway entrance. Time had become irrelevant. I had to find that archive. I'd read Geraldine's article later on.

"Stand clear of the closing doors." The announcement sounded mere seconds before I slithered into the subway car and grabbed a seat opposite an old man dozing in the corner, his cap pressing down a mass of snowy hair. The stench of wilted French fries lingered inexplicably in the atmosphere. I studied the advertisements high above the seats. "Train for an exciting career in computers," urged a sprawling invitation from Worldwide Technical Institute.

As the train rumbled from station to station, Geraldine's words replayed over and over in my mind. "Join the club, Emma. You have a great project." Was this true? Or was I just filling my time with nonsense when I should be job hunting or doing volunteer work or training for a new career at Worldwide Technical Institute?

The farther the train went, the larger my doubts grew. What did I know about real research anyway? Or history, for that matter? I had no formal training or experience. If this place was the real deal, then I'd be totally out of my depth and laughed at by serious scholars with solid credentials and projects to match. Wasn't that why I was reluctant to ask for real help at New York Public Library? At least there was safety in numbers there. However, Geraldine said we were all hybrids and urged me to just jump in. But she was probably crazy.

The train screeched to a halt at my stop, breaking

into my jumbled thoughts. I exited onto the gloomy platform and headed for the stairway. With each step, I felt more foolish.

Drawing a deep breath after reaching the open air, I began walking. The farther I went, the fewer the people, stores, and street action. Buildings weren't as tall or as new, the ghostly reminder of another era. One place was abandoned. A door hung off the hinges of another.

"Hey, lady!" A disheveled man, stains dotting his rumpled jacket, shouted from the corner of a crumbling doorway. He held out a filthy cup. I continued walking.

Clouds masked the skyscrapers that now seemed so very far away.

A sliver of anxiety began creeping along my spine, only overshadowed by the shame I felt at being so gullible.

Then, abruptly, it was there in front of me—a worn, orange-red brick façade with tall windows, slightly peeling. A short, black iron fence ran its width, meeting a matching handrailing that lined deep stone steps. A sturdy, cream-colored door, bordered by two pillars, was topped by a generously curving arch. All reminders of long-gone days of elegance.

As I faced the building, I studied the boarded-up structure to its left, graffiti its only decoration. To the right stood an empty lot, the restraining fence broken and the ground littered with the fractured remnants of a demolition—part of a porcelain sink, a half-broken stone bench, some torn cushions. I pondered all of it for a moment. A horn blared in the far distance.

There was no obvious sign in front. Double checking the address, I wondered if it was just a plain, empty building. Further evidence of my total lapse in judgement. On closer look, though, there was a small bronze plaque at the top of the stairs near the door. I had to squint to make out the ornate script identifying *The Bauwers Archive*. So, it really existed.

Now what? Should I climb those aging stone stairs and ring a bell?

Plagued by indecision, I shifted from one foot to the other until the front door opened. A fifty-something man in dark blue work clothes came outside. We were both startled.

"This is the Bauwers Archive?" My words tumbled out in anxiety. "A friend told me it was here and I wasn't sure if I got the right place." *And since when in the past few hours had eccentric Geraldine been raised to the status of a friend?* I rambled on, feeling the desperate need to explain my presence on this otherwise deserted street. Then I stopped abruptly. The man didn't even look like a researcher or a library type. Maybe he had just robbed the place.

He offered a genuine smile. "You got it. The Bauwers place." He walked down the steps. "I'm Joe. I do maintenance for them. Probably the only person in the place without his nose in a book or a dusty file. It's after closing time, so I get to lock up today."

Joe had kind brown eyes that smiled when he did. I relaxed a little and laughed with relief. My fears of him being a burglar evaporated. "I'm Emma. I don't know much about the archive, except that it might help my research into 1903 or 4 or so. Maybe I'm not even qualified to have access." There I was, rambling once more, again to a total stranger.

"You'll be fine, Emma. Believe me, they want people to use the place. Look, do you have their phone number?"

I nodded.

"Good. So, first thing tomorrow morning, call and ask for Meghan. She'll set up an appointment with the director. It's just a formality. You'll talk to her and sign a statement that you won't pilfer any old books or papers. Oh, yeah. They'll hit you up for about fifty bucks for membership. Before you know it, you'll be a card-carrying Bauwers researcher."

"Wow. Okay, then. Thanks, Joe."

"No problem. Good luck. Be seeing you soon." He waved and headed north.

Joe sounded like the voice of reason. And maybe Geraldine wasn't so crazy after all. This could be fun and just what I needed to help me find what I was looking for.

Dusk was growing quickly, and when I reached the corner, I turned to take in the street once more. The block felt even quieter than before, frozen in time. I could only make out the hum of a few random car engines and the metallic slam of a rolling security gate on a nearby street. In a few years, though, the area would probably be studded with modern buildings, its decaying charm vanished along with any lingering traces of history.

Just as I gave the building one final glance, a light flickered in one of its top floor windows. At first, I thought it might be an automatic security device of some sort. But then a shadow moved slowly across the light. It seemed as if someone was watching.

Chapter Seven

Della and I huddled in a corner table at Reese's, sipping steaming mugs of hot chocolate as I described the previous day's events in minute detail.

"Am I crazy? I just walked out of one of the most respected libraries on earth to hunt down some obscure building. All on the say-so of a total stranger. Dell, am I losing it?"

Della laughed so hard that a dollop of whipped cream landed on her nose. "Don't be ridiculous! Look, you found the place, and it seems on the up and up."

"Yeah, according to strangers. Whatever happened to not talking to strangers?"

"But you liked them, and they made some sense. It's an adventure. This could be what you're looking for—and need."

I grinned and nodded. "Okay, okay. You're right. But it's still pretty bizarre."

The familiar *quack-quack* resonated from deep inside my pocketbook. My brother.

"Ralph. I'm at Reese's with Della. I'll have to call you later."

"Just need your ear for a minute." Right-to-the-point Ralph again. "I had a brainstorm. Why don't you invite Cousin Louise to our Halloween party? Then you two could talk about what's in the boxes, and we could all reconnect. And she probably likes pumpkin cookies."

"So then why don't *you* call and invite her. I tried getting in touch a couple of days ago. They said she's away on a trip with friends or something. And I didn't forget about the cookies."

"Swell. I'll try calling her then. She'll love those cookies."

"Jeez! Do you want to see me or just make sure that I bring the pumpkin cookies?"

"I'm wounded," Ralph replied in mock horror. "I just want to see my favorite sister."

"I'm your only sister."

"Right. Well, I'll give Louise a call. This'll be fun."

"Bye, Ralph."

Della laughed and pushed a green-streaked wisp out of her eyes. "Ralph? Ha! There must be some devious plan afoot, and it involves more pumpkin cookies?"

I told Della the gist of it. "Actually, I'm glad he came up with the idea about asking Louise. It'd be nice to see her. Good memories. I remember one time she made us little sock puppets when we were kids. They smelled like her perfume—*Amaze* or *Astound* or something. Anyway, I've called and she's still away. Maybe Ralph'll have more luck."

"Any other close relatives?" asked Della.

"A few distant cousins, but we all lost touch. Ralph and I are her great-niece and nephew, I think. Everyone from her generation is long gone, and her husband died young. But Louise had a ton of close friends who were just like family. They all looked out for each other."

"And why does the king of wicked plans want her

at his Halloween party?"

"Just to make sure that I come and bring pumpkin cookies?"

"Ha!" laughed Della. "Knowing Ralph, that's possible."

"Still, I could talk to her about the stuff in the boxes. Oh, Dell, I almost forgot! Ralph invited you to his party, too. Sunday before Halloween. I hope you can come. It'll be fun."

"I'd love to go. Your brother is always entertaining."

"Great! Better think of costume possibilities."

"I'm way ahead of you on this." Della gave me an evil grin.

Chapter Eight

"And just how did you hear about us?" Ms. Tipton, the Director of the Bauwers Archive, posed her question with crisp formality. Her piercing brown eyes scrutinized my face with an intensity that was unnerving. Well-shaped, decisive brows added to the effect.

"An acquaintance from New York Public Library," I answered, smoothing my carefully selected soft gray skirt. It would have been embarrassing to divulge that I'd just accidentally met Geraldine, spending only a mere twenty minutes with her.

"Hmm," she responded with a slight nod. Her squarish face loomed large, accentuated by dark, pulled-back hair, neatly arranged in a 1940s-style hair roll. Ms. Tipton, however, was somewhere in middle age, far from having lived in that era. She exuded the venerable maturity of my most intimidating grammar school teachers. I felt as if I was twelve years old again.

"Please tell me about your project and what you hope to discover here."

Fortunately, I'd rehearsed this on my way to the appointment. "I want to find the identities of people mentioned in some diary pages that were among my family's belongings and get background on their lives. There's also some jewelry in this collection. It might possibly belong to the descendants of another family. If so, I'd like to return the pieces to the rightful heirs." I took a deep breath.

If Ms. Tipton found any of this unusual, she didn't show it.

"And what makes you think this jewelry didn't belong to your own family?"

"Just that some of the written materials suggested they might have been given to someone in my family for safekeeping." I hoped this sounded high-toned enough for the occasion. I couldn't confess my worries that a theft, or possibly several thefts and related crimes, might be involved, even if they had taken place over a century ago. After all, I could be wrong. Once more I began to worry that this entire adventure was silly, a pathetic quest to fill my expansive free time.

There was a timid knock at the door.

"Yes?" called Ms. Tipton. A slender young man entered. His wrinkled tan shirt almost matched his light brown hair. Swallowing audibly, he handed a large, official-looking envelope to her, a corner of his shirt escaping from worn black jeans. "You asked me to bring this as soon as it came." He gave me a sideways glance and nodded.

"Thank you, Baxter." Ms. Tipton took the envelope and Baxter retreated through the doorway.

Ms. Tipton studied my face once again, as if the answers to additional questions might be etched there. Then she looked down at the envelope. An uncomfortable silence followed during which I studied the intricate pattern of scratches on her well-worn desktop. Somewhere in the room a clock ticked faintly. I was sure she was getting ready to have me escorted from the building. By this time, even to me, the explanation of my project seemed far-fetched. It wasn't scholarly; it rather resembled the plot of some Grade B, late-night movie. Right at that moment, I vowed I'd get rid of the whole miserable pile of family hand-me-downs, just like Ralph did. I'd donate or throw it all away and go back to my classes and crosswords and make a real attempt at running. At the same time, I'd find a job, any job, all just so I'd be busy and come back to earth again.

Ms. Tipton adjusted her neat, but solid form into a more comfortable position. When she looked up and finally spoke, I stifled a gasp.

"All right. I'm quite sure you'll find some helpful details in our collection." She glanced down at the envelope and continued. Her voice was still serious but with a softer edge to it.

"We charge a fee of fifty dollars every six months for unlimited use of the archive. And you must sign this form." She pushed a single sheet of paper across the desk in my direction. "By signing this, you swear that you will not deface or remove any of our materials."

I nodded. "Yes, I understand." *Only fifty dollars? And a promise to behave like a decent person?* Joe had been right. And now, I was actually getting permission to use the archive.

"Once we've completed this paperwork, you're free to begin using our books and materials immediately during all of our regular hours. Our two research assistants, Meghan and Baxter, are here to help with your questions."

She paused for a few seconds. A single ray of sun broke through the faded lace curtains. It illuminated a glass-enclosed bookcase nearby, an array of fingerprints outlined there in dusty relief.

Ms. Tipton continued. "There are study desks and tables interspersed throughout our premises for the use of all our researchers. The stacks are open as are the regular files. The specialized materials, such as rare diaries and documents, are available upon request. You must use these in the main room. Any questions?"

"No, thank you." I had all but folded my hands and bowed my head in gratitude. *That was all there was to the process?*

I signed the paper with just my contact information, a few words about my research interests, and a promise that I wouldn't harm anything. After I handed her my check for fifty dollars, Ms. Tipton gave me a printed list of rules and regulations. There was even a nice floor plan of the building attached. It all seemed so simple and so impossible at the same time.

"Meghan will take you on a brief tour now." The young woman appeared at the door as if by magic.

Ms. Tipton stood and so did I. She formally shook my hand with a grip as firm and decisive as those eyebrows.

"Welcome to the Bauwers Archive."

\*\*\*\*

"C'mon. We'll start downstairs and work our way up." Meghan tucked a strand of shoulder-length auburn hair behind her ear. One of the two research assistants at the archive, she had a bright smile and a sweet face with deep bangs casually sweeping her forehead. None of this matched the air of authority she exuded.

I followed Meghan down the hallway, the hardwood floor creaking rhythmically under our feet as we walked past plain walls dotted with an occasional antique sconce. It was a challenge to keep up with Meghan's swift, willowy moves, almost like those of a dancer. At the end of the hall, she opened a door leading to a steep flight of cement stairs. I gratefully noted the sturdy hand railings.

"We also have an elevator that goes to each level." Meghan indicated a small door nearby, almost as an afterthought. Obviously, this detail was only for informational purposes since she was already leading the way down the dimly lit staircase.

At the bottom of the stairs, a compelling aroma of dust and mold greeted us. I was stunned at the sizeable space there, entirely crammed with books. They lined the walls and were tightly packed into a vast labyrinth of ceiling-high gray metal shelves.

"Voila! The open stacks." Meghan laughed and waved her hand at the space in front of us. Then she pointed to a small study table with a gooseneck lamp on its surface—one of a number, she assured me, which were squirreled cozily into various random corners. "You're always free to use these. Our researchers like the quiet down here."

The desks in my immediate sightline were empty.

Meghan continued. "Believe it or not, you can find all the titles and authors in an old-fashioned card catalog. Been a while since you've seen one of those, right?"

"Right. But it's sort of comforting."

"Then this is your place. We have computer access, too, but most people seem to prefer the cards." She gestured in the direction of the ceiling. "Everything's upstairs by the main room. We keep cross-referenced cards for rare documents and photographs and even for non-print items stored in boxes, like commemorative thimbles and bronze plaques. There's plenty there, and Miss Bauwers wanted all of it available."

I was curious to know more about Miss Bauwers, the woman who founded the place. I didn't have to wait long before Meghan launched into her commentary on the subject.

"There's a display room on the second floor. Our little museum. There's lots of artifacts there from the family and others. They were prominent in turn-of-the-century New York, and Miss Bauwers insisted on preserving details from this important time in the city's history."

I nodded. So far, I had learned all of this from Geraldine.

"She planned everything herself?"

"Yes, she was quite a force of nature."

Another voice, a deeper one, suddenly joined in. "And a force with the finances to back it up."

Meghan turned to face the speaker, responding with cautious formality. "Well, Mr. Renleigh. I didn't realize you were here."

A tall, nicely dressed man, especially for one rubbing shoulders with so many dusty books, appeared from behind a row of shelves. Mr. Renleigh was around my age with well-styled hair morphing gently from brown to gray. He had a handsome face, and his close-cropped beard was both distinguished and boyishly charming. With fluid elegance, he introduced himself.

"Please call me Alan." He smiled, shook my hand, and held it longer than necessary. "And you are?"

"Emma Streyt."

"Welcome, Emma."

Meghan quickly jumped in. "Mr. Renleigh is one of our regular researchers. He's studying special-interest organizations in New York at the turn of the century."

Alan Renleigh's face lit up. "I've been asked to write a series of articles on the subject."

*Was everyone researching and writing articles about some arcane subject? And where were they going to be published? Weren't there fewer magazines now?* Alan's topic sure beat Geraldine's horrifying flu epidemic, though. I supposed it was as good as any if a publication was willing to pay for it. Maybe if someone would pay me to write about family artifacts, I'd feel a little more confident about my project. But would anyone be interested?

"So, what research brings you here, Emma?" Alan seemed genuinely curious, so I gave him the little speech I'd rehearsed for Ms. Tipton.

"Wonderful," he responded. "I'm sure we'll be seeing a lot more of each other." He glanced at Meghan, who was shuffling from one foot to the other, impatient to continue our tour.

"We need to get going," she prompted with business-like efficiency.

"Emma," continued Alan, seemingly loath to end our conversation, "I hope we can sit down sometime soon and compare notes on our research."

"Okay," I said, my face growing red at the marked attention from this attractive man.

"Till then." He finished with a winning smile before vanishing into the stacks once more.

Meghan and I marched back up the cement steps and into the main research room, obviously a centerpiece of the building. Tall windows illuminated several long, polished wooden tables. Each had inviting leather chairs, now occupied by only a few researchers, heads bowed in close inspection of a book or manuscript.

I glanced quickly at these individuals. One woman carefully pored over photographs, gingerly holding them with white-gloved hands, a stark contrast to her drab olive sweater. She didn't look up, nor did the older man with whiskers that lined only the sides of his face, or the younger woman with a magnifying glass who was scrutinizing an oversized manuscript with the intensity of Sherlock Holmes on the hunt for clues.

At the front of the room was an enormous oak desk where a semi-bald man appeared to be bent in deep concentration over a mass of books and papers. However, he frequently raised his eyelids a fraction above the black rims of his glasses, carefully observing the researchers so intent upon their work. We approached him quietly.

"Mr. Winthrop." Meghan's voice was a respectful whisper. "Our new researcher."

He raised his small, portly frame from the chair to shake hands. I found it hard to take my eyes off his prominent burgundy bow tie.

The intimate atmosphere of the place was comforting in comparison to New York Public Library's vast and confusing hive of activity. *But shouldn't there be more people here?*

Next, Meghan led me into a plain kitchen with several small tables, reminiscent of those my grandmother once owned. A refrigerator, microwave, and efficiency sink completed the room. Meghan waved me toward one of the chairs. "Tea?" she asked.

I nodded. Meghan selected two packets and filled cardboard cups with hot water from a simple dispenser on the countertop. "Free tea and coffee," she announced and then added, "not exactly gourmet, but it's fresh." As we dipped our tea bags in the water, I studied the room.

As an eating space, the room had a certain utilitarian charm. Its framed pictures of old New York added an appealing touch to the otherwise spare walls, especially the Currier and Ives reproduction of people enjoying a long-ago winter evening in Central Park.

My concentration on the picture was abruptly broken when a figure hurriedly swept into the room. She stopped and gasped audibly, seemingly startled to find anyone else here.

It was the woman from the research area with the drab sweater, now without white gloves, who'd been studying photographs with such intensity. She seemed frazzled.

"Oh...hello," she began. "I didn't mean to interrupt. I just need some water."

With that, she bee-lined toward the sink and grabbed a small paper cup, filling it with tap water. Viewed from the back, her sweater seemed even more drab, oversized, and slightly misshapen. A wisp of salt-and-pepper hair escaped over her ear. She silently drained the cup and then turned to face us. Her plain oxford shoes squeaked against the floor's smooth surface.

"Millicent," began Meghan, trying her best to smile. "I'd like you to meet Emma. She's a new researcher here. I've just been giving her the grand tour."

Millicent approached the table. A pair of calm, intelligent brown eyes met mine. With unexpected poise, she extended her hand in formal greeting. Her clear gaze and solid handshake were at odds with her previous demeanor—that of a flustered, rabbit-like individual.

As she withdrew her hand, she must have noticed the slight wince of discomfort on my face at her more than firm handshake. "I'm so sorry," she said, immediately looking down at her hand. "My ring must have slipped around by accident. I hope I didn't hurt you."

I assured her I was fine and caught a quick glimpse of two round glittering stones, one red and one deep blue, set opposite each other in an unusual design. She made no move, though, to turn the ring back away from her palm. Then, in an instant, she returned to flustered mode, mumbling a "nice meeting you" and leaving as quickly as she arrived.

Meghan grinned. "Some of our researchers are quite dedicated, and slightly eccentric."

I subtly checked the palm of my hand. It showed the diagonal imprint of the two stones from Millicent's ring. "Quite some handshake," I commented, rubbing my palm. We both laughed, and then Meghan returned to talking about the kitchen's facilities.

"You're welcome to bring your lunch and snacks and store them in the refrigerator. It pays to have lunch onsite if you're going to spend the day. You've probably noticed there's not much in the way of good eats anywhere really close by."

She took a mouthful of tea and shifted

uncomfortably. "Speaking of the area, I need to tell you that basically the neighborhood's quiet, but okay." She paused, considering her words carefully. "There were two muggings recently. But they were well after dark," she added hastily. "I figure you should know. We don't want to over-react, but we want everyone to be safe."

"Thanks for telling me," I responded. "I guess it's good to be cautious anywhere." It wasn't hard to imagine a mugging given the desolate feel of the area, especially after dark.

She continued. "Both times it happened *well* after the archive was closed."

Meghan looked at a framed map on the wall and then into her empty cup. I had a sense there was more she wanted to say. I waited, worried about what was coming next.

"The last time was more serious than a purse snatching."

*What did that mean?* She seemed to be struggling to compose herself.

Meghan's voice caught as she continued. "They never found the person who did it."

"Oh," was all I could manage. *Was there more to this? Was it connected to the archive?*

She avoided my eyes. "Just, please be careful," she cautioned before quickly closing the subject and suggesting we continue our tour. *But she never explained what "more serious" meant.*

"Here's where Baxter and I work." Meghan quickly ushered me past a small, cluttered office with two desks liberally scattered with papers, mismatched bookcases, worn cabinets, and files everywhere. It was as if our previous conversation never happened.

"We're both research assistants. We answer outside requests for information and, of course, we're here for our researchers. You can come in anytime if you need help." She indicated the office with a sweep of her hand. There sat the thin, earnest-looking young man who came into Ms. Tipton's office earlier. He pressed a phone to his ear, running a free hand through his hair and then down to stroke his throat. Baxter waved, offering a distracted smile. Meghan and I waved back and returned to the hallway.

Meghan pointed to a small table and chair near the front door. "We have a college intern who sits here part of the time when she's not helping with filing. When she or no one else is at the table, we try to remember to lock the door. Just ring the bell and someone will let you in."

I asked Meghan about the cute little sitting room I noticed when I came in earlier.

"C'mon, I'll show you," she answered genially.

A Victorian sofa, several chairs, and a small writing desk filled this charming room. Sunshine poured through filmy curtains, saturating the colors of the rug with a soft brilliance.

"You can come here and read or go through your notes, especially if you'd like to breathe in some clear air after a few hours in the dusty stacks," said Meghan. "Also, if someone's going to meet you when you're finished, they can wait here. Just let us know they'll be coming."

I immediately planned on asking Della to meet me here soon. She'd love it.

"One last thing." Meghan indicated another flight of stairs. Unlike the steps down to the open stacks, these were wooden, their surface partially covered with tasteful carpeting. We began our climb to the second floor. I ran my fingers over the cool, lustrous wooden banister, admiring the elegant portraits that lined the left-hand wall on the way.

"The Bauwers family," commented Meghan, seeing my interest. Their faces seemed alive. The artist had been a master. I made a mental note to study each portrait at another time.

At the top of the stairs was a double wooden door. It was so grand and imposing that I almost didn't notice several other closed doors off the hallway.

Meghan opened the big door, revealing a generous space with cream-colored walls and high windows dressed with sweeping crimson draperies. Old-fashioned museum cases were spread over the center of the room. Glass-enclosed cabinets lined the walls, and another small elevator door was tucked between two of them. A crystal chandelier twinkled gently overhead.

"This is our little museum. I'll just show you a few highlights," volunteered Meghan. "You're free to come here any time and take a closer look."

The cases were chock-full of items with neatly typed descriptions. The array was staggering—maps, beribboned medals, a chunk of an old building. All a mini-history in itself.

"Most of this, but not everything, dates from the 1890s to just before World War I," explained Meghan. "There's a lot of memorabilia from the Bauwers family and their close friends. You could literally spend days here and still not catch every detail."

She smiled. "You have access to all of downstairs and to the museum room here, but nothing else on this floor or beyond. Our rarities are stored there and, also, Mr. Bauwers has his apartment upstairs. He's the founder's nephew." She paused. "Don't worry. It's all on your building chart."

"Thanks, Meghan. I think I'll spend a little time here now with the exhibits. Then I'll be back soon to officially start my research." *My research.* The words alone were exciting.

Meghan smiled again. "That's terrific. We'll all look forward to seeing you." She grasped my hand warmly and shook it in parting. Then she left me to my wanderings.

I leisurely browsed the cases at random, too excited to concentrate. I just wanted to graze through the displays now and get a sense of everything.

A dollhouse in one of the wall cabinets housed intricately carved furniture and exquisite figures of people. A silver service caught the light along with memorial tributes in softly tinted mattings. Several elegant books, frayed but reasonably well-preserved, drew my attention.

While I was deciphering book titles, a creaking sound startled me. A thin, bent man in a worn tweed jacket entered through the little elevator door. Shuffling in my direction, he nodded in a slow rhythm—whether voluntarily or not, I couldn't say. The only sound was the tap of his cane on the hardwood floor. I spied the tufts of yellowing white hair hanging over each ear. Glasses with fine gold rims were perched on a hawk-like nose. He stared at me through thick lenses. When he spoke, the words were slow, the sound of a once regal voice now diminished.

"You are the new researcher," he stated, rather than

asked, his tone quite formal.

My voice caught before I could reply.

"I am Harlan Bauwers."

Chapter Nine

Nestled in my seat on the train ride home that afternoon, I tried to concentrate on a crossword puzzle book I picked up in Grand Central. It was useless. I kept replaying the events of the day, right through my surprise meeting with the elderly Mr. Bauwers. He'd offered a monosyllabic "welcome" and a skeletal handshake before retracing his path to the small elevator door. Startled, both by his sudden appearance and his obvious frailty, I'd managed to eke out my name and a thank you. It had seemed enough.

When I got home, I called Della.

"So, how was your day at Chez Bauwers?" she asked.

"Weird, but good," I answered. "It's like going back in time."

I filled Della in on everything. What continued to stand out in my mind, though, was the relative ease with which I'd been accepted as a researcher by the inscrutable Ms. Tipton as well as how few people seemed to be using the archive. Della didn't find this strange at all.

"I'm sure they're thrilled," she commented, echoing what Joe, the maintenance guy, said during our chance meeting. "With people continually surfing the internet for everything, they're probably happy that anyone wants to use a real archive. Your project is a genuine one, and Ms. Tipton can see you're a responsible person. It's all good, Em. Just go with the flow."

Reassured, I continued sharing every detail I could remember, including Meaghan's unsettling news about muggings in the area. What had she meant by the last one having been "more serious"? Complicated circumstances? A severe injury or...murder? *No, not that.*

"I think there was more she wanted to tell me about that second mugging but she was, I don't know, holding something back or afraid to say anything else. She seemed upset."

"Meghan might tell you more when she gets to know you better. The important thing is to please be careful, Em," cautioned Della. "I hate to think they haven't caught the person yet."

"I'll be careful, and I only plan to be there during the day anyway, so it should be all right," I promised, quickly getting off the subject.

"So, what's next?"

"I'm going back to start my real research. I can feel it, Dell. The answers to my questions are there. Besides, the archive is easier to navigate than New York Public Library."

We signed off, and I headed for the kitchen just as the low rumble of a car engine sounded in the driveway. Obviously, Steve was home from the endless stream of clients and work. When he trudged into the room, I again noticed the dark circles underscoring his blue eyes.

"Chicken-avocado sandwich?" I offered, just starting to fix one for myself. Despite my worries about

Steve, I felt calmer than I had in weeks. *The side effects of my time with Ms. Tipton, Meghan, and the whole archive crew?*

Steve looked at me somberly. "Okay. I'd like that."

Wordlessly, I gestured to the table and began gathering the fixings for the sandwiches.

"Good day today?" Steve asked.

I spoke while slicing the avocado and arranging slices of chicken on thick multi-grain bread. "Very. I was accepted at the Bauwers Archive. Tomorrow, I start my research." I placed two sandwich plates and side salads on our cheerful ivy-patterned placemats. "Would you like some wine?"

"That'd be nice."

I decided to fill Steve in on my day, letting him relax first before asking him anything about work, a topic that seemed to be the catalyst for his fatigue and my frustration lately.

For a brief moment, the only sound was the faint ripple of chardonnay filling the slender wine glasses. It was comforting, almost like a small fountain trickling in a quiet garden. I brought the glasses to the table before speaking again.

"I really haven't had a chance to fill you in. Long story, but someone at New York Public Library told me about a private archive downtown. It's like walking back in time. Probably just what I need to solve the mystery of the diary and the jewelry."

As he took a tentative bite of his sandwich, Steve raised an eyebrow in question. I picked up my glass and clinked it against his with a mysterious smile. Then I launched into my story.

"There was so much in those boxes and that trunk

from Ralph," I began. "But what I found most intriguing were some random papers that looked like they came out of a diary." After a quick sip of wine, I continued. "The person who wrote those pages was in the middle of a lot of action. She was given something important to keep by somebody named Abigail."

Completely swept up in my narrative now, I intermittently punctuated the air with my salad fork for additional emphasis as I spun my tale of stolen jewelry, tragedy, historic newspaper articles, and modern-day rightful heirs.

Steve finished the last of his sandwich. "How could you trace the jewelry and prove who it belonged to, though? And figure out if any type of crime was committed at all?"

"My research at the archive will give me more information to help figure this out. Wouldn't you feel the same as I do if you were in my shoes?"

Steve looked perplexed. "I guess so, and there could be something to it. But, Emma, it was so long ago, and there are a lot of questions…"

"*But*," I interrupted, "those newspaper articles that were circled and the jewelry itself really seem linked to the diary pages. I'm just investigating further."

I had no idea of where I was going with this, but a newfound sense of purpose propelled me forward. I moved to the refrigerator and took out two small dishes of my chocolate studded vanilla mousse for dessert. Truthfully, I'd planned on eating both as a reward for getting through today. Now, I plopped a dish on each of our placemats.

"When there are more details and things get figured out," I added quickly, "I want to write an article about the stories behind the diary *and* about my research." *When did I decide this? Was I already channeling Geraldine or even that guy Alan from the archive's stacks?*

Steve looked surprised. Not quite as surprised as I was myself.

"Sounds like a good idea." He was trying to be supportive, but I could see he'd been distracted the whole time I'd been talking. Or maybe he was just being polite and thought my entire project was a wild and crazy goose chase.

"Okay," he said, hesitating a moment before abruptly changing the subject. "Emma, we really have to talk. I know I've been working so late…"

"Yeah, you *have* been working late," I interrupted unintentionally, my exasperation with this bubbling to the surface. "Can't you hire more people to help?"

There was an awkward silence. I made no attempt to fill it.

"I'd like to, and I will," he continued. "But there's more to it than that."

His serious expression made me stop short. Suddenly, our dessert was forgotten.

He readjusted his position in the chair. "I accidentally stumbled on something at work."

I now ran my thumb over the little raised flower pattern on the handle of my dessert spoon. My enthusiasm of a few minutes ago settled into quiet anxiety.

Steve took a sip of his remaining wine. "It really started with a question from the accountant a couple of weeks ago. Then I started looking further. I almost thought I was imagining things but…"

This time, it was the doorbell that interrupted Steve.

We both jumped and looked at each other.

"Don't answer it," said Steve, closing his eyes as if in pain.

The bell rang again several times, more insistently. A loud pounding and a muffled shout followed.

We looked at each other again. Whoever was there was not going away.

"I'll get it," I said finally.

Reluctantly, I made my way to the front hall, hoping to quickly get rid of whoever was there. Steve was right behind me. When I opened the door, there was old Mrs. Ryan, our next-door neighbor. She looked totally bedraggled. Tears streamed down her face, spilling onto the collar of her worn brown raincoat. She clutched a red leather leash as if her life depended on it.

"It's Chester...Chester ran away." She choked out this news in the midst of a sob.

This wasn't the first time that feisty Chester, an aging Yorkie mix, had slipped his leash to explore the greater outside world. Why did he have to choose tonight for a repeat adventure?

"Don't worry, Mrs. Ryan." For a fleeting moment, I almost forgot my frustration at this ill-timed interruption. She was totally distraught. It would have been heartless to do nothing.

Steve was already tossing on his windbreaker. "We'll go look for him."

"Thank...you." Another sob punctuated her words. She clutched the leash even closer.

"It's okay, Mrs. Ryan." We were the only sympathetic neighbors she could turn to. "You stay on your front porch in case Chester comes back by himself. We'll find him."

I put my arm around the woman, leading her outside. "Steve and I will search for him. You stay by your door and be on the lookout."

She nodded through her tears and walked back to her house.

The crisp fall evening had turned decidedly chilly, and I regretted running out the door without a jacket. I hugged my thin blue sweatshirt closer.

I soon shivered from the cold and frustration over the evening's turn of events. But then I remembered Mrs. Ryan's heartbreaking sobs. Chester was all she had.

Both Steve and I kept calling "Chester...here Chester" while rounding several corners past an array of Halloween decorations from grinning jack-o-lanterns to inflatable ghosts. We finally stopped in front of a charming colonial, its inviting front porch laden with strings of pumpkin lights. We'd been gone for about twenty minutes. Still, no Chester.

With hands on hips, Steve's gaze continued taking in the surrounding lawns. "Let's go back and see how Mrs. Ryan's doing," he finally suggested.

Now the only sound was the scrunch of newly fallen autumn leaves under foot. Finally, unable to contain myself any longer, I broke the silence. "What is it, Steve? What's wrong?"

He took a long, deep breath. "It looks like Hank's been taking money from the business."

"What?" My exclamation punctured the chill night air.

"Emma, I *want* to be wrong, but everything's

pointing to this. That's why I ran back to work the other night. The accountant had more details. He said he really needed to talk to me right then. I've hoped for some logical explanation for the discrepancies. But there just doesn't seem to be any."

I was stunned. "But why didn't you say something to me before?"

Steve's voice cracked. "I'm sorry, Emma. I was praying it might have just been a glitch in the books. I've spent the past few weeks going over everything, even trying to draw Hank out about client situations. We'll be at the conference this week, and I'll have to confront him."

"But why, Steve? Why would he do this? The business is doing great, right? If Hank needed extra, why didn't he just come to you and talk about it?"

"I don't know. I need an explanation for the facts the accountant gave me. I can't go over it anymore. It's time to talk honestly with Hank. Maybe it's all a mistake."

I paused a moment. "But you don't think so, do you?"

Steve looked away for a moment, then shook his head before answering.

"Truthfully, the facts don't seem to lie. It's not that the business itself is in trouble financially. We're busier than ever. But if he's doing something that's..." He hesitated before continuing, "that's not right, then there's more than money at stake here, isn't there?"

We arrived at our neighbor's house just in time to spy Chester doing a ten-yard dash across the lawn into the waiting arms of Mrs. Ryan and the cluster of his favorite treats she'd been frantically waving into the cool night air. We approached the reunited duo, relieved.

I stopped for a minute before we reached the pair.

"But, Steve, why didn't you tell me?"

"Because I didn't want to believe it. Because I felt terrible saying the words out loud. And, Emma, suppose I'm wrong? Suppose the accountant's wrong?"

I looked at him sadly. "But suppose you're both right?"

Chapter Ten

The next morning as I walked down the desolate street for my first full day at the archive, I tried hard to bury my emotions from the previous night. Angry at Hank, I concluded he must be guilty or else the accountant wouldn't have so clearly called the discrepancies to light. And I was angry at Steve for not telling me about the situation sooner and, truthfully, for seeming to have more sorrow than rage over the whole thing.

By the time I marched up the archive's chipped stone steps, I grabbed the brass doorknob and charged through the entrance with more force than necessary. The figure at the front table jumped in horrified surprise. It was Baxter, Meghan's fellow research assistant, whom I'd seen briefly the day before.

"I'm so sorry," I burst out. "I didn't mean to startle you." I paused to let him catch his breath. "Baxter? I'm Emma."

I thrust out my hand in greeting. Baxter responded with a tepid shake.

"Nice meeting you. Meghan said you'd be starting your research today." He ran his hand over his throat, just as he'd done when I'd seen him at his desk.

"I'm looking forward to beginning." I smiled, hoping to set him at ease.

"Good. I guess you already know where to hang

your coat." He indicated the closet down the hall. "If there's anything you need, just let me know."

I thanked him, shed my coat, and went into the kitchen to put my name-labeled lunch bag in the refrigerator. It joined at least four others, also well-marked.

Next, I headed for the research room and its neat rows of card catalogs. The place was silent. Millicent closely studied her photographs. A drab brown sweater replaced the drab olive one of yesterday, her white gloves offering a stunning contrast and hiding her ring. Only three other people dotted the room, all studiously absorbed. I knew, though, that Mr. Winthrop at the main research desk was well aware of their every move, as well as mine.

I hurried to the card catalogs, thrilled to feel the tiny grains of its walnut surface and to fit my index finger into the little curved brass ring handles on the drawers. Inside was the once familiar sight of aging, beige-colored cards, their typewritten details faded with time and use.

For the next half hour, I copied down the titles of materials to check in the open stacks downstairs, a good place to begin. Maybe I'd request some rare items from Mr. Winthrop in the future. But now, I walked down the hallway toward the cement staircase to the basement.

Ms. Tipton appeared immediately, looking crisp and orderly in a navy-blue suit that fit her matronly figure remarkably well. Not one wisp of her 1940s hair roll moved out of place.

"Good morning, Emma. I'm glad to see you're starting your research."

"Hello, Ms. Tipton. I couldn't have waited another day."

She seemed quite approachable at the moment. Maybe I was just feeling more confident now as an official Bauwers researcher.

She smiled in return. "Please keep me abreast of what you find." She studied my face carefully. "I'm *quite* interested to hear about your discoveries."

*Was she this interested in everyone?* Maybe this line was just another part of her job.

I scurried down the stairs to hunt for my books. The scent of mold was strong, and my fingers were soon smudged from grasping the decaying volumes. The lights were dim in a few of the aisles, and I hoped Joe would soon replace some of those high, lengthy lighting tubes.

Sliding into one of the desk tables tucked into a random corner, I spread my books and papers out as best as I could. Soon I was reading and taking notes from *A Concise History of New York City*. Its chronologically organized information matched the broader topics in a few of my circled newspaper articles. Details relating to others remained a mystery. Nothing helped me figure the significance of such perplexing headlines as "Marry to Escape the Law."

Other books carried in-depth stories about disasters, memorable events, and short biographies of locally important people from the early 1900s. I scribbled some notes for myself, enthralled with the topics, but still far from getting specific answers to my questions. Could the page from the diary about Greta and her babies be linked to the *General Slocum* disaster or was the paragraph about brilliant lights of a new era connected to New Year's Eve as the city welcomed in the year 1900? And what about the man with the sparkly object in his cravat? I plunged deeper into this absorbing world. It was all that mattered to me at that moment.

Then, without warning, a light tap on my shoulder hurtled me back to the present. I gasped, accidentally knocking several books to the floor. Their resounding *thwack* sent clouds of dust flying in every direction. I looked up with a jolt.

"Hello, Emma."

Alan Renleigh smiled down at me.

"I'm *so* sorry, Emma." Alan swept my books off the floor with the graceful flourish of a professional tennis player.

"I was lost in the last century," I stammered, trying to regain my composure. *How long had he been staring at me?*

"*Great Events of the Early Twentieth Century*," he read, putting the first weighty volume back on my small desk. Alan studied each title carefully. "Some pretty intense works here." His pale-blue shirt cuffs were spotless despite the dust and grime in the surrounding book stacks. "Looks as if you're really getting serious about our archive."

"I'm finding a lot of helpful things."

"This is a very helpful place," Alan said, holding my gaze for an uncomfortable moment. "I just wanted to say hello but, please, let's get together soon and compare notes."

"Sounds good, Alan." I lowered my eyes to the books in front of me, politely ending our discussion and happy he didn't push his point further.

Why would Alan be interested in my family sleuthing? And I couldn't get excited about his research into the role and impact of social organizations in bygone days, although I supposed there might be some details worth exchanging. I also couldn't ignore his flirtatious mannerisms. Flattering though this might be, his attention was unnerving.

I returned to my reading, checking the information against my carefully prepared list of diary topics and circled headlines. Someone went to great pains to identify those headlines. I needed to find more specifics from diaries, interviews, and personal accounts. Perhaps these were among Mr. Winthrop's carefully guarded items in the research room upstairs.

Eventually, my stomach began to grumble. Time for lunch. I headed upstairs to the kitchen. Meghan and Joe greeted me there.

"I see that things worked out." Joe smiled. "Glad you're here."

"Thanks to you, Joe. You steered me to Meghan, and it's all gone smoothly from there."

I joined them at the small table, its old-fashioned Formica surface clean but worn. We chatted sociably for a while. Meghan revealed she was going to night school to study fine art and hoped to combine it with archival research. Her current job at the Bauwers, as well as some previous summer internships, all opened up another world for her.

"Being here opens up new things for me, too," joked Joe. "Including holes in the plumbing. The water leak last week left a wicked puddle behind one of the wall shelves. I had to pull everything out. You haven't lived until you've smelled a combo of basement mildew, soggy books, and mold." His frustrations with keeping the old building in good shape were obvious.

Soon, and with a crunch of her sandwich wrapper, Meghan stood. "Time to get back to the mountain on my desk. See you guys later."

This left Joe and me together for a few minutes to finish our sandwiches.

"So, you're finding everything okay?"

I had a nagging feeling that there was something more to Joe's question. *But what could it be?* I tried to sound casual as I answered. "Oh, absolutely. I can already see that a lot of what I need will be here."

"Good." Joe paused, a fleeting shadow of concern crossing his face. "If anything seems amiss, just let me know, okay? I'm always around the building."

"Sure, thanks."

He stood to leave. "Back to work. Glad you're here, Emma. Enjoy your research."

When Joe left, I stared at my sandwich wrapper. What had he meant by *if anything seems amiss*? Another water leak? A serious crack in the stairs? Or was Joe just another eccentric? *Or did it have something to do with those muggings—especially the second one?*

While I pondered this, Mr. Winthrop charged in, nodded a brusque greeting, retrieved his lunch bag, and made a hasty exit. No idle chatter for him.

"He barely leaves his desk." I was surprised to see Meghan again, just seconds after Mr. Winthrop scurried out. "Makes you wonder if he ever takes a bathroom break."

We both laughed.

"I didn't realize how much I needed more coffee to

get me through the afternoon," she confessed, filling the floral mug she brought with her. Before leaving, she turned for a brief moment, lowering her voice. "By the way, have you run into Mr. Renleigh again?"

I nodded. "Yes, he stopped to say hello when I was downstairs."

"Quite the charmer, isn't he?"

"I guess so. We only chatted for a minute or two, though." His particular brand of charm made me uncomfortable, but I was reluctant to confess this to Meghan.

"I'm sure you'll be seeing more of him," Meghan said. "Well, back to work." With this, she headed out again with her graceful dancer's glide.

*What was that about?*

It was time to go back to my books. Everyone was just a little puzzling here. In a way, history seemed far more logical than real life.

I shrugged as I returned downstairs. Before long, I was again lost in the early 1900s.

## Chapter Eleven

I left the archive a little while before closing time. It was at a convenient stopping point. Tomorrow I'd continue and soon it would be time to head for Mr. Winthrop's rare research room.

Going home immediately would drop me into the start of commuter rush and, anyway, Steve left for the conference earlier and the house would be empty. Della was busy with the Butterflies tonight. Taking a long walk to a more populated neighborhood and hunting down a huge piece of chocolate cake sounded like a good plan.

First, and on an impulse, I wedged into a nearby doorway and fished Geraldine's business card from my purse. I sent her a brief text, saying I'd been accepted at the archive and asking if I could phone her later in the evening or over the next few days to ask some questions about the place. After all, she said to let her know how things worked out. That done, I set off on my walk in search of chocolate cake.

After only a few steps, though, Geraldine responded.

*—r u downtown? drink in half hour?—*

This was much better than chocolate cake. *—yes— just left archive—*

A return text with a location quickly followed.

\*\*\*\*

The Big City Café was anything but big. It was on one of those half streets that was no doubt popular a century ago but had been in hiding ever since, now known only to the local crowd. A long bar with a pitted, yet nicely polished mahogany surface commanded a room warmly lit with strings of 1950s holiday lights. A chaotic mixture of blackboard specials and drinking memorabilia filled the wall behind the bar. The menu's old traditional standbys were etched for eternity on beige walls, providing an eye-catching backdrop to the dozen or so tables scattered throughout the cozy room, their tops neatly dotted with small candles.

The bartender looked in my direction, raising an eyebrow in question. It was only late afternoon and still quiet. I felt a bit out of place.

"I'm meeting a friend," I began.

No more explanation was necessary. At that moment, Geraldine swung through the entrance with energetic force, her emerald tote bag smacking noisily into the doorframe. Her sharp green eyes found me in an instant.

"Emma! Over here," she called out in greeting, indicating one of the miniscule tables by the wall. Nodding to the bartender, she held up two fingers. Obviously, she was no stranger here.

"They make a killer Stormy Hurricane. You'll like it."

*What was a Stormy Hurricane and why was I agreeing to drink it?*

We settled into our chairs. "So how are things in 1918?" I asked, remembering Geraldine's research.

"Ghastly, but good," she replied. "Nothing like a client who's willing to pay me well to stun his readers with such a dreadful subject. At least my landlord is getting the rent on time."

"Maybe your next assignment will be a little more upbeat," I said hopefully.

"Definitely will be. I've got it lined up already—a short history of circus posters. Clowns and elephants after my bout with germs and fever." Geraldine grinned.

"Good for you." I smiled back.

Our drinks arrived, a generous amount of sparkling amber liquid over plump ice cubes.

"So, you're one of the Bauwers crowd now," Geraldine commented as she raised her glass in a toast. "To the Bauwers." She clinked her glass against mine.

"I knew it was the place for you," she continued. "What do you think?"

"I like it." Again, I was surprised at how definite I was. "It's a bit unusual, though."

I took a tentative sip of my Stormy Hurricane. It was surprisingly good, with a snappy tang, maybe ginger, and enough kick to announce its alcoholic content on no uncertain terms.

After a long sip, Geraldine continued. "You're being too nice, Emma. It's more than a bit unusual. They're definitely an odd bunch."

*A bit of irony coming from Geraldine.*

"You probably want the low-down on the major players," she said, smiling appreciatively at her glass.

I nodded. It was almost as if no time had passed at all since our conversation at New York Public Library. Geraldine launched into the subject. There was no need for prompting.

"It's been a while since I was there to get the scoop

for my article, but I do remember them well. A few people really stood out. I'm assuming you've spent time with Ms. Tipton."

Again, I nodded, more relaxed as a few sips of the Stormy Hurricane started to take hold. The flickering candle on the table added to the drink's calming effect.

"The joke was that her first name is 'Ms.' " Geraldine laughed generously. "She was born to be in that place. Interviews everyone. Wants to know what they're working on, what they've found, what it means. Makes you wonder if she has any outside life."

*And what would that outside life be like?*

She continued. "Well, ditto Mr. Winthrop. He probably sleeps there. It wouldn't shock me if he keeps some of the rare items in a big box with a mousetrap attached. The man is obsessed, always worrying about someone pilfering something valuable. As if there are hordes of people desperate to lift a fan used by Mrs. Vanderbilt or one of Lucretia Bauwers' corsets."

I was beginning to enjoy Geraldine's entertaining monologue. Or maybe it was the Stormy Hurricane kicking in.

"Ms. Tipton and Mr. Winthrop seem totally dedicated," I commented. "They can't be in it for the salaries. I doubt those are too high."

"You'd think," responded Geraldine. "But it seems that old Miss Bauwers planned to provide quite well for some of those pivotal staff positions. A letter to this effect is in one of the display cases somewhere. You should take a look."

She signaled for another round. It seemed that Thom, the bartender, regularly provided bar-to-table service for Geraldine. While we waited, I launched into my story of checking out the display room, only to be surprised by Harlan Bauwers. She gave a substantial whoop of laughter. A weathered guy at the end of the bar momentarily jolted upright at the sound. The next minute, though, he sank back into the depths of his coat collar, returning total concentration to his drink.

"That's a good one. Yes, old Harlan Bauwers keeps close watch and has been known to do the surprise entrance. Probably fancies himself a latter-day Barrymore." Geraldine gestured into the atmosphere, her silver bracelet glinting in the candlelight. "Take a careful look at the displays. You'll have better sense of it all. How's your research going anyway?"

"I'm just beginning. I spent some time in the stacks, but I'm going to begin reading through some diaries in rare research. A few belonged to people whose names were circled in the newspapers I found in my family's things."

"Find anything useful in the stacks?"

"Not a lot. But it's a start. It's like going through a long, confusing tunnel."

"Keep going," counseled Geraldine. "There'll be a light at the end, and it might come as a total shock." She sipped her drink thoughtfully. "Also, instead of only concentrating on the names and events in the circled articles, why don't you read some of the other pieces in those issues and look up some of those people and places. Sometimes that random type of thing can point you in a good direction. You'll find answers to questions you never even thought to ask."

"Thanks. I'll give that a try."

By now I was totally relaxed. We were happily sailing through Stormy Hurricane number two and had put a sizeable dent in the bowl of spicy pretzels that Thom brought for us.

It was easy to fill Geraldine in on everything now. She seemed extremely interested in the goings-on at the Bauwers.

"So Alan Renleigh is still researching his social organizations?"

"You mean he was doing that when you were there?"

"He's probably been using the archive forever," Geraldine said. "If you ask me, he should have enough material for three books on the subject by now. I figure he's just a rich guy who likes old, dusty places. Who knows what he's actually written, if anything." Geraldine dismissed the idea with an idle shake of her head.

"Oh." That was a curious tidbit.

"Same with the Lady of the White Gloves. Heaven knows what she's been doing with those photographs, but I'm guessing it's some sort of obsession. She and Renleigh are probably bored, or just a little cracked, or both."

I laughed as Geraldine continued.

"How's Hedgehog?"

"Who?" I asked, perplexed.

"The guy with the weird whiskers."

"Oh, right. I know who you mean. I saw him in the research room."

Geraldine smiled. "I have no idea what his real name is, but I think he's researching Teddy Roosevelt." She was obviously enjoying her reminiscences about the Bauwers people.

"Who's the woman with the magnifying glass?

Sort of a female Sherlock Holmes?"

"She must be new," suggested Geraldine. "And I'm glad they're getting new people. Otherwise, I really do wonder how they keep going. They've got to be running low on funds by now, and I doubt that they've had much in the way of grants or new contributions."

We continued munching on the delicious, spicy pretzels, washing them down with our drinks. I filled her in on my tour with Meghan and on Joe's many problems with building repairs.

"Joe must also be new. He wasn't there a few months ago when I brought in a finished copy of my article. There was some older guy in that job who might have retired or died. I remember Meghan, though. She seems like a nice enough sort. Maybe she's got a crush on Alan Renleigh. You know—the smooth, older guy thing. It wouldn't be a first for that kind of deal."

We were nearing the end of our Stormy Hurricanes and pretzels. This made me sad.

"So tell me, has Baxter worn off his Adam's Apple yet?"

"No," I answered, thinking about his nervous throat stroking, "but he's trying hard."

Again, we both started laughing. By now, the weathered guy at the bar was used to our raucous outbursts. He didn't even look up.

"Baxter is afraid of his own shadow and, more likely, he's intimidated by his own family's shadows. Evidently his parents are high-powered academic types, and Baxter has been desperately trying to measure up and finish his dissertation before—what's the deadline these days—twenty years?" Geraldine chuckled at her own joke before continuing. "Sure hope he nails it before he expires of anxiety." She readjusted her thick black braid. It caught a red glint from one of the strings of overhead Christmas bulbs.

"What's it about?" I asked, genuinely curious. "We haven't had a chance to talk yet."

"You will. He's anxious to be helpful. His topic's urban transportation at the turn of the century. You know, horse and buggy meets automobile and subway."

Geraldine glanced at her watch and motioned to Thom. "I need to get going," she announced suddenly. "Off to a lecture on historic medical practices. I might pick up some useful details for my article."

I reached for my wallet but she waved me away.

"This one's mine. We're discussing research, right? Tax deductible for me." Geraldine's green eyes sparkled. "Keep in touch, Emma. And keep your eyes open in that den of oddballs."

Then Geraldine strode off, her thick braid swinging buoyantly. Only then did I realize I had forgotten to mention the muggings.

My sleep that night, if you could call it that, was filled with shadowy dreams of a party in the archive's open stacks. Thom, the bartender from the Big City Café, was giving out enormous glasses of Stormy Hurricanes, tangy bubbles floating high above their rims. The Lady of the White Gloves stared at her gloveless hands; and Baxter paged through an oddly shaped book while continuously stroking his throat. Meghan asked everyone in a hushed voice, "Where is Mr. Renleigh?" My neighbor's dog Chester appeared at the end of every aisle, but when I ran to him, Mr. Winthrop took his place, looking over the top of his thick glasses.

"You're searching for the wrong thing," he told me sternly.

Chapter Twelve

"I guess you're Emma." The young woman seated at the table inside the archive's front door raised her prominent fake eyelashes and slightly lowered the paperback novel she was reading. Judging by its cover—a sun-drenched scene featuring a passionately embracing couple—its contents had little to do with scholarly research.

"Hi, I'm Ashley," she continued.

Ah, the college intern.

After returning her greeting, I told her that my friend would be coming to the archive before closing time and would wait for me in the Victorian parlor. Ashley made a note of it, lowered her eyelashes, and went back to her book.

It was already 9:00 a.m. sharp, and I was determined to fully use every moment of the Saturday half-day hours. Della was excited to meet me here later. We'd then go uptown for a late lunch and then window shopping. Now I barreled down the hallway, eager to get started. I was halfway toward the research room when Baxter and I abruptly collided.

"Oh! I'm so sorry, Emma!"

"It's okay. No problem." He seemed genuinely flustered, and I had the urge to pat his arm to make him feel better.

"I'm on my way to the research room," I continued

cheerily. "Maybe you could help me. It'll be my first time requesting materials there. I've been mainly using the open stacks till now."

Baxter eagerly jumped at this opportunity to help.

"Of course. We'll need to fill out the request forms with the proper details."

Was Baxter really this excited about routine rules and procedures? It appeared so.

"There's a few old diaries I'd like to read," I said. "But I don't know if it would take several hours or several days to go through them."

"No problem, no problem." Baxter liked to repeat himself. "Mr. Winthrop can set aside any research items you're not finished with until the next time you're here. They'll be safe."

I had no doubt about this.

Baxter proved to be quite helpful and within a short space of time, I joined ranks with Millicent—a.k.a., Lady of the White Gloves—Hedgehog, and Sherlock Lady in the research room, all under the watchful scrutiny of Mr. Winthrop. Each time I looked up, his words from my dream echoed in my head: "You're searching for the wrong thing."

I shook off the dream memory and stared at the two time-worn diaries now in front of me. Each was small and rather dainty, the edges of their brown pages crumpled with time. The elaborate handwriting inside was of the same vintage as the diary pages in my possession. Although I was becoming better at interpreting this style of penmanship, it still offered a challenge, especially with ink fading over the years.

Each of these diaries matched names circled in the newspaper articles. Though I'd never heard of these people before, I thought their words might offer some solid clues about my own diary pages and perhaps help me uncover the identities of Abigail, Greta, and the diarist herself.

The first volume belonged to someone who'd obviously led a wealthy and privileged existence. But she only offered a retelling of the everyday life of social gatherings and innocuous family gossip. No familiar events or individuals were mentioned. No possible clues or connections. Disappointed, I set it aside and plunged into the next.

In Diary Number Two, a woman named Carrie wrote of a far more fascinating life than that of her socialite counterpart. From a well-off Midwestern family, she came to New York to seek adventure. Her job in a department store brought her in touch with some intriguing people. And she seemed well versed on the latest trends in fashion, home décor, and the arts. Her name had been circled in a 1903 marriage announcement in my old newspapers. *But what did it mean?*

I jotted down a few notes, more out of personal curiosity than anything else. Why were their names circled in the first place? There were no details about jewelry or events or anything else that would have been useful, leaving me with more questions than answers.

The morning dwindled quickly, and the archive closed at 1:00 p.m. Everything else would have to wait until Monday. I returned the diaries to a solemn Mr. Winthrop.

"How did you do? Did you find anything that was helpful?" asked Baxter, who suddenly appeared behind me when I reached the main hallway.

"Not yet. I'm still looking for connections." I then shared some additional details about the items I'd inherited.

Baxter pondered for a moment, stroking his throat. I found it difficult to remain serious while he was doing this as I recalled Geraldine's comments. At the same time, I felt sorry for him. He appeared awkward and somewhat lost. But he was genuinely interested in my cast of characters and most willing to help me. Of course, this was his job.

"I'll play with some of these names in our holdings and on the internet and see if I can come up with anything that might be useful," he offered. He pulled out an index card from a small assortment in his shirt pocket and jotted down some details as well as additional notes on some of my family memorabilia, including a couple of the circled headlines. I doubted he'd find much with the limited information I offered.

"I don't want to put you to any trouble," I told him. "I'm afraid I don't have a lot of solid facts to go on."

"That's what we're here for." Baxter smiled. He certainly was dedicated to his job.

I headed for the Victorian parlor. Della was already there, sitting on the pretty floral sofa, the green streaks in her side-swept bangs softly glowing in sunlight that shone through the lacy curtains. Next to her sat Joe. They were deep in conversation.

"Hi, I see you found it!" I said by way of greeting my friend.

Then I turned to Joe. "Thanks for keeping Della company."

"No problem at all," he said with a bright smile.

"I'll go grab my jacket and be back in a minute." I

fled down the hall, feeling awkward.

Della and Joe looked so happily engrossed in their conversation that I felt guilty about making them cut it short. On the other hand, it was almost Saturday closing time at the archive. Others in the building were already heading toward the front door.

I slowed and then pulled out my mauve-colored corduroy jacket, taking extra time to button it up. When I couldn't dawdle any more, I turned at the precise moment Alan appeared.

"Emma! I had no idea you were here today. What a wonderful surprise." He smoothly grasped both my hands as I stepped aside to allow him access to the closet.

"Were you in the research room today? I didn't see you down in the stacks."

"Yes. I needed to check out some diaries," I answered quickly. His way of showing interest in everything I had to say was both engaging and awkward.

"We really do need to sit down and chat. Are you heading out now?"

"A friend is waiting for me… Maybe some other time."

"Next week, then. Promise?"

I managed a wordless smile, feeling even more awkward now.

"Here," continued Alan, smoothly guiding me by the elbow. "Let me walk you down the hall." Meghan and Baxter now followed right behind us.

When we all arrived at the Victorian parlor, Della and Joe still lingered in conversation. Thrust into the role of mistress of ceremonies, I quickly introduced

Della.

"You must be the friend with the very lively grandchildren," smiled Meghan. "Emma's told all of us how great they are."

Della was beaming. "They certainly are energetic," she said. "But they're a lot of fun."

Ms. Tipton peered into the room on her way out, her gaze lingering a moment on Della. She waved briefly but didn't stop to talk. It was closing time, and we all said our goodbyes.

Della and I headed to the subway. We decided on having lunch at a small restaurant uptown, a place we'd been eager to try for a while.

"Ah," began Della the moment we grabbed among the last of the remaining subway seats. The lilt of humor in her voice was clear, even over the roar of the train. "So that's Alan. Quite handsome, and quite taken with you."

"Which is making me extremely uncomfortable," I confessed.

"I can imagine." Della was trying hard to suppress a smile.

"Why is he so anxious to get together and 'compare notes'?" I asked, making imaginary quotation marks with my fingers.

"Maybe it's not research notes that he wants to compare," joked Della.

"Very funny," I said, adjusting the sleeve of my jacket and then tilting my head a little farther in Della's direction so she could hear me over the train's rumble. "Looks as if you and Joe hit it off well." Now it was my turn to flash my brightest smile.

Della responded immediately. "Joe is such a nice

guy. I got to the archive early, and he happened to pass by the parlor, and we got to talking." She paused for a minute until a muffled announcement ended. "Did you know he likes old movies? And baseball? And he has a couple of grandchildren around the same age as the Butterflies. His wife died a few years ago, and he spends a lot of time with those kids now." She took a deep breath. "We really hit it off…"

"I sense there's an *and* to your sentence?"

Della smiled almost shyly. "Okay, okay. *And* we're going out to dinner next week."

The train screeched to a halt, punctuating Della's last words. We quickly exited.

"Wow!" It was hard to hide my surprise. "You guys must have really clicked."

Della didn't trust easily and didn't go on dates often since her divorce several years ago. When she did, the men rarely passed muster. She just met Joe. This was a true first for her.

"We really did, Emma. For once, I didn't have warning bells going off in my head."

We started up the stairway, trailing others who'd also gotten off at this stop. When we reached the street, I grabbed her hand and squeezed it.

"I like him, Dell. It'll be fun for you two to go out to dinner together."

We continued to chat about Joe until we reached the restaurant. By the time we sat down, the conversation turned to the craziness of my project and my impromptu cocktails with Geraldine. Then Della filled me in about the latest news with the Butterflies. After this, it was an afternoon to put aside any serious talk and just enjoy a nice post-lunch walk and some window shopping in the beautiful fall weather.

****

*Quack-quack!* I'd barely reached the front door that night when my cell phone sounded its distinctive ring. Ralph.

"Did you forget about me? Didn't you get my voicemail?" Ralph always wanted instant responses to his calls. Make that instant responses to everything.

"I was busy today, Ralph. It didn't sound urgent. I went to the archive and then out to lunch in the city with Della."

"Well, not urgent, I guess. First, you remember about our Halloween party, right?"

"Yes, yes. I remember. And, yes, Ralph, I also remember that if I don't bring several dozen pumpkin cookies to the party, then Dracula or Frankenstein or both will carry me off, or something like that." I kicked off my shoes and settled comfortably into a corner of the sofa.

"Very funny. Yeah, that's about it. Now, there's one other thing."

"What other thing?"

Ralph hesitated for a beat and then his voice took on a more serious tone. "It's Cousin Louise... She's sort of, um, missing."

"*What?*"

"So, here's the story. I called, like I said I would, to invite her to the Halloween party. Her regular phone always goes to voicemail. Then I called the desk at the senior apartment complex where she lives. I got the same sort of run-around you did when you called. There was a private group vacation tour, so forth and so on. But now the trip's over. And here's the thing. Louise didn't come back with the main group."

I jumped up from the sofa and paced from the living room to the kitchen and back again.

"Well, Ralph, didn't you ask where they went? I mean, she's a senior citizen, and she went on an organized group trip. She can't just vanish." I was getting frustrated with Ralph, even though I knew this was unfair. He was just the messenger bearing perplexing news, even if he was my annoying brother.

"Emma, get real. No one said she vanished. And remember, she's a senior citizen, not a prisoner. This is an apartment complex for independent people who just happen to be older. It's not a hospital or a nursing home or anything."

"All right. But she didn't return with the people from the trip?"

Ralph's frustrated sigh was audible. "Not exactly, although it seems as if individual trip extensions sometimes happen." And now Ralph mimicked the woman's voice from the desk. "*I am not at liberty to say anything further.*"

"That could mean anything. Does Louise have a cell phone? We could call her on that."

"The woman didn't say much. As it was, she probably said more than she should have. Basically, it comes down to a privacy issue."

"But we're family."

Ralph sighed again. "Come into the twenty-first century, Em. Being family doesn't count for much unless we're formally named as primary contacts. The apartment complex can't give out information or cell phone numbers, even if she has one. We could just be *saying* we're family. And some people don't even want to hear from their families."

I was floored. I took a moment to digest this information.

"Well, I'm sure she'd want to hear from us. And, Ralph, doesn't it seem odd that Louise disappeared at the very moment we're trying to reconnect with her? And when the whole subject of family memorabilia is a major issue?"

"No." Ralph didn't hesitate. "And she didn't disappear!" Ralph was clearly regretting his choice of the word "missing" earlier in the call. It had a more sinister implication than if he'd just said she didn't return with the original trip group.

"Remember," he continued, "she's been living her own independent life just fine for years. We're sort of walking into the middle of the story. And family memorabilia is only a major issue for you. You're reading way too much into this."

"Jeez, Ralph. Just think about all the possibilities for a minute."

I stared out the front window at the lengthening shadows of dusk. Why hadn't we kept in touch with Louise over the past couple of years? And now Louise was lost. Maybe kidnapped. Maybe being held somewhere for something.

Ralph broke into my riotous thoughts. "Em, I can almost hear you thinking. Before you start jumping to conclusions and dreaming up wild scenarios, just remember there's probably a reasonable explanation for all of this. Okay? Louise is an adult and is obviously able to look out for herself."

I crossed my arms and bit my lip in frustration. I was angry, partially because Ralph could read me so well and, partially, because I knew he was right. Still, I was worried.

"So, what do we do now?" I asked in clipped tones. "What's the exact plan?"

I dug my toes into the carpet. Why was Ralph chiding me for my worries, especially when he seemed concerned, too? And it had been *his* suggestion to reconnect with Louise and, also, to invite her to *his* Halloween party. *He* should be the one to come up with a master plan. Not that I wasn't already thinking of one myself.

Ralph sensed the annoyance in my voice. "Well, I'm not totally sure, but maybe we should check out her apartment complex in person sometime soon. Chat up some of the people who know Louise. Be nice to the powers-that-be and see what we can find out. And I repeat, it's not like she's been reported kidnapped or anything. It's only that she didn't return with the original tour group. No one is worried, but they're not allowed to give out information." He paused for a beat. "Really, I'm not worried. But maybe we should follow up."

"All right, Ralph. How about tomorrow?"

"Tomorrow?"

The pause was significant. There were probably social complications on Ralph's part.

"Tomorrow's Sunday." Ralph hesitated before continuing. "Okay, let's do it early. Louise's place isn't too far for either of us. Why don't we meet there at 12:30?" Again, a pause. "I need to be home before 4:00."

"More seasonal doings?"

A heavy sigh. "My next-door neighbor's football

party."

"Ah." *Football party? Since when was Ralph into football?*

"And just remember, Em. There's a logical explanation for all of this." Ralph was eager to get off the topic of football.

"Well, if it's so logical, then why are we charging to the rescue?"

"We're not rescuing anyone. We're just trying to be good people and good relatives."

"Like we should have been all along," I commented sadly.

Ralph ignored this. "I'll text you the driving directions. Oh, and I'll bring you that envelope of papers and other stuff. See you at 12:30 tomorrow."

I kept pacing through the house after Ralph's call. When was the last time I saw Louise? It seemed like ages ago at some large family reunion-type gathering. Just about everyone there was now either gone, moved, or had drifted away over time. What was once a connected network of people had dwindled to almost nothing.

Louise had been a favorite cousin of my mother's, but my mother passed away a few years ago. *Why did we let our contact with Louise fade? Were we so busy with kids and jobs that we couldn't make a phone call once in a while?* At the same time, though, Louise was building a new life at the apartment complex where she lived after downsizing from her house. *Did everyone downsize?* And if this was the natural flow of things and a story familiar to many families, why did I feel so bad about it?

Chapter Thirteen

"And, again, what is your exact relationship to Mrs. Haley?"

The woman at the gleaming mahogany reception desk spoke in crisp, business-like tones. There was no smile on her face or in her voice. Dressed in a sleek blue suit, her blonde hair in a perfect chignon, she stared disapprovingly at my brown corduroy jacket. Thank goodness I hadn't worn my orange running shoes.

Ralph quickly picked up the conversational ball, eager to be ingratiating.

"Louise and our mother were cousins. They were very close before Mom passed away." He smiled, tilting his head toward the woman in an attempt to establish a friendly connection. The collar of his striped polo shirt looked crumpled. Had he used a comb this morning or just opted for running his fingers through those unruly brown curls?

"I see," said the woman frostily, setting her mouth in a hard line. Ralph's attempt at charm only made it worse. She probably thought we were con artists trying to pull a scam.

"Let me page the weekend manager," she continued. "Perhaps he can clarify this situation. In the meantime, why don't you have a seat in our lounge." She waved us toward a skylight-illuminated sitting area dotted with comfortable couches upholstered in relaxing earth tones. We trudged over to the couch farthest from the reception desk, a perfect spot to view the inviting fireplace. I was impressed. Elegant, both inside and out, the place was clearly well run. There was even a shiny ebony grand piano nearby, a dramatic centerpiece to the room.

"So much for your idea of chatting up the locals," I hissed. "This place is up on their security. They'd have us in handcuffs if we tried talking to anyone without permission."

"You're way too uptight, Em." Ralph smiled in my direction. "I think our friend at the desk likes me. After all, she's getting the manager to talk to us."

"That's ridiculous!" It was all I could do to keep my voice down. "She's probably getting the manager to have us thrown out. You won't be smiling then."

"Everything I said is true. Mom and Louise were close."

"Yeah, but then why does it sound so phony?" I now simmered in a quiet rage.

"Because you're feeling bad we got involved with our own lives and didn't stay in touch with Louise. Did it ever occur to you that Louise got involved with her own life, too, and lost touch with us? And that you, or me, or Louise shouldn't feel bad because that's just what happens sometimes with families?"

I looked up at the skylight and sighed. Ralph was right, although I hated to admit it. "Then why are we here?"

Ralph paused dramatically. "Because if you remember, *you* got so involved with the boxes that I thought it could be good to reconnect with Louise and get her input. And there's nothing wrong with that either."

"And that led *you* to adding Louise to *your* Halloween party list," I countered. "Probably as another reminder to me about the pumpkin cookies."

Ralph burst out laughing and, in spite of myself, so did I.

And then it all happened at once. The woman at the desk rose as a tall man strode briskly out of the administrative offices in our direction. He was all business in his well-cut suit. Within seconds, the automatic glass doors at the entrance parted and several people bustled into the lobby. Two young uniformed men appeared and rushed toward them.

Startled, Ralph and I scrambled to our feet, not sure where to look first.

"May I help you?" the tall man from administration asked of us. He had a most officious voice until mere seconds later, however, when he bellowed, "Hey, wait!"

Ralph ignored the man and grabbed my hand, dragging me to the front door.

"It's okay...thanks," I managed to mumble over my shoulder in a ridiculous effort to be polite, at the same time attempting to wrench my hand from my brother's iron grasp.

I was furious.

"Ralph! What are you doing? Let go! They'll have us arrested." I was ready to kill him. "Let go!" I demanded, yanking my hand free.

"Listen to me, Emma," Ralph said in a quiet, measured tone, "and look over there." He still stared ahead.

"Just a moment," barked the frosty woman from the front desk. She stood firm in our path in an attempt to stop us from reaching the mélange of people at the front door.

"Sorry, sweetheart," Ralph told her, dropping his charm act with the woman. He was all business now. "We know them."

*Sweetheart?*

I looked in the direction Ralph was staring, suddenly realizing that he saw in an instant what I'd missed in my mixture of anger and anxiety.

At the front door two women were being warmly greeted by the young men in uniforms.

"Welcome home, ladies," greeted the first of the pair, as they all shook hands.

"Don't worry," said the other man, possibly to the driver of the car just visible outside the glass door. "We'll bring in their suitcases." The men exited.

By this time, the tall man from administration regained his composure, not to mention his superior tone. "One moment, please," he began. He caught up to us and stood shoulder-to-shoulder with the desk woman. An imposing pair. "You're not authorized…"

"I believe we are," said Ralph, calmly meeting his gaze. Ralph had enough of being treated like a kid or a criminal, or both, by this pair of gatekeepers.

The woman near the door in the chic hot-pink suit circled beyond their ranks. A pair of glittery silver earrings caught the light, complementing her beautifully styled silver pageboy. She flashed a broad smile at both of us.

"Emma? Ralph? What a fabulous surprise!"

*Was it possible?*

She held out her arms, and we both ran to her for a hug. I realized at that moment just how much I'd missed Louise. *And how happy I was that she hadn't disappeared.* Seeing her again brought back so many youthful memories. A single tear ran down my cheek.

"They're family," she calmly told Tall Man and Desk Woman. "Emma and Ralph. We're cousins once removed or twice reconnected. I could never get that family tree jargon straight."

"We're so sorry," said Tall Man, although he didn't look it.

"It's okay." Louise winked at us. "They do a good job of keeping things in order."

The man and woman retreated.

"Here, let me look at the two of you." Louise studied us. "I'd know you anywhere. So, what brings you here? Is everything all right?"

Ralph jumped in. "We tried calling a few times but you were away. I wanted to invite you to come to a Halloween party Sheila and I are having at our new condo. And then we have some questions about some family memorabilia."

"A party? I love parties." Louise was positively glowing.

Parties? How old was she now anyway? I felt twice whatever the age.

"I'm coming," announced Louise. "And what's this about family memorabilia?"

"Oh, Louise. Now isn't the time. You just got home from your trip," I said. Personally, I'd be exhausted from any trip, but Louise looked like a million dollars.

Louise sensed my discomfort. "How about this.

Let's get together for lunch soon, and we'll talk about everything. Sound good?"

Nodding enthusiastically, we all happily agreed and made plans.

****

Later, after getting home, I sat in the family room for a long while and stared out the window thinking about the afternoon. The large catalog envelope Ralph gave me when we met sat unopened in my lap.

Louise seemed so vibrant, so full of life, the same Louise I remembered. She was warm and friendly with us today, as if no time had passed at all. *What had I expected?*

Then I heard Steve's car. The conference was over and so was his time with Hank.

I forgot about Ralph's envelope and ran to the front door. I tried to push away the feeling of dread that was beginning to sweep over me. Steve called briefly over the weekend to say he'd share what was happening, but it was better done in person and not over the phone.

Now I opened the door and watched as Steve walked up the driveway. He made his way slowly, his head bent as if carrying the weight of a trunk instead of his light overnight bag.

"Steve?" I stopped, taken aback by the lines of sorrow on his face.

Dropping his overnight bag to the floor, he hugged me for a long moment.

I insisted he sit and relax. I brought in some red wine for us to sip until he was ready to talk. We settled into the velour cushions of our couch. I ran my fingers slowly over its surface, trying to seek comfort from the soft material. I took a tiny sip of my wine, barely tasting it.

Finally, Steve began. "He admitted it. Hank stole from the business." He let out a heavy sigh before continuing.

"It was pretty intense." He was obviously reliving the scene as he told me the story. "Hank totally broke down. He said he and Susan were having problems, and he started spending money he didn't have on lavish things to win her back. He was desperate." By now Steve's face twisted in pain. "Desperate enough to risk everything professionally and personally."

"But why didn't he just come to you? Why didn't he tell you what was going on?"

"He said he was ashamed." Steve paused. "But it didn't stop him."

I clutched the edge of the sofa cushion so tightly now that I was afraid I might rip out a handful of fabric. I was so angry at Hank for hurting Steve like this.

A tear rolled down my cheek. "I'm so sorry, Steve. I'm so sorry."

Then Steve buried his face in his hands and kept saying over and over, "I never knew."

Chapter Fourteen

Baxter and I collided at the kitchen door, each of us ready to grab our lunch bags from the refrigerator. We were always awkwardly bumping into each other somewhere.

It was a little early for lunch, but concentrating on my research this morning had been a challenge. I couldn't stop thinking about yesterday's events. What a rollercoaster ride after happily reconnecting with Louise to hearing Steve's devastating revelations about Hank. Steve and I talked until almost midnight. The business itself would survive, although Steve would certainly need additional staff. But the partnership, tainted by Hank's outright betrayal, would have to end. And their long-term friendship was in shreds.

Now, Baxter was a welcome interruption to my swirling thoughts.

"Want to eat outside?" he asked. "It's a perfect summer day for autumn." He smiled.

This suggestion seemed quite spontaneous for Baxter who usually ate his bland-looking sandwich quickly and returned to his desk. For such a young man, his face had a pallor that suggested little time spent outdoors, rain or shine. But I was happy for the invitation.

"Okay. Where can we eat?" I asked.

It was a logical question. There was no park nearby

or even a little patch of grass near the building. No seating of any sort lined the street, and the dirty, rubble-strewn empty lot next door wasn't even an option.

Baxter smiled again, a rarity for him. "The front stoop."

"Okay, sounds good," I responded.

We headed outside, waving to Ashley, who was on duty at the front table. She barely acknowledged us, her face buried in the latest tale of romance. The couple on the front cover looked suspiciously the same as the one from the previous novel, although this time the background scene was moonrise on a tropical beach.

Baxter led the way to the middle of the chipped steps outside. We brushed aside some random leaves and found places to sit and securely rest our coffee cups. Then, carefully balancing our brown bags in our laps, we ate. It was a joy to feel the unseasonably warm sun against my face. Even the dilapidated buildings across the street looked appealing, the panes of several broken windows artfully reflecting prisms of blue sky in the noontime light.

"How's your dissertation going?" I asked. Baxter's struggles while working on his project, not to mention his occasional differences of opinion with his academic adviser, were common knowledge at the archive. It made me shudder to think of my daughter Leeann as she began her own graduate studies. I hoped her experience would be more pleasant.

Baxter made a face. "Trust me, it's been slow. If I could change advisers, I'd do it."

"Why can't you?" I surmised that his work on the project was anything but fun. I doubted he was making much progress either. "Maybe a change of adviser could make a real difference."

"Everyone would lose face," he responded dejectedly. "Word would get around, and another professor wouldn't take me on and ruffle the feathers of a colleague. Plus, both my parents are pretty high profile at the school, and it wouldn't look good if I made waves." He sipped his coffee thoughtfully. "I'm sort of trapped at this point."

"That *is* tough," I sympathized. "I hope you can figure it out with the adviser soon."

"That would be nice, but it seems that big clashes over small scholarly issues are common sport in academia."

"Hang in there, Baxter." It seemed as if he needed a friendly ear today.

"I'm trying."

Baxter took a bite of his sandwich and we both sat quietly for a moment. He broke the silence first. "How's your research going? I wanted to tell you I'm sorry I haven't been able to come up with anything too helpful for you yet. There's not a lot to go on at this point."

"I totally understand. Maybe it would help if I fill you in on a little more of what I've been thinking." I took a sip of my coffee. "It almost seems silly, doesn't it? I mean, I told you that I wanted to find the identities of some almost nameless people in my diary pages and connect them to the memorabilia."

"A lot of research seems silly at the beginning," Baxter reassured me.

"Okay," I continued. "But I'm more and more convinced that there were thefts involved way back in the past. I didn't say too much about this before. I was worried. Embarrassed, I guess, that someone way back in my family might have been involved with a criminal."

"Thefts?" Baxter lowered his sandwich for a moment and looked at me closely. "Why do you think that's the case?"

I filled him in more about the circled news articles and the lion head, the pocket watch, and the u-shaped pin. Finally, I leaned forward. "Baxter, this is going to sound crazy, but I think the woman named Abigail stole that jewelry and gave it to one of my ancestors for safekeeping. I guess a lot of it's conjecture." I paused. "But there are a fair amount of coincidences with the jewelry, the diary, and the newspapers."

Baxter continued eating his sandwich as he listened.

A horn sounded in the distance as I continued. "Okay, maybe my 'creature' pin isn't a lion. And I could be over-reacting in making that connection. But listen to this. There was a newspaper article circled about the opening day of the subway in 1904. There was a theft." I paused to take a gulp of my own coffee.

"Sounds no different than today," Baxter commented.

"True. But this was supposedly the first theft in the subway's history, and a man's expensive diamond stickpin was taken. It was shaped like a horseshoe and that's the same as u-shaped, right? I can't find any evidence that it was ever found or if the thief was ever caught."

Baxter didn't register surprise at this event. "Henry Barrett, right? Got on at the 28th Street station and immediately realized his stickpin was gone."

"You know about it?" It had only gotten a couple of sentences in the newspapers. On the other hand, Baxter was studying various forms of turn-of-the-century transportation for his dissertation so he probably knew a lot of random stories like this one.

"Sure. Somewhere I read that it was worth about five hundred dollars back then. I guess that it'd be a lot more today, both monetarily and historically." He looked at me. "Emma, are you saying you think you have *that* stickpin?" His skepticism was obvious. "What would give you that idea?"

"Look, it's just a possibility I've thought about. The pages in the diary mentioned someone watching a man under a streetlight with something gleaming in his...his cravat."

As was his usual habit, Baxter stroked his throat in concentration.

"And," I continued, "there was another entry about someone, maybe a young woman, clutching a ticket of some sort. Well, couldn't it have been a ticket for a first day ride? Plus..." I was warming up now. "The paragraph in the news article about the theft was circled. And that person in the diary named Abigail said she stole something and pressed it into the diarist's hand for safekeeping. And she gave her some other pieces, too. Suppose something happened to Abigail or the diarist, and the stolen items were never identified or returned?"

Baxter looked out at the street. "Are there dates on those diary pages?"

"A couple of them have 1904 and 1905 penciled in at the bottom."

I pulled out my cell phone and scrolled through the

photos of the jewelry. "Look, I know I didn't give you a lot of information before this. But here's a picture of the diamond u-shaped pin. Scroll forward to the photos of the jewels. They seem to match up with some of the other articles." I pointed. "See? That's the creature, or lion's head. And there's the pocket watch."

Baxter scrolled through the photos carefully. Then he looked up. "Sort of intriguing. I don't know about the lion's head, but since my dissertation is about early urban transportation, I could point you to some resources about the subway. Maybe they'll say something about the pin. It's a long shot that it's the real deal. And proving it would be next to impossible. But if your research uncovers some interesting side details, it would make a fine endnote in my project."

*An endnote?* "Thanks," I said as he smiled and handed me the phone.

"Of course, you'd have to trace Abigail's and Barrett's families and so forth."

"Yeah. That's where I could really use your help."

"Tracing that jewelry to old thefts could be a wild goose chase."

"But it's still worth a try, right?" I asked hopefully.

"Maybe." Baxter paused skeptically. "By the way, have you taken the diamond pin and the other pieces to a jeweler to get them assessed for authenticity and value?"

I hadn't thought of this.

We were so engrossed in our conversation that we both jumped when another voice from the bottom of the steps chimed in.

"Diamonds?"

It was Alan Renleigh, speaking casually and with a cheerful smile.

Chapter Fifteen

The next morning, I leafed through historic scrapbooks in the research room. It was slightly easier to concentrate after Steve and I talked again last night. It was a relief to hear about his upcoming meetings with the accountant and lawyer and their practical plans to help—certainly a start, even in the midst of his turbulent personal feelings and mine, as well.

Now, I focused on the scrapbooks. The first belonged to a singer whose name was circled in one of my newspapers. After a modestly successful career, she gave it all up to get married. There were yellowed concert notices and some lovely letters from friends signed by Elsie, Anna, and Josie. But no Abigail. I just couldn't figure out why the scrapbook woman's name was circled. With a frustrated sigh, I decided it was time for lunch.

I was pondering the scrapbook as I poured some coffee and took my lunch to the last available seat in the kitchen. Suddenly, there was a shout.

"I won!" Ashley ran in, waving her hands with the enthusiasm of a cheerleader.

Everyone looked up in surprise. This was probably the most noise the archive had heard in over half a century and also the most crowded I'd seen the kitchen at lunchtime since starting my research here. A captive audience eagerly waited for Ashley's exciting revelation.

"C'mon, tell us," prompted Meghan, her spoon poised in mid-air over a small container of raspberry-flecked yogurt.

"Five hundred dollars! I won five hundred dollars in the lottery!" Ashley's announcement vibrated with excitement.

Applause rang out at this good news.

"You're going to need an armed escort going home," commented Joe between bites of another of his usual mouthwatering hero sandwiches—today, roast beef and spicy cheese.

Ashley stopped short. "Uh, I never thought about that." Then she brightened as she reached over her shoulder, pointing to her overstuffed backpack. "This isn't leaving my sight. And going home, people will never know what's hidden there besides my schoolbooks."

"So, what will you do with your newfound wealth?" Hedgehog made a rare appearance in the kitchen to get a glass of water. All of that research into Teddy Roosevelt must have made him thirsty. I tried not to stare at his long-outmoded facial whiskers.

Ashley scrunched up her face in thought. "I'll do all my holiday shopping...and get some new clothes...and I'm going to buy a few more lottery tickets. Maybe I'll get *really* lucky next time."

Hedgehog toasted these ideas with his water cup and left after draining its contents.

"So if you won really big, what *would* you do?" Meghan posed her question thoughtfully, scooping up the remains of her yogurt.

"Quit school and go on a grand vacation to one of

those tropical islands…"

"Like the ones in those books you read?" asked Joe. We all had to smile at this, having seen the covers of the many romance novels Ashley devoured every chance she got.

"You bet," she said enthusiastically. "And then I'd have adventures."

"Sounds like a plan," said Joe.

"You know what I'd do if I won big?" Meghan seemed caught up in lottery fever now. "I'd go to school full time and then open my own business. Either a gallery or else an art and antique research and appraisal company."

She turned to me now. "Emma, what would you do?"

"Good question. Maybe go to a few conferences for researchers and then set up a nice home office for myself where I could study and write." *Wow! Where did this come from?*

"Baxter," I asked, watching him finish his tuna fish sandwich and neatly capture rye bread crumbs before they spilled onto the floor. "What would you do?"

"Forget my dissertation and not worry about starving on the salary of those academic jobs that appear to be in my future." He gave an ironic laugh.

"I'll bet my college professors would say the same thing," commented Ashley. "What about you, Joe?"

"Get away from it all and take my grandkids on nice trips."

"Sounds like what Emma's friend Della would do for her grandchildren," said Ashley, who'd also heard stories around the lunch table about the twins.

Joe smiled appreciatively at the mention of Della's

name.

Ms. Tipton listened to the conversation while getting a cup of coffee. Now she seemed eager to weigh in on the topic. "I'd renovate the archive if I won a big lottery jackpot. Restore the original charm to the building, and then set up an endowment fund for it."

"That's a really nice idea," I told her, breaking the momentary silence from the group.

Then Ms. Tipton smiled at Ashley. "Congratulations! Use your winnings wisely."

****

Alan turned up later on as I headed for the hall closet to grab my coat. Meghan was already there. Alan helped her into a stylish, smoky-gray jacket.

"Emma! Here, let me help you, too." He removed my coat from the hanger and held it out with a flourish.

"I have an excellent idea," Alan began as the three of us moved toward the front door. "It's still early and if you're both not in a rush, please let me treat you to coffee. There's a new little café a few blocks away."

Frankly, I was surprised there was any sort of café in the immediate area.

Meghan's face lit up, and she answered quickly. "That'd be great!"

Alan turned to me. I was about to say that I had some sort of appointment, but my protective side emerged. I was reluctant to see Meghan go off alone with Alan, even though she was an intelligent young woman. She was around Leeann's age and seemed quite taken with him. I wondered about Alan's motives. *Silly me. It's just my mother instincts kicking in.*

But with this realization, I answered, "Sure, thanks," trying to sound upbeat.

The three of us left the archive and walked a few blocks, the dreary blend of old buildings continuing as we dodged soiled food wrappers the breeze sent in our direction. Thankfully, I'd worn sturdy shoes as broken glass crunched underfoot. *Why would anyone open a café here?*

Without many people on the street, it was easier than usual to keep up our three-way conversation as we walked.

"I can't wait to tell you what I've found, Emma." Alan was enthusiastic.

He really did seem involved with his research into social organizations at the turn of the century. Still, I remembered what Geraldine said about him just being a rich guy with time on his hands.

"It sounds exciting." Meghan was beaming.

"You'll be interested in this, too, Meghan, since you seem to be developing a real affinity for close research and analysis."

*What did he mean by that?*

"And, Emma, I hope you don't mind, but I couldn't help overhearing you tell Baxter about that young thief who is mentioned in your family diary."

*Yeah, it was obvious he'd taken to eavesdropping, just like my brother.*

Alan continued talking as we descended a few steps to the lower level of an old brownstone building where the Café Alabaster was located. Living up to its name, the narrow front window displayed a milky white sculpture—a square sitting on a triangle topped with a lightbulb-shaped form. Art at its most confusing.

"Emma, I believe I found a social organization that can help with Abigail's identity."

I froze at this sudden news. So did Meghan. *He even overheard Abigail's name.*

"Do you mean a women's association or something like that?" I asked, unable to fathom how his research could have had any connection to *my* Abigail.

"Hardly." Alan winked at me. "A women's organization of thieves."

Meghan was quick to respond. "Like a turn-of-the-century girl gang?" Her comment hung in the air as we entered.

The inside of the café did not disappoint. Large, inexplicable alabaster sculptures grew out of alabaster walls—a mask, a flower, a star, an ear, a nose.

We took seats at a small table, and Alan ordered the house specialty for each of us. It had the look and consistency of paint. In reality, it was a smooth, creamy vanilla latte served in large, oblong glasses. I took a sip, eager to get back to our conversation.

"So, Alan," I began, "what was this organization of women thieves?"

"Just that, Emma."

Meghan frowned. "Something like this couldn't really be called an organization in the true sense of the word," she commented, as we tackled our drinks. "At least not the kind of organization you've been researching." She took another sip of her latte. "And you haven't been researching thieves from what you've mentioned before."

Meghan certainly seemed informed on the subject—and on Alan's research.

"But they were organized, weren't they?" continued Alan. "And good at what they did."

"In the last century and a half, this sort of thing

was pretty rampant. Organized in its own way, yes. But not in a traditional sense." Meghan spoke forcefully. "By traditional organizations, I would think of a music society or a gardening club. Not a gang of girl thieves." At the moment, she didn't seem all that taken with Alan and his unusual pronouncements.

I turned to Alan. "You think that someone in a criminal organization of women…umm, girls…might have stolen the jewels that are part of my memorabilia?"

"I'm saying it's a possibility."

Meghan's frustration was clearly visible. "Look." She drummed a finger on the top of the table and studied the surface of her latte for a minute. "From everything Emma's said, nothing would point to this being the work of a gang member. Abigail didn't fit the profile. Also, depending upon the gang, there would have been serious complications getting an outsider involved like the diarist. Especially if the loot had to be turned over to a leader such as the Queen of Thieves, the woman who ran a school for street urchins to learn petty crime. And the dates for that certainly don't match either." Meghan looked at me. "It still seems more likely that Abigail was working out a personal situation, not doing hard core theft. There had to have been more to her story."

I was ashamed to have thought Meghan needed a chaperone. It was obvious that she had knowledge and opinions, and she wasn't afraid of speaking up. Meghan could hold her own.

But why was an art student and archive assistant knowledgeable on this subject? *Could Meghan have been in a modern-day girl gang?* I shook off this appalling thought as ridiculous.

Alan seemed at a loss for words, and I was beginning to think that his big revelation was nothing more than an excuse to socialize, not to offer any really helpful research. *And why was he so desperate to socialize?* Meghan seemed offended by his premise and lack of solid details.

I felt it was up to me to say something to ease the situation.

"Hey, thanks, Meghan. It's sort of a relief to know that Abigail doesn't appear to have been a lifelong thief. My diarist either."

Meghan gave me a grateful glance, brushed aside her bangs, and finished her latte.

Then I turned to Alan. "I really appreciate your taking time to think about my research and trying to come up with a connection for me."

He flashed a somewhat deflated smile. "My pleasure, Emma. I'll keep trying. Maybe I'll have better luck next time."

Then Alan turned to Meghan. For once, it was difficult to read the tone of his words. His charming façade dropped for a moment.

"You certainly seem to know a lot about gangs and crime."

Meghan shot back quickly, "You'd be surprised at what you learn working in an archive."

Chapter Sixteen

"Did you hear what happened?"

I'd just waved to Ashley and began pulling my right arm from my coat sleeve when Alan approached. He seemed genuinely agitated. Perhaps over yesterday afternoon's conversation about girl gangs? But when Ms. Tipton marched down the hall in our direction, I realized that it must be something far more serious.

"Something happened?"

"I just found out. Poor old Mr. Bauwers..." began Alan.

Ms. Tipton joined us and picked up the conversation from there. Her intense brown eyes were serious and fixed on me. "Mr. Bauwers was taken to the hospital last night."

"I'm so sorry." I'd only met the elderly man once and still pictured him slowly making his way over to formally introduce himself to me, his cane steadying the path.

"Please keep him in your thoughts," Ms. Tipton said. "I need to tell the others." She abruptly turned and left.

Alan reached out and took my hand. Like all of Alan's gestures, it made me uneasy.

"I'm worried about him, of course," he began. "But I'm also thinking about how this will affect the archive."

Harlan Bauwers' love of the archive was well known.

"What do you mean?" I wanted to move away, but curiosity kept me at a standstill.

"Well, he's one of the main reasons this has stayed open for so long."

"Alan," I replied, removing my hand and resting it casually on the doorknob of the coat closet. "Why is the archive dependent on Mr. Bauwers?"

"Because he's the last of the original family. I mean, there's his son, but he isn't interested in archives. What's going to happen now if Mr. Bauwers can't come home here?"

I thought back to my original conversation with Geraldine. She'd mentioned that Harlan Bauwers' son would probably sell the building and property when his father was gone. But Harlan wasn't gone; he was only in the hospital. Maybe it was temporary. And what business was it of mine to get too involved in the whole thing? *And what business was it of Alan's?*

Baxter and Millicent came out of the research room and walked solemnly in our direction. Millicent clutched her hands together tightly. The stones of her unusual ring were still invisible, probably turned toward her palm as they had been that first day I met her.

"You heard?" Baxter half-asked and half-stated.

"We did," I said. "I hope he'll be better soon." What else was there to say?

"He will be greatly missed," commented Millicent, almost as if Harlan had departed permanently. She seemed visibly upset. "It was all so sudden." *What did that mean?*

"Come, Millicent," urged Baxter. "Let me get you

a cup of tea."

They walked toward the kitchen, just as Meghan and Hedgehog joined us.

"Sad news," said Hedgehog, shaking his head, the motion emphasizing his bushy whiskers. "I really liked the man."

*Why was everyone speaking as if Harlan Bauwers was dead?*

"He's quite elderly, Emma," Alan persisted. "You knew he had a helper who came in to clean and cook for him several days a week?"

"No, but you've got to remember that I've only been here for a very short time."

"Well, he did have help. She just came in through a private entrance. And I overheard this morning that she's probably not coming back."

"You might have overheard wrong," Meghan quickly interjected. "Eavesdropping rarely tells the full story."

The previous day's discomfort between the two seemed alive and well. And who had Alan been eavesdropping on? And why? Didn't he want to concentrate on his research?

"Look," I broke in. "I'm sure we'll find out more in the next few days. Why don't we all go back to our research. It'll take our mind off things. There's really nothing we can do."

Alan nodded. "You're right, Emma." Then he reluctantly headed down the hall and disappeared through the door to the stacks without responding to Meghan's previous retort.

"He's only worried about the status of the archive," commented Meghan.

"So I gathered."

Our conversation was cut short as Sherlock Lady walked past us shaking her head.

"Shocking! Such a nice old man." With that she headed toward the restroom. I'd never heard her utter a word before. Obviously, Harlan Bauwers was much loved as an individual or as the main reason for the archive's existence. Either way, the situation seemed tenuous.

I passed Ms. Tipton's office on my way down the hall. She was sitting quietly and staring into space. Shaking my head, I hurried to the research room, hoping to look at a few more scrapbooks before leaving a little earlier for an appointment to have the jewelry assessed.

Even though I was clueless about the details, it seemed quite clear that Harlan Bauwers' situation had a far-reaching impact, one that went deep beneath the surface. *And what exactly had been the cause of his sudden admission to the hospital?* In turn, this reminded me that I'd never learned anything about that second mugging that made Meghan so uncomfortable.

Chapter Seventeen

"I'm an idiot!"

Della's eyebrows shot up at my dramatic greeting. I slid into the empty chair opposite her at Reese's and buried my face in my hands.

"Can't be that bad," she responded calmly, pouring me a cup of hot cocoa from the steaming pot she'd just ordered. Based on the text I sent earlier, Della already had a clue as to what was wrong.

"I was so sure they were the real thing. Della, they're all fake. Really fake! Not just the diamond pin. The pocket watch, too! And the creature...lion...alien...whatever. This is beyond embarrassing." I slid my hands down my face, smudges of makeup coloring my palms.

"Hot chocolate will definitely help." Della pointed to my cup, urging me to drink. "Let's review the facts here. There's been no natural disaster, no injury, or no..."

"Theft," I finished for her. "There was no theft! Or else the thief was an even bigger idiot than me."

I took a sip of hot chocolate. Its warmth together with Della's calm presence was comforting. Still, facts were facts. The jewels were fake.

"And after all my research, what do I have to show for it? Nothing! What kind of theft was this? How much do you want to bet that the diary was just the work of a kid who was goofing around. Like me when I was ten. I wrote in my diary that a pirate lived in our backyard. Maybe this was a child entertaining herself, and I've just gone on an idiotic wild goose chase."

"It's not idiotic," Della said. "I wrote in my diary that I was a princess in disguise as a regular kid in Yonkers. But I was really on a mission to save the world from an invasion by creatures from another planet."

I had to smile in spite of myself. "That was pretty good."

Della smiled and went on. "Oh, and in another two or three years, I forgot about saving the world and started writing that Raymond—the kid with the curly blond hair who sat in the next row in math class—was madly in love with me. Now *that* was imaginary!"

I sighed. "Okay. We both did the same sort of thing. I don't know about you, but I tore up all the pages of those diaries and threw them away. I certainly didn't want anyone reading my ridiculous entries a year later, no less a hundred years later." I sipped some more hot chocolate.

"Seriously, Emma. Stop to think about it. The contents of the diary pages you found had some pretty serious stuff in it. No princesses or pirates. Greta and her babies didn't come from the imagination of a ten-year-old," said Della.

"That's true," I agreed, thinking of that heart-wrenching entry.

"Em, you still have a mystery. Even if the jewelry's fake, there's got to be some good explanation for the pages and the circled newspaper articles, and how the jewelry, fake or not, figures in. It's still worth researching. There's more to it than that."

Della had a point. I still had my mystery along with a big helping of embarrassment.

I twisted my floral paper napkin in frustration. Della waited for me to go on.

"At least I had solid reasons for thinking the jewelry was stolen. But now they seem about as solid as the reasons I had for saying there was a pirate living in my backyard."

Della smiled. "Even your pirate idea probably had solid reasons at the time."

I sighed. She was right, of course, but now I had another worry.

"I'll tell you what's not fake. The reactions I'll get when I go back to the Bauwers and confess that I've been on a ridiculous mission to return stolen jewels that aren't even real. Especially when I tell Baxter. He suggested getting them assessed by a jeweler. You'd think this would have been the first thing that would have occurred to me when I started." I tapped the table in frustration. "Of course, I was better off when I started because I hadn't talked about the whole possible theft thing. In the beginning, all I said was that I was trying to trace some ancestors and possibly return some items to the heirs of some of their friends. Leave it to me to go and share my complete theft-and-intrigue story and turn out to be an *idiot* in the process!"

Della leaned forward. "I understand how you feel, but you don't have to tell any of them right away. Remember, you're still trying to discover the identities of the diarist and Abigail and how they relate to your family." She paused. "There's more going on here, Emma. There's a piece of the puzzle we're both missing. I still think the diary pages and the jewelry, even if it's fake, mean something. Although I do have to say, it all looks pretty real."

"You're probably right, Dell, but, for the life of me, I can't figure out what it means. And the jewelry does shine so beautifully under the light, too. It looks so authentic and expensive. But I guess there's just no figuring."

We sat quietly for a few moments, grasping the handles of our floral cups and staring into their depths, as if the answer lurked in those last drops of hot chocolate.

Chapter Eighteen

The warmth in her eyes was magnetic, radiating a quiet compassion and fully lighting up a plain, yet appealing face. The high neckline of her modest, long-sleeved black dress was accentuated with only a single coral brooch. One hand rested in her lap, gracefully displaying a unique twin-stoned ring. But it was the expression in her eyes that drew me in.

I'd been heading up the stairs to revisit the display room. Truthfully, I needed a place to think after the startling revelation about the worth of the jewelry, or lack of it. *What had I been thinking when I dreamed up this fantasy of stolen jewelry, rightful heirs, and historic intrigue?*

If I hadn't specifically requested some materials from Mr. Winthrop in advance, I might have stayed home today. Despite Della's logical encouragement, I was deflated and planned to quietly drift away from the archive. But since I promised to come in today anyway, I wanted another look around, especially in the display room, before I was willing to let it all go.

I'd seen the Bauwers' family portrait gallery before, of course, but today that first compelling portrait stopped me. Her compassion seemed to reach out, even though more than a century separated us. Underneath was a simple brass nameplate: Elizabeth Bauwers.

I contemplated Elizabeth for a full few moments before moving on, eager to take a closer look at the others. What struck me was the sharp distinction between Elizabeth's likeness and that of Lucretia Bauwers, several steps higher on the ascending side wall. The difference was in the contrasting personalities of the individuals themselves that radiated through their faces.

Lucretia's eyes were also brown; yet they met the viewer with unabashed determination. Like Elizabeth, she was young, and they both had the same aquiline nose and dark, pulled-back hair. In Lucretia's case, though, these features blended together with an almost regal force. She was dressed in a fashionable black gown, its low, square-cut neckline set off with an unusual blue-stoned pendant that sparkled prominently against flawless skin. Short sleeves highlighted her slender forearms. They formed a striking pose, her long, elegant fingers clasped together and decorated with several jewel-encrusted rings.

Lucretia had been the driving force behind the archive. Her strong personality seemed to transcend the canvas. In addition to her brass nameplate, a short, descriptive paragraph displayed on the wall next to her portrait stated that she had "created this archive for the continuing research and study into the vast and enriching history of turn-of-the-century New York City."

Yet, what of Elizabeth? No descriptive material accompanied her portrait. Who was she? A sister? Probably Lucretia's sister. The facial features were similar.

Ashley broke into my reverie as she swung around

the upstairs corner, swiftly heading down the stairs in my direction. Her arms embraced a thick batch of file folders.

"This'll take a year for that guy to read through," she fumed.

"Who?" I asked, curious.

"You know, the guy with the weird whiskers. Mr. Winthrop said to get these for him *pronto*. As if the files were going to run away. He's got enough to read already."

I laughed.

"I mean, it's all stuff about Teddy Roosevelt. How long has he been dead anyway?" Ashley didn't even pause before answering her own question. "Probably over a hundred years. So what's the big rush?"

"The man must be a dedicated researcher," I offered, amused by Ashley's annoyance—probably more with Mr. Winthrop's edict of "pronto" than with the researcher's request. I assumed that the researcher in question was "Hedgehog," so aptly code named by Geraldine.

"Oh, he's dedicated," continued Ashley, taking a few more steps down the stairs. "There are at least twenty pounds of files here. And they don't usually let me go into the rare storage rooms, but these files had already been pulled, and they needed a packhorse to carry them."

She stopped for a brief moment to catch her breath. "Looking at those paintings?" she asked. She inclined her head in the direction of the third and final portrait closest to the top of the stairs. "That guy gives me the creeps."

With that, Ashley ran down the remaining stairs

with a breezy, "see you later, Emma."

I turned to look at Prescott Bauwers, a formidable individual. Seated bolt upright in a sturdy chair, his dark frock coat, high forehead, and stern expression all screamed no-nonsense. He looked harshly in the direction in which his chair was facing. Was he observing something or someone who posed a threat? Or was this just his way, humorless and maybe even a touch ruthless? The description accompanying his portrait identified him somewhat vaguely as "a leading businessman, industrialist, and member of New York society."

The artist for father and daughters was certainly a master as well as an astute judge of human nature. He brought the singular essence of each of his subjects to vivid life.

I pried myself away and headed for the display room, trying to shake off the lingering impact of the portraits. More than compelling, they were disturbingly haunting.

Chapter Nineteen

"Nothing makes sense," I complained, almost oblivious to the stunning backdrop of autumn leaves and unusual warmth of the October morning sun in the park.

Della and I agreed to spend an hour with the Butterflies in the kids' playground. We chatted as I pushed Joy on one of the swings while Della took charge of Julie on another.

"Cents!" screamed Joy, after hearing me say "sense" and drawing the conclusion that coins were the topic of the day. "I have ten cents in Mr. Piggy Bank."

"Me, too! Me, too!" Julie joined in the chorus.

"That's nice, ladies," laughed Della. "You just keep doing a great job on the swings."

"But we want to play with the animals now." The girls spied some green plastic dinosaurs and suddenly lost interest in the swings.

"Animals!"

"Yay!"

We helped them off the swings and brought them to the sandy plot where several small dinosaurs of varying species smilingly awaited. They climbed on the animals, holding animated conversations with them, certain the dinosaurs fully comprehended. This allowed Della and me a few minutes to chat on a nearby bench.

"Ralph gave me a huge envelope of stuff on

Sunday," I began with a sigh, noting the caked dirt on my orange running shoes, which had done little running up to this point.

"Stuff? That sure sounds like a Ralph-ism."

"You're right about that. He said he found some more miscellaneous things when he and Sheila moved, including some embroidered handkerchiefs and a big catalog envelope filled with scraps of paper. It didn't sound like much, and I guess I sort of forgot about it on Sunday after we met Louise and then Steve came home. Now I'm not even sure I want to look at it."

"Wait a minute." Della was taken aback. "You haven't opened any of it yet?"

I lowered my eyes. "I guess I'm still upset after finding out about the jewelry being fake. And then I went back to the archive yesterday to take one more look. I think it's time to call it quits." I paused to take a deep breath of lovely autumn air.

"Emma! You can't call it quits! Forget about the jewelry. You still have research to do. Open that envelope!!! Do *not* give up on this!" Several people turned at Della's emphatic words.

"I don't know. Suppose it's just what it appears to be? A batch of old stuff. Moldy papers and scraps of fabric and fake things that mean nothing to anyone anymore."

"C'mon," said Della, more quietly. "You know that's not true. You have to keep going."

Della was vigorous in her support, even after the jewels were assessed as fake. Much as I appreciated this, it was hard to get over my gloom.

"Dell, it's probably time for me to get back to everyday life and get another job or volunteer

*"Of course."*

*"But first, I must ask, what is that lovely bowl with the golden scallops on the highest shelf?"*

*"That is to be used for decorative purposes or as an accompaniment to an elegant afternoon tea."*

*"May I see it, please? And you must tell me. If you were to receive a gift of this nature, which would you choose—a fashionable vase or the beautiful scalloped bowl?"*

"Wait a minute!" Della shouted. "A bowl with golden scallops? Just like…"

"The one over there," I finished for her, pointing toward a bowl near the wall.

"And a fashionable vase?" she continued.

"Yeah, there's a vase." I again pointed. "Would that be considered fashionable?"

A whoop of laughter rang out from the girls. "Look at us!"

Now they picked up the pace, trying on hats and then playing with the glittery masks.

"Please be careful," pleaded Della, torn between keeping an eye on the twins and looking at the papers from the envelope. Glitter drifted lazily from the masks.

Della was frantic now. The girls were hovering seriously close to some breakable objects. "Why don't you draw a picture of yourselves wearing the hats?" she called out.

Even though they began drawing, we knew it wouldn't be for long.

Soon, a shout pierced the air as the twins ran toward us. "Look at our hats," said Julie, waving her drawing. Joy followed but tripped over a tall pile of magazines from the trunk. She fell face-first on the carpet, and magazines scattered in all directions. A small whimper sounded.

Della scrambled off the floor and raced over. Joy wasn't hurt, but she was startled and crying softly. Della picked her up and spoke to her quietly.

I ran over to them. "Are you okay, Joy?"

The little girl nodded. "I'm sorry," she said pitifully.

"It's all right," I assured her. "You and Julie want some more cookie treats?"

Joy brightened. So did Julie, who'd been watching the action with interest.

"Here, let me help you pick these up," said Della, heading for the magazines. "And then it's time for us to leave. Cookies will have to be for the road. Sorry for the mess, Emma."

"Don't worry about it, Dell. It's okay. I'll straighten up later. Not a problem. And, anyway, I have to leave soon for our lunch with Louise."

We gathered the drawings, and I gave the girls some cookies. Then I hugged all of them.

"Keep on going," whispered Della at the door.

I didn't have much time, so I picked up a few scattered magazines, closing some that fell open when Joy tripped.

With a quick glance, I could see that the tables of contents were filled with titles echoing another century. I had to laugh as I read a few, closed the covers, and replaced them in the pile.

That was when one of the titles caught my eye. I froze. It was a story entitled "The Boarding House" by A. E. Waters.

Chapter Twenty

Luminaire was charming. Soft candles and delicate pink and white flowers set in sparklingly clear glass bowls decorated the muted rose-colored tablecloths. Polite servers kept a subtle, yet attentive distance, allowing us to chat comfortably. A soothing piano recording lingered unobtrusively in the air, providing a relaxing background for our lunch.

"So, Louise." Ralph spoke first. "Tell us about your trip." Part of Ralph's game plan consisted of getting Louise to talk first so he could concentrate on the delicious hot popovers that accompanied our appetizer salads.

Louise smiled benevolently. "Savannah was wonderful. The architecture and the fountains were a sight to see." She took a bite of popover before continuing. "We visited inside a few historic houses, but my absolute favorites were the ghost tours."

Ralph's eyebrows shot up. "You went on a ghost tour?"

"That's pretty much a necessity in America's most haunted city, don't you think?" Louise's eyes twinkled at Ralph's surprise. "I really did like the nighttime cemetery visit and the moonlit haunted street tour. That one ended with a pub crawl."

"A pub crawl?" By now, Ralph was spellbound and, for once, speechless, although that might have been because he was on his third popover.

Watching Ralph's reaction to Louise's traveling adventures was extremely entertaining. I grabbed another popover myself and settled back to enjoy the show.

Louise filled us in on the ghosts and mansions of Savannah. Then there was the extension trip that four of them took to Charleston, the reason for her late arrival back home.

"We couldn't miss seeing those plantations and taking a sunset boat ride."

Louise certainly didn't fit the central casting definition of her chronologically advanced years in looks, actions, or words. Ralph's surprise was obvious, and Louise was reveling in it. So was I. This was giving me a much-needed lift. Walking cobblestone streets and quaffing local beer at a ghost tour afterglow? Impressive. So much for the myth of slowing down with age.

Generous plates of quiche arrived with huge slices of melon and fresh strawberries. Our slender glasses of champagne were refilled, and Louise raised hers.

"Here's to reconnecting with each other!"

We clinked glasses and began eating. The quiche was magnificent.

"What's this about family memorabilia, Emma? Are you doing genealogical research?"

I took a deep breath and began explaining everything that had gone on so far. Given this morning's unusual discovery in the magazine, I had more to tell and to ask. Even with Ralph there, annoying as he could be, I felt comfortable telling my entire story. He was beginning to look at me with surprise, too. It was the first time he'd heard as much about Geraldine, the archive, and my bogus ideas of stolen jewelry from a century ago. And now, the magazine. Could this be the same A.E. Waters? Like the initials on the handkerchief?

Louise listened carefully as we ate.

"How much do both of you know about our family's history?" she asked. "Or maybe I should ask how much do you know about Antonia Emmaline Waters?"

"Nothing really," I answered. "We know some names, and her name, but they all lived so long ago that I guess we never asked much when Mom and Dad were here."

Louise nodded. "Sometimes when we're young, we don't know what to ask. When we're old enough to be interested, there isn't the opportunity or the right people left to tell the stories."

Ralph suddenly jumped in with the enthusiasm of a schoolboy who had just thought of the correct answer in a class discussion. "I once overheard Mom say that some ancestors liked to use their initials instead of signing their full names."

*Ah, Ralph! He learned family history from eavesdropping.*

Louise burst out laughing. "I think you're right. I heard that somewhere, too."

"Does that mean she was the one in the magazine?" It was just too much of a coincidence to be anything else.

"Yes, Emma. And there's much more to the story."

Then Louise looked at Ralph seriously. "And thank you, Ralph, for finding a good home for the memorabilia with Emma. Some of this fills in missing pieces for me, as well."

She then turned to me. "Emma, I'm proud of everything you've done. You didn't have much to go on and your conclusions were totally logical."

I sighed with relief. Maybe I wasn't crazy after all.

"I didn't realize some of those items still existed. It was before my time, so what I know was told to me when I was young." She smiled at Ralph. "And some of it I overheard, too."

She cut a piece of her melon and then continued. "A lot of what you've described very likely belonged to Antonia Emmaline."

"You mean those diary pages were hers?" I asked.

"They weren't diary pages, Emma. They were something even more special, and you discovered a key part of it this morning."

\*\*\*\*

Louise's apartment was lovely. Her couch burst with a gorgeous floral pattern, and the sunshine pouring through sparkling windows emphasized each colorful bloom. Plus, it was comfortable, a feature that Ralph was enjoying as he nestled into a corner perch. Louise set out a plate of delicate sugar cookies, and Ralph was not shy about helping himself, although we had eaten quite well at Luminaire. He totally ignored my evil stares at the crumbs on his shirt and the implied suggestion that he eat with a little more finesse.

Louise placed some books and photos on the coffee table before sitting down on an elegant wing chair that matched the couch. Her apartment radiated tranquility, even with my brother spreading cookie crumbs over everything.

"First, let me tell you a little about Antonia Emmaline. Then the contents of the boxes will begin to make sense." Louise paused to sip from one of the tall glasses of iced tea she had poured for all of us. "Antonia was in her late teens at the turn of the century. Even though that era was old-fashioned by today's standards, it was a time of change. Women were starting to seek activities of their own. They still had a long way to go, but many began setting the bar higher."

Ralph reached for one of the glasses of iced tea. Out of the side of my eye, I saw a cascade of crumbs go with him. If Louise noticed, she didn't let on.

"Antonia was one of five siblings, and their branch of the family was well off. Plus, they encouraged her to follow her passions—acting and writing."

"Acting?" I was startled.

Louise smiled. "There was a lot of theater back then as well as performance venues of all types. Antonia loved the theater, and she began taking small parts in a number of shows."

Louise carefully took a scrapbook from the pile on the table and handed it to me. "Here are a few of the more memorable productions she was in. I have others if you're interested."

Ralph leaned in to see as I half tilted the aging book in his direction.

"She never had any major roles," Louise continued, "because she started to turn to her real love, and that was writing. She was inspired by several women who wrote stories, articles, poems, and, especially, plays."

"Women wrote plays back then?" asked Ralph, incredulous. "Plays that were produced?"

"More than you'd realize." Again, Louise was

amused by Ralph's surprise.

"Opportunities were starting to open up. Theater was expanding and women were a part of it, onstage and off. Antonia Emmaline loved theater, and she loved writing. And she was one of a number of women who diversified their writing. It wasn't just plays. There were lots of magazines to write for. And newspapers ran contests for stories and plays, and women entered these. That's not to say it was easy, but things were starting to change for women."

"So, about Antonia…" I paused to finish a cookie, worried that I would start dropping crumbs like Ralph. "She wrote plays *and* stories, too? And the plays were produced?"

Louise beamed. "Yes. Here. Take a look." She handed us several magazines. Antonia's name was listed as A. E. Waters, her pen name as a writer, I presumed. Her acting credits gave her name in full. "Some of her stories are in these, too. Like the one you found this morning."

"And here are some of the plays." She indicated more copies of works on the table. "Often the plays were published as well as produced."

I thumbed through the pile, Ralph and I trading with each other. "There were a lot of magazines and theater programs in those boxes. I'll bet that…"

Ralph finished for me. "Antonia's in those, too."

We exchanged startled glances.

"And since she wrote as A. E. Waters," I continued, "I wouldn't have noticed her name as quickly. And I guess I never looked at the theater programs." *But how could I have missed such obvious things? Because my attention was focused on jewelry theft instead.*

Louise smiled. She was thoroughly enjoying herself.

"But what about those pages I thought were a diary?" I asked.

"And those scraps of paper that were in the envelope?" Ralph chimed in, drawn to the story as much as I was.

"From the photos you've shown me, they were random pages with notes, parts of drafts, snatches of dialogue, and miscellaneous reminders to get in touch with some other playwrights. I have a few of them, too."

"But a lot of the pages seemed to be about real incidents," I continued. "And the newspapers had articles circled, too."

"Antonia and many others enjoyed getting their plotlines from the newspapers and current events and then building on them. Abigail, your desperate thief, came from her imagination. Take a look in that second magazine over there. Antonia wrote a short story about a young woman who stole some jewelry to help her sister who was ill. Part of that came from a news article and the rest was about someone she knew on her street. The plots were based on real incidents and then fictionalized from there. Crime and retribution. Hardship and triumph."

"But, Louise," I asked. "What about the jewelry and other things I found in the boxes? The jewelry that turned out to be fake?"

"Some of those jewelry pieces were props for plays and some of the clothes were costumes. Remember, back then things weren't as complicated as they are now. The playwright could get to suggest props, depending on the circumstances of the production. And, of course, some of the things you have were just family memorabilia."

Ralph had been busy leafing through the bound books of individual plays. "Hey, look!"

He held up one that was titled *The Busy Shopgirl and the Gentleman Customer*. "Isn't that like the page in the envelope? Where the guy picked out vases and fancy dishes for a gift?"

"I think you're right, Ralph." I nodded, pleased that he had taken such an interest.

"So, there was no diary?" I asked Louise.

Louise rose gracefully out of the wing chair and went to a glass-enclosed bookcase at the side of the expansive room. She carefully slid open the doors and removed three bound volumes from one of the shelves. Turning, she brought them over to where we sat.

"*These* are her diaries, or at least the ones that still remain." Louise held them out in my direction. My eyes widened in awe.

I took them reverently from her outstretched hands. Gingerly opening the first pages, I recognized the familiar handwriting. Dates headed the tops of the pages. My eyes open in surprise, I read a few of the opening sentences out loud.

*Margaret Mayo encouraged me from the very beginning. She invited me to see her play and told me about the contest in the newspaper after reading my work in* Story Journal *magazine. I also wanted to write plays, just as she had done. With your acting experience and writing talent, she told me, it would be a shame not to try. I was flattered and, also, a bit frightened. What if my play wasn't good? What if I disappoint Margaret and the others? And, yet, I must try this. What if I succeed?*

I looked up at Louise, tears in my eyes. Antonia Emmaline felt real now. She spoke plainly of her fears and, at the same time, of her enthusiasm.

Louise nodded in understanding. Even Ralph seemed moved by these words.

"Antonia knew some women writers and playwrights, like Edith Ellis, Lottie Blair Parker, and Eleanor Maud Crane," said Louise. "I learned that by the end of the first decade of the twentieth century, about a third of onstage plays in New York were written by women. And there was even a group for women dramatists." Louise looked at Emma. "Why don't you take all of these with you. Read them and you'll find out a lot more about those items in the trunk."

"But, Louise," I protested. "These are yours; they're so valuable…"

Louise shook her head. "Emma, they're only valuable if they're used. They're no good to anyone if they stay locked in a glass bookcase turning to dust. Something tells me that they'll open a new door for you." Then she smiled directly. "Besides, I remember something about your mother liking the name Emmaline, and I'll bet that's where you got your name from. I believe this was something I once overheard." She winked at Ralph. *Ah, a fellow eavesdropper.*

"How can I thank you for trusting me with these?" I asked her.

"No thanks necessary. Enjoy finding out a little more about Antonia Emmaline's life. I've always

151

thought that the more we read about others' lives, the more we understand our own."

My enthusiasm had been reawakened. What a wonder to have reconnected with Louise and to borrow the books and diaries of my ancestor. I would study them carefully. And my research would change. I would search for more background about Antonia and the other women from her time. Maybe shine some light on their importance, then and now.

Ralph looked up suddenly at Louise. "You said that Antonia did a lot of things in her young life. What about her older life? What did she do then?"

Louise paused for a moment. Her face was serious. "Unfortunately, she never got to live an older life. Antonia died in a streetcar accident. She was only thirty-two years old."

Chapter Twenty-One

Rain had been threatening all morning, the darkening sky now a deep steely gray. When the first drops began, they sounded a soft, ghostly whisper outside the tall windows of the otherwise silent research room. More insistent now, their metallic pelting became increasingly hard to ignore. The sound drew my attention away from the materials in front of me and for several minutes, I stared at the high windowpanes, mesmerized by the vicious pounding of the now full-blown storm.

Louise's revelations filled me with fresh energy, and my research suddenly took on a whole new meaning. After already staying up late for several nights to study the volumes from Louise, I now returned to the archive to read copies of *The Theatre* and the *New York Clipper,* absorbing their details on long-vanished people and productions. Their musty pages held the promise of real discovery and support for my new purpose. I wanted to find background information about Antonia Emmaline's life and work as well as that of the other women writers of her time. From there, I planned on creating a whole new project for myself.

A little after noon, I decided to take a break. Quietly pushing back my chair, I indicated to Mr. Winthrop that I would return and then headed for the kitchen. The pungent aroma of Joe's thick, rich meatloaf hero greeted me the moment I walked through the door, a reminder of just how hungry I was.

After retrieving my tuna fish sandwich from the refrigerator, I joined Joe, Meghan, and Ashley, already huddled over their lunches. Weather was the topic of the moment.

"Maybe I should skip class this afternoon." Ashley took a gulp of her fizzy green soda. She looked up hopefully, anticipating unanimous support for her idea. "It's pouring, and you know how many blocks I'll have to walk to get the bus." She pushed her freshly brushed hair away from the collar of her shirt, making eye contact with each of us in turn.

The most direct way for Ashley to reach school was via a bus that was a fair distance east of the archive. The long, soaking walk was one thing. But today the bus would move at a snail's pace because of the weather, its interior crammed with irritable passengers, annoyed about getting to their destinations late. And the stench of their soggy raincoats and canvas tote bags would be unbearable.

"Have you missed other classes this semester?" asked Meghan.

"Two, maybe three." Ashley was clearly hedging.

"It's just rain," responded Meghan. "You should go to class and save the cut for something more fun."

Ashley frowned. I knew she would have preferred to stay at the front table and delve into another of her steamy romance novels. And on a day like today, I couldn't say I blamed her.

"Do you need an umbrella?" asked Joe. "We've got a couple of extras in the hall closet."

"Nah," she replied. "It'll just blow inside out. Thanks anyway." She waited a moment, still harboring a glimmer of hope that at least one of us would insist she stay.

Finally, and with a slight pout, she rose from her chair. "Well, I'm off," she announced. "To Sociology—and the storm."

Gathering her backpack with a dramatic sigh, she gave us a brief wave and was off.

We returned to our lunches.

"Poor Ashley. Maybe she should have cut class," I mused out loud, starting to worry about her plight and wondering if I should have cast a vote in favor of her idea. "She sure wouldn't be the only one skipping class today."

Meghan nodded. "But school's important. And she won't remember getting wet on a rainy day by the time she graduates."

"This rain's pretty intense, though," added Joe, as we continued to eat.

While we spoke, the rain increased its brutal attack on the building. The deafening noise grew louder. It was amazing that we heard it at all from the windowless kitchen.

Finally, Meghan gathered her lunch wrappers. "Well, I guess it's back to work," she said, rising from the table and heading for the trash bin.

At that moment, a bloodcurdling scream rang out as the heavy front door violently crashed into the wall. Meghan whirled around in shock, her coffee mug shattering on the floor. The three of us ran as the panicked screams continued.

It was Ashley—running down the hall toward us,

her face contorted in terror. She was soaked, her thin purple raincoat plastered to her body. It fell back, revealing hair now tangled in a knotty web from the torrents of water. She gulped for air in between her cries.

Ashley threw her arms around a bewildered Meghan, clinging as if for dear life. Big heaving sobs wracked her body.

Her screams brought everyone into the hallway.

A frantic Ms. Tipton ran out of her office and began shouting. "What's wrong?"

For a stunned moment, we were all at a loss, not knowing what to do next.

Ashley was close to incoherent.

"Out...side...in the lot," was all she could manage to utter.

Without saying a word, Joe and I both raced to the wide-open doorway and down the cracked front steps. *Was someone outside hurt?*

The storm hit me like a brutal tidal wave, rain smashing against my face, its force instantly drenching my hair and clothing. Still, I ran, following Joe next door to the abandoned demolition site.

There, only a few feet from the sidewalk, barely inside the vacant lot, lay a figure sprawled face-down on the ground. The drab sweater, now soaked, was so familiar. Her naked hands were splayed out beside her, palms down.

It was Millicent, the Lady of the White Gloves.

Joe knelt down next to her in the muddy, dirty rubble of building scraps. I held my breath for what seemed an eternity as Joe felt for her pulse. Then he closed his eyes and shook his head sadly.

## Chapter Twenty-Two

The usually desolate street now burst with police activity. Their vans and cars lined the curb, lights flashing out of sync with each other in a surreal, rainy haze. Teams of officials were checking every inch of the filthy, abandoned lot and its surroundings with a complicated mix of equipment. And despite the weather, everyone from the archive finally came outside, anxious to see for themselves what was happening.

Several uniformed officers quickly herded us back indoors where there was shelter from the unrelenting storm. We were then told we'd each be separately interviewed by a detective.

Thankfully, someone found a blanket for Ashley and wrapped it around her. She was inconsolable, barely able to answer questions for the police when it was her turn. Afterwards, Meghan put an arm around the shivering young woman and brought her into the kitchen for some tea, hoping to calm her down.

Police interviews were being held in the Victorian parlor. In the meantime, several of us congregated in the hallway while waiting our turns to get to the closet and grab coats and sweaters, whatever would help take the chill from our rain-soaked clothes and skin.

I grabbed my coat, drawing whatever warmth I could from its thin lining. Baxter was right behind me.

He pulled his own jacket closer than I thought humanly possible.

"This is hideous." Baxter spoke with muted frustration through clenched teeth. "Millicent shouldn't have died."

Mr. Winthrop, in a rare foray into conversational mode, solemnly commented. "This is truly a tragedy." Nervously adjusting his gold bow tie, now wilted from exposure to the weather, he slid a worn tan raincoat off its wire hanger. "The mugger is getting more brazen."

My name was called, and I walked down the hall slowly, pondering Mr. Winthrop's curious comment. When I arrived at the parlor, I looked around sadly. Just so recently, Della and Joe had happily gotten to know each other here, sitting in the bright autumn sun that poured through the large, curtained windows. Now, the entire room, even the once cheerful sofa pattern, took on a sinister tone.

Detective Reynolds was in charge, a middle-aged man with a weary face. He invited me to sit opposite him, indicating one of several folding chairs retrieved to spare the room's nicely upholstered furniture. His dark-blue jacket looked uncomfortably rain-soaked. A lanky, younger associate, whose name I didn't catch, stood nearby. After asking for my basic information as well as about my purpose for being at the archive, the detective began his real questioning.

"Please, Mrs. Streyt," he began. "Tell me what happened."

"Well, we were eating lunch in the kitchen…"

"And who is 'we'?" he interrupted.

This should have been obvious, since he'd already spoken to Ashley, Meghan, and Joe. Perhaps he needed to be sure that our stories matched.

He nodded as I repeated their names and told him of the events as I remembered them.

"Ashley really didn't want to go to school. The weather was horrible. But we urged her not to cut her class." Now I was sorry about this. Someone would have found Millicent, but did it have to be our carefree, young college intern?

"Go on," prompted the detective, fixing his tired brown eyes on me.

"After she left, it only seemed like a minute or two before we heard the front door smash into the wall and then Ashley ran down the hall screaming."

He leaned forward and studied my face. I could see the circles under his eyes. Deep fatigue, just like Steve. "Then what?"

"It all happened so fast," I said, fully recounting how the sobbing Ashley clung to Meghan while Joe and I ran outside.

"And why did you go outside in all of the rain?" He certainly didn't miss any detail.

"Because just about all Ashley could say was 'outside in the lot.' Maybe someone had gotten hurt...I don't know. Joe and I just ran."

"Was anyone else outside?" Despite his fatigue, the detective was scrupulous. His fellow detective remained silent, occasionally glancing at a rain-spotted windowpane.

"I didn't see anyone already out there. But then people came out of the archive after we did when they heard Ashley's screams. I'm sorry, Detective, I was just too stunned to notice much more. Except...except for Joe feeling for Millicent's pulse. And when he shook his head…I knew…"

Detective Reynolds nodded quietly.

The door opened abruptly, and a uniformed officer motioned to the two detectives.

"Excuse us for just a moment."

There was a brief, hushed exchange in the hallway. Flashing red lights from outside filtered through the curtains, and I wondered if they had taken Millicent away.

The creak of the door opening signaled the return of the two men.

"All right," Detective Reynolds continued, sitting down and checking his notes. "Do you know of any reason anyone would want to harm Mrs. Bauwers?"

"*What?*" It was impossible to hide my shock. "*Mrs. Bauwers?*"

"Is something wrong?"

"No, no. It's just…just that I never knew her last name or that it was the same as the name of the archive. She was introduced to me as 'Millicent'. I only spoke with her once, briefly, on my first day here. But, of course, I always saw her in the research room at the table." I breathed in sharply, still stunned by this revelation. "And, no, I haven't any idea who would want to hurt her."

Once more, the detective nodded. "Okay. I suppose you know there have been a few muggings in this area recently?"

"Yes, I heard something about this."

"It's possible the mugger might have struck again. Mrs. Bauwers' wallet was just now found in the lot. Her money was gone."

"Oh. May I ask how she died?"

"We won't know that for sure until we've investigated further." He sighed.

For the first time, the other detective spoke.

"Since her money was gone, this is probably another in a string of muggings. We both suggest that you be very careful and not linger here after dark." *A string of muggings?*

"Yes, I certainly understand. But why was Millicent here after dark and in the lot?" I couldn't comprehend any of this and was now beginning to just think out loud.

"We have no idea," said the standing detective.

Detective Reynolds shot him a look.

"Wait," I interrupted. "If this was a mugging, did they take her ring?"

The men exchanged glances.

"And how do you know about her ring?"

I explained about our handshake on that first day.

"The ring was still there," Detective Reynolds admitted. "Maybe someone or something frightened the mugger or maybe he didn't even notice it."

"Oh. I always thought muggers checked for jewelry. It looked sort of expensive."

He suppressed a smile.

"With muggers, it's anyone's guess. This one wanted money. It fits the pattern. And he must have wanted it quickly. That's a number one priority for criminals around here."

He thanked me and rose.

I left the room and walked down the hall to the kitchen where some people were randomly gathered. *Mrs. Bauwers?*

Hedgehog stood next to Sherlock Lady, solemnly

examining the contents of his coffee cup. *What were their real names, anyway?* Mr. Winthrop, his wilted bow tie and tan raincoat only adding to his forlorn look, sat at a table with Baxter and Meghan. Alan Renleigh, alone at the other table, leapt to his feet to pull back the remaining empty chair for me when I entered.

"Emma," he said, placing a hand on my shoulder as I sat. "Are you all right?"

"Yes, thank you," I replied, shaking off his hand as I turned to look at Ms. Tipton, who was now framed in the doorway.

Her penetrating gaze surveyed each one of us in turn before she spoke.

"This has been a terrible tragedy. We will all miss Millicent." She looked at the Currier & Ives print on the far wall as if for guidance. "The police just told me you're free to go home now if you've talked with them. Please get some rest. We are going to go on as best as we can here in the days ahead. Millicent would have wanted it that way."

*Had she known that Millicent's last name was Bauwers before the police revealed it? Of course, she did. She interviewed every researcher before they joined the archive. Unless there was some other explanation.*

No one spoke for a moment, frozen in place, as if waiting for some signal.

Ms. Tipton continued. "Ashley's family just came for her. She's safe with them."

She turned to leave, paused, and then looked back. "And please use extra caution when walking in and around the neighborhood," she said formally. And then she was gone.

Sherlock Lady was the first to move, wordlessly walking out the door. Mr. Winthrop rose, shook his head, and soon followed.

Alan turned to me. "Emma, would you like me to walk you out?"

"Thanks, Alan, but I need to sit for a while."

He nodded, my silence inviting no further conversation. He reluctantly said his goodbyes and left. Hedgehog remained with his coffee cup. I joined Meghan and Baxter at their table.

"I had no idea." Meghan brushed back the deep bangs from her forehead and looked down at her hands. There was a pause before she spoke again. "I didn't know that Millicent was from the Bauwers family." She hugged her damp sweater closer.

"How was she related?" I asked.

"Ms. Tipton just told me that she's—she was—Harlan Bauwers' daughter-in-law."

We all took a moment to digest this information.

"It seems strange that she kept it a secret," I continued. "And it's also strange that she was in the abandoned lot. Was she there at night? What was that about? And no one noticed she was on the ground, even in the morning?" This was unbelievable, although the lot was in a less traveled part of the street, and most of us walked to the archive from the opposite direction.

Hedgehog offered his thoughts. "The weather was pretty bad," he said. "It would have meant even fewer people on the street than usual. And it's not a busy place to begin with." He shook his head sadly, his whiskers moving at their own pace.

"I don't want to sound mean, but maybe anyone walking by might have assumed she was homeless," commented Meghan.

*Possible, and a chilling thought. Suppose she'd still been alive?*

"But sleeping in the rain?" Hedgehog asked. "Wouldn't anyone have wondered why a homeless person hadn't tried to find some shelter in a doorway and then called for help?"

"Sometimes people just don't want to get involved," added Meghan.

Hedgehog sighed. "I'll miss her," he commented. "She was dedicated to her research."

*But just what was she researching?*

Hedgehog disposed of his coffee cup and said goodbye.

A long moment of silence followed after he left. Then Baxter spoke.

"Well, it's a desolate block with no video cameras," he began. "And there's certainly enough crime in the area. She was mugged in an abandoned lot and her money was taken. It was probably just an addict who needed cash."

Meghan choked on a sob and then unleashed her fury on Baxter.

"*Why* was Millicent in that lot? She never stayed after hours. All these crimes happen after hours. We can't just write it off to some robbery by an addict."

"Well, that's what the police seem to be thinking," he shot back defensively.

"Don't you even care what happened to her? And why? That poor woman, dead in that awful muddy place. Doesn't it matter to you?"

Baxter was visibly taken aback.

"I'm sorry. It's just that I guess I'm looking for the

most reasonable explanation."

Interesting how Meghan lashed out at Baxter, just as she had done with Alan at the café.

Meghan looked up as a tear ran down her cheek. "And I didn't even have a really good idea of what she was working on."

This was surprising, given that both she and Baxter pulled files and helped with requests.

"I'm sorry, Meghan. Really sorry," said Baxter, remorsefully stroking his throat in his usual nervous fashion. "But we also need to think about a very real threat here. Someone is roaming the neighborhood looking to mug people, to hurt them if they don't give up their money. We should all be afraid."

A chill ran down my back. I was suddenly terror-stricken at the idea of being in the archive's neighborhood at night. Winter was fast on its way and darkness was coming earlier, getting nearer to closing time. It would be even more desolate then. And more dangerous. *And what exactly had been the story behind the previous crimes?*

There was something odd about all of this. I couldn't help wondering why no one seemed to know much about Millicent's research, except that it focused on old photographs. And it was beyond odd that no one seemed to know that her last name was Bauwers. Well, Ms. Tipton knew, or had she only found out after the police discovered her moneyless wallet?

"I can't imagine why she never let on that her last name was Bauwers." Meghan echoed my thoughts. "Evidently, she used her maiden name instead of her married one when she signed her application for research—Millicent Fenmore. What was the big secret?

It wouldn't have mattered." Then Meghan looked directly at each of us in turn, brushing away another tear. She hesitated before speaking. "You realize this might not have been random."

Baxter's eyes widened in terror. "Are you suggesting she was murdered? Why?"

The question hung in the air as Joe walked in, halting this turn in the conversation. He pulled up a chair and joined us.

"What's this about murder?" he asked.

"I'm just saying we can't rule out that this might have been intentional," said Meghan.

"But it happened off the premises, and the police seem to believe it was a random mugging," chimed in Baxter. "If it had been pre-meditated, wouldn't it have happened inside here or somewhere else, like where Millicent lived?"

"A reasonable assumption, I suppose," Joe answered, glancing away.

"We don't even know how she was killed," I added.

It was Joe who responded to this. "She hit her head on that awful ruin of a stone bench. At least that's what the detective mentioned."

*Why did Joe know this? The detective didn't answer me when I'd asked. Joe knew more than he was saying. Should I be nervous? After all, he was starting to date my best friend.*

"Maybe it was an accident?" I ventured, processing this new information.

"You mean maybe she fell while being mugged?" asked Meghan.

"Who knows? All we can do is keep our eyes and

ears open," Joe interjected. "And see if the cops come up with anything new."

But the thought of intentional murder was in the air now and it wouldn't go away, even though a random mugging or an accidental fall seemed logical. But murder?

And yet, the details didn't add up. Millicent was "Mrs. Bauwers." The mugger didn't take her ring. And she was in that awful lot at night. For what reason?

"Please, let's all be careful," I said, looking at Meghan, Baxter, and Joe in turn.

As soon as I uttered the words, it hit me. *I hoped I wasn't speaking to a murderer.*

Chapter Twenty-Three

Snatching one of the throw pillows from a nearby chair, I hugged it close, burying my face in its soft contours. This still didn't stop recent events at the archive from rushing into my mind, even now in the warm security of my family room. They haunted me. It was hard to forget Ashley's screams of terror. Or the vision of Millicent, face down in the muddy rubble, with Joe shaking his head sorrowfully next to her.

Steve walked into the room with two mugs of coffee.

"Doing okay this morning?" Steve was visibly shaken after he'd heard about Millicent. I now sensed that he was going to bring up the subject once more with renewed vigor. He wanted me to leave the archive. He'd said so last night, and I knew this wasn't going to be the last of the discussion.

Trying for my brightest smile, I toasted with the coffee mug. "Doing much better with this. Thanks! I'm beyond grateful for more caffeine."

"Will you be okay if I go to the office for a while today?" I don't know why he thought otherwise, but I sensed this was just a conversational lead-in to the main topic.

"Of course. I'm going to read through more of Louise's things and check some of my old newspapers. Oh, and go on the computer, too. You know, it'll be relaxing." I tried to sound casual, lighthearted even. "Maybe talk to Della again. And I owe Geraldine a call. Then you and I can have a quiet dinner later. You must have so much you need to do."

We sipped our coffee in silence for a few minutes.

"Em, about the archive," began Steve.

*Here we go.*

"Please! I know you're worried, but…"

"Emma, listen to me. A woman is dead…"

"I'm *well* aware of that, Steve," I bristled in frustration. "You don't need to lecture me."

"I'm sorry, Emma, but the cops even told you there's a lot of crime in the area. This wasn't just an ordinary mugging, which is bad enough. She's dead."

Of course, I neglected to mention to Steve that a few of us suspected Millicent's death might not have been quite so simple.

"And she was mugged and killed after dark," I reminded him in an effort to bring some logic into the conversation. "After the archive closed. And I'm there during the day."

"But suppose the mugger starts up in the daytime? Criminals can be desperate."

"You can suppose anything, Steve. Suppose we get mugged on our front lawn or getting into our car in the driveway?"

"That's highly unlikely, Emma," commented Steve, slightly rolling his eyes.

"Steve, I know you want me to leave the archive, but I can't…"

"What about New York Public Library? They should have more than everything you need. And we have a fine library right here in town."

*Ha!*

"The Bauwers has the specific things I want and need right now, and from the specific time period I'm looking into. And they're easier to access there. I can't leave until I've checked out everything." *And until I find out why Millicent was murdered. And who murdered her. I had to know. I felt like a part of the place now.*

"Emma, be reasonable. It's not safe."

"I'm perfectly safe, and now I'm sure there'll be more police around trying to catch that criminal. And he might have been scared away from the area by this time anyway. And I don't stay around there after dark. I just made a breakthrough in my research, Steve. I can't stop. And I don't want to stop."

Steve raised an eyebrow. He knew I was trying to minimize the gravity of the situation. And he also knew that I was not going to give in.

"Emma." He took my hand. "Please think about this. I'm worried about you."

"I'll be fine." I squeezed his hand in return, hoping for an end to this tug of war over my presence at the archive. "And I'm worried about you, too," I said, in an attempt to dodge the spotlight. "You've had a terrible shock, Steve. You really should be careful of your health."

"I'll be fine," he said. "Look, Emma. Please promise me you'll think about it."

"Yeah, I'll think about it." *Right.*

Steve reluctantly left the family room.

Indignantly, I turned to the stack of yellowed newspapers. It was time to work. Get back to business. The newspapers were closest to me so I decided to start there by checking out some of the non-circled articles as Geraldine suggested. It would sharpen my concentration so I could focus more on the books from Louise once my anger simmered down. I picked up the issue at the top of the pile, frayed snippets of its edges sailing into my lap.

Geraldine was right, urging me to read everything in those old issues. You never know what other interesting details you might find, she'd said. I was only getting around to taking her advice now. And since I wasn't looking for jewel thieves and tragedies, my attention was now not only on general news, but especially on old theater reviews and gossip from the stage. It was at the center of my great-great-aunt Antonia Emmaline's world so many years ago. What had that world been like?

I was thrilled to find a theatrical column that cited her as the playwright for a production featured on a small New York stage and to see her name again as a cast member in a play written by another woman. I'd started devouring her stories, scrapbooks, and plays that Louise had given me. Now those newspapers were filling in the flavor of her entire era.

Another of Geraldine's ideas was beginning to seem more reasonable, too—of writing about my family or about something new I might discover while researching them. It didn't seem so far-fetched anymore. "You could write about your experiences digging into your family's past," she'd said. "Or share stories about something special from that time." Geraldine's enthusiasm encouraged me. And now I knew I was looking for turn-of-the-century women writers, playwrights in particular—what they wrote, what their lives were like, and how they made a difference.

Journalism from those years was entertaining once you got into it, and it was the perfect distraction for me. The articles and advertisements were certainly eclectic. From serious to charming, they had a style all their own. I skimmed through news of boxing and baseball, cholera outbreaks abroad, rooms for rent, and natural disasters. There were ads for handkerchiefs, rheumatism cures, fine chocolates, and silverware. Short poems occasionally appeared at random. Advice on maintaining a good complexion could be found inches away from notes on the social gatherings of the well-to-do. Occasional line sketches of important individuals added variety to columns of text.

Antonia and her peers had so many themes to choose from, and they let their imaginations run wild from these basic facts as they spun them into absorbing fiction for both page and stage. I wanted to follow up on one or two stories so I moved to the computer to try and locate some additional issues at an online historic newspaper site.

Just then, Steve poked his head into the family room before he left for the office.

"Looks like you're lost in cyberspace," he commented, noticing my eyes riveted on the computer.

I jumped, so intent upon the screen in front of me that I didn't hear him enter the room.

"More like I'm lost in another century." I smiled now, my anger having taken a backseat to my fascination with the words and pictures in the old papers. "Steve, you won't believe the stuff in these newspapers. Some of the ads are hilarious—fashionable carriages, shorthand and typewriting schools, lace corset-cover yokes…"

"Yes, that's definitely from another century." He drummed his fingers on the doorframe for a moment. "Well, I'm taking my 'fashionable carriage' out to get gas now and then on to the office." He smiled. "We'll talk later."

"Okay," I said. It was nice to see Steve smile. He seemed a tiny bit more relaxed since the situation with Hank was out in the open and he was able to talk about it. But I still saw him looking sadly or angrily into space in a quiet moment. On the other hand, his worries about my safety after Millicent's death had given him his own diversion of sorts, and I truly wished it had been a happier one. I also wished he'd go back to thinking about his own work problems and leave his anti-archive crusade out of the picture.

Turning back to the computer screen and continuing to read, my new plan filled me with a growing sense of excitement. I planned to research and write about Antonia Emmaline and the other women playwrights, many of them now forgotten, and bring their contributions to light. I was anxious to begin organizing my developing ideas.

While looking for specific stories, I became sidetracked by the various columns of other miscellaneous news and announcements. Scrolling randomly through these old issues, I saw ads for hats, a poem about holidays, news of ships arriving…

And that's when I saw it.

I stopped and read word for word.

It was an obituary, modest in length and fanfare, especially for someone called one of New York's notable business magnates and financiers. A long-time leader of his company, his many accomplishments were listed, some related to finance and others to transportation. A few surviving family members and other deceased individuals were acknowledged.

At the very end, though, the piece mentioned an early partnership in which the deceased had been involved. Most people in the current century would probably never have read so far down that column. Would never notice that brief final sentence or pick up on that one small detail. The one stating that early in his career, Prescott Bauwers was a founding partner in the firm of Bauwers & Tipton.

Chapter Twenty-Four

"Something is horribly wrong, Dell. I can feel it."

Della and I cruised the fresh fruit and vegetable section at the supermarket, discussing what I'd found in those old newspapers—specifically, the obituary for Prescott Bauwers. There wasn't much to go on, but those few facts increased my growing fear that something was terribly amiss at the archive, something making Millicent's death seem more and more like murder, as Meghan suggested.

"It was the obituary that got me started. But two smaller articles I found later about the dissolution of the Bauwers & Tipton partnership hinted that there was bad blood between them, probably money. Well, about business and real estate, which I guess means money."

"And then there's the name 'Tipton' adding to the intrigue," said Della as we continued circling rows of fruits and vegetables.

My cart bumped into a display of caramel apple kits, sending three of them toppling to the floor. I swooped down and retrieved them.

"Em, that was over a century ago," pointed out Della, selecting some fresh apples and then removing one of the boxes from my hand. She studied the side panel instructions. "Think I'll give this a try."

I half-heartedly picked up an orange, thought better of it, and plunked it back in the bin.

"Yeah, but let's look at the facts. There's a Tipton basically running the archive and a Bauwers, well a Bauwers-by-marriage, who just got murdered."

"Shhh," cautioned Della. "People will hear you."

We looked around quickly. Fortunately, the only ones in earshot were a sobbing toddler and her frantic mother. The little girl grabbed two packages of organic brussels sprouts and wouldn't let go.

"And, besides," continued Della, picking up a red pepper before pausing to speak. "The police think it was just another mugging."

"But what do *you* think?" I asked her.

She turned the pepper over in her hands and then looked up at me. "Emma, I think something's not right. And I don't want you putting yourself in danger trying to figure it out."

"You're starting to sound like Steve," I shot back as Della motioned me toward the cereal aisle. We retreated to a quiet spot in front of a display of fruit-flavored crunchies shaped like farm animals. Della picked up a box and pretended to study the green cows and orange horses on the front, continuing the conversation in hushed tones.

"If someone really murdered Millicent, you better be careful. I'm worried about you."

"Okay, Dell. I'm a little worried about me, too, but please don't say anything to Steve if you see him."

"I won't. But, Emma…"

"Look, I don't have any information that would harm anyone. Right?"

"But you're poking into it. That's enough to attract attention."

"I'm only listening and asking some questions.

You know, the curious type of questions that anyone would ask."

Della exchanged the animal-shaped nuggets for a box of chocolate monsters.

"Too many questions can put the wrong people on alert," she cautioned, sending a pleading glance in my direction. "Watch who you talk to."

"Well, I'm certainly not talking to Ms. Tipton. Now that I know she's somehow or other connected to the Bauwers family. You don't think…"

"Emma, I don't know what to think, but *please be careful.*"

I pulled my jacket closer and took a deep breath as we reached the checkout line.

"Della, I'm scared." There. I'd admitted it. Out loud.

The woman ahead of me on the checkout line turned in my direction with a quizzical look. I smiled sweetly and nodded in the direction of the threatening headline on a nearby pulp magazine—"Invasion of Extraterrestrial Geese Predicted." Della suppressed a laugh, shaking her feathered earrings. The woman scowled. At least it broke the tension.

"Listen, Joe and I are going out to dinner again tomorrow night," Della began the moment we were in the car and I started the engine. "Maybe he could shed some light on the situation."

"I don't want to drag you into this. I like Joe and, well, obviously, so do you. Umm…"

I was afraid to ask if we could trust him, but my unspoken question hung in the air.

Fortunately, Della didn't let me keep on talking before she blurted out, "Joe's a good guy! I have radar for the bad ones by now."

"Okay, but please don't ask too many leading questions. I'm sure he *is* a good guy."

*Geraldine said he was new at the archive. Did this mean something?*

I continued, trying to shake off my worries. "But I don't want to put you or Joe in danger, just because of my curiosity."

Della was quiet for a moment. Unlike the Della I knew.

When she finally continued asking questions, I breathed a sigh of relief.

"And what about you? How do you plan on staying out of danger? Or maybe the better question is: what's next?"

"I'm meeting Geraldine for dinner tomorrow night. She was the one who got me into this in the first place. I'm figuring she'll share some insights."

"How do you know that you can trust *her*?"

"She's not involved with the archive; she was only on assignment there." *But was this really true?* Guilt seemed to be pointing a finger at everyone. "What would she have to gain by murdering Millicent?"

*But what would anyone have to gain by murdering Millicent?*

Chapter Twenty-Five

The soothing lights and sounds of the Big City Café were comforting as I headed inside from the brisk fall evening. I waved to Thom, the bartender, and grabbed a corner table with a view of the time-honored menu inscriptions on the wall. I shed my jacket and got settled just as Geraldine strode through the door. She, too, waved to Thom as I held up two fingers for Stormy Hurricanes, copying Geraldine's signal at our last meeting here.

"You read my mind." She smiled, joining me at the table.

"I see that one of the favorites is a Killer Mile-High Burger," I began, reading off the tempting description of one of the house specialties. Tonight, we agreed to meet for both drinks and dinner. My treat. I had plenty to discuss with my unusual new friend, and I wanted time with her. "Drinks, first, though. There's a lot to talk about."

"Something tells me this is more intriguing than research." She gave a knowing look.

"Intriguing would be putting it mildly," I began as Thom arrived with our drinks. We each took a welcome sip.

"You've probably heard about the killing in the vacant lot. The police think it was the same mugger as before. This time it went wrong."

"I just caught something about the victim being a woman…"

"Millicent. The Lady of the White Gloves," I broke in, unable to contain my growing terror as I began my story. I looked down at my hands, gripping the glass. They trembled ever so slightly.

Geraldine looked up in surprise.

"How much did you know about her when you were doing the research for your article?" I asked, waiting to tell her the real surprise.

"Just that she looked like she had a thing for old photos. So, there she sat with her damned white gloves continually going through stacks of them." Geraldine paused to take another sip of her Stormy Hurricane. "Remember, I only spent two mornings there. I had five places I was researching for my piece and had to get to them all before I started writing."

"You never knew her name?"

"No, but I sense this is leading somewhere." Geraldine studied me carefully.

"Yeah, it is. I don't think…well, a few of us don't think this was any random thing. We don't care what the cops say."

Geraldine waited patiently for me to continue.

"I met her—Millicent—in the kitchen on my first day. When she came over to say hello, she seemed different. Everyone sort of wrote her off as an eccentric, dowdy person."

"That did seem to fit," commented Geraldine.

Then I told her about the handshake and how the ring made a visible impression on my hand. Plus, there was the very non-eccentric impression I had of her up close.

"So, what's your point, Emma? Lots of eccentrics are intelligent and have nice manners and wear rings."

"Yeah, but her ring looked awfully similar to the one Elizabeth Bauwers was wearing in that portrait." This only occurred to me a few days ago after carefully studying the painting and beginning to make such connections. It also dawned on me that those three paintings on the stairwell at the archive represented a lot of past secrets that could be related to Millicent's murder—if, indeed, that's what it was—as well as the current-day inner workings of the archive itself.

"Get this," I continued, pausing for emphasis before revealing my next bit of news. "Evidently, Millicent registered at the archive as Millicent Fenmore, but when the police questioned us, we found out that her full name was Millicent Fenmore Bauwers."

"What?" Geraldine gave a low whistle. "Whoa! Now that really does make you wonder. And why do you think it was murder?"

I sighed and continued. "For one thing, the ring was still on her finger, not the gloves, but the ring."

"Perp could have been scared off before he took more than her money," concluded Geraldine.

"That's what the cops said."

"Okay, but why was she in the vacant lot?"

I shrugged. "I don't know. And, evidently, she was there at night."

"Which Bauwers was she?" Geraldine asked.

"Harlan's daughter-in-law."

"Well, that's curious. Why would she need to do research there incognito? And research into what?" asked Geraldine.

"That's my pressing question."

"And no one knows?"

"No one I've talked to," I answered.

Thom arrived with a second round of drinks, and we each decided to go with the Killer Mile-High Burger, although I felt bad about eating a dish with killer in its name.

"There's probably a lot more going on at the archive underneath the surface," I continued. "I can't figure it out, though. And here's another disturbing thing."

I then told her about discovering Prescott Bauwers' obituary and its mention of an early partnership in the firm of Bauwers and Tipton. "Then I searched the internet even more. There was another small news item that said Prescott Bauwers and Morgan Tipton parted ways over some sort of business and real estate issues. Probably boils down to money. Don't you think? So, can it just be coincidental that a 'Ms. Tipton' is now working at the archive? Wouldn't it seem logical she's connected somehow?"

Geraldine sipped her Stormy Hurricane thoughtfully before replying. "Possibly." She fixed me directly with her perceptive green eyes. "Are you suggesting that she might have been settling an old family score? And somehow this involved Millicent?" She took a deep breath. "Okay, I'll say it. Do you think Ms. Tipton murdered Millicent?"

I looked down. Geraldine directly said what I'd been thinking. "It crossed my mind. Well, yeah, it more than crossed my mind, and now I'm freaked out."

"Understandable."

Thom arrived with our enormous burgers, each

with a generous portion of thick fries. Suddenly this didn't look so tempting as I thought about Ms. Tipton as a possible suspect. I took a gulp of Stormy Hurricane. Geraldine, however, plunged right into her meal and into more of her questions and speculations.

"And here's something else," said Geraldine in between bites. "Wouldn't it have sent up a red flag when Ms. Tipton got the job? When they saw her last name?"

"I was wondering that, too, but then Meghan told me all of the business affairs and hiring had been done by an independent legal firm for years. You know, one of those large places with someone on staff who handles things in the museum and cultural sector. Lucretia Bauwers stipulated this in her will. Maybe they just didn't know some of the finer details of history. Maybe they didn't come across the name 'Tipton' in anything that was remotely current. I'm figuring Harlan Bauwers knew but, then again, how much do any of us really know about our family's history? Or maybe there's some other reasonable explanation."

Finally, spurred on by Geraldine's obvious gusto for the meal at hand, I took a bite of my burger. It was surprisingly warm and comforting, considering my emotions at the moment.

"True," said Geraldine, demolishing several fries with abandon. "And here's something else to think about. If Prescott Bauwers only had two daughters—Lucretia and Elizabeth—and no sons, then how does Harlan fit in? His last name is Bauwers. Is he a descendant of some other family member?"

"I have no idea."

By now, I had to admit my burger was really good. And the pickles on the side were amazing. Juice rolled down my wrist as I bit into the first one.

"Let's get back to Millicent Bauwers and Ms. Tipton," said Geraldine. "What does it all mean? And why should it equal murder?"

"Well, we have to study the connection between the two. Maybe it's nothing," I ventured, mopping up the last of the ketchup on my plate with two thick fries.

"You don't honestly believe that," smiled Geraldine, finishing off the last of her Stormy Hurricane, ice rattling noisily in her glass.

"No, I don't. I think there's lots more going on at the archive now, and maybe that's gone on in the past. More than we've even started to imagine. Trouble is, how do I even start to figure this all out?"

We sat and discussed it for a while, agreeing on Irish coffees in place of dessert.

"Look," said Geraldine. "I'd like to do a little digging for some info, and here's what I propose." She was in her true element now. "I'll check around for a few days, and you keep your eyes and ears open. Then let's get together again and compare notes. If Millicent really was murdered by someone at the archive, we'll be doing a public service by finding out. And if it really was just a random mugging, then let's hope they find who did it. In the meantime, Emma, be careful, and make sure you have a can of mace or something in your bag."

\*\*\*\*

Two nights later, my cell phone sounded its usual loud *quack-quack*. I was tempted not to answer, my total attention on reading and researching Antonia's world. *It better not be Ralph prodding me about pumpkin cookies.*

I looked at the number. Geraldine.

"Hold onto your hat," she began in her typical style.

*She'd found something already?*

"What is it?" I asked, still amazed at how friendly we'd become in the brief few weeks we'd known each other.

"I did some quick digging after we got together. Did you know that probated wills are a part of public record?"

"No, I didn't."

Geraldine continued. "I have a friend who's been very helpful with this type of research in the past. Speeds things up. And terrific for finding out dry, but useful details about various business and private institutions." She took a breath and continued. "Anyway, just on the surface, there are some things in Lucretia's last wishes that you will find more than captivating."

"Wait a minute, Geraldine. You read her will? I mean, that's great and all, but why?"

"Isn't it obvious?" she asked. Actually not, but I allowed her to plow ahead anyway.

"Emma, I got you into this whole murder mess."

*So Geraldine also believed that Millicent was murdered.*

"To be truthful," she continued after a pause, "I'm curious. There's got to be a great story here." *Ah, the crux of the matter.* "We'll divvy it up when the time comes."

"What?"

Geraldine was relishing every moment of revealing her research tidbits and, at the same time, calculating a substantial bonanza in terms of future articles and potential freelance connections that could result. She now launched into her tale with conviction.

"Time's close to being up on the archive and the property if they haven't been able to get some sort of grants or private funds to help keep it going. And from what you've told me, I suspect they haven't gotten more than a thimbleful recently. There were certain financial stipulations spelled out clearly in addition to the personal ones. Look, it's the age of the internet and all. Little archives and libraries are not as attractive as before. Even the bigger places are busy hustling money. But the archive's property is another matter. It's got to be worth a bundle."

"The property?" I paused a minute as something occurred to me. "If property is worth so much in that neighborhood, then why is that empty lot next door just sitting there? Why isn't someone already building an office or an apartment building or something?"

"I have a theory on that," replied Geraldine, not missing a beat. "Whoever owns it is waiting for the Bauwers place to go on the market. Then maybe they'll snatch it up and have two properties and the chance to build some mega-thing. That would be a lot more lucrative. And it would show there's a trend for development on that street."

"I don't suppose you know who owns the lot?" I asked, intrigued by Geraldine's idea.

"Patience, patience," she chided. "I'm working on it. And I'm only giving you the short form of the story right now. Can you meet me tomorrow around 4:30 for coffee? I have an evening meeting but I'll spend a little while really bringing you up to speed. I'm literally running out the door now."

Geraldine was always running someplace or other. "Sure."

"Oh, and I'll leave you with a tantalizing little detail. When the property is eventually sold for megabucks, it looks like the descendants of the original property owners get the bulk of the loot."

"Harlan Bauwers?" I asked, offering the most logical conclusion.

"The Bauwers and—" She paused dramatically. "—Tipton families."

Chapter Twenty-Six

Gloom and fear radiated from the walls of the archive. The police seemed to have all but vanished from the area, as well. As Baxter quickly pointed out, theirs was a busy precinct and they were probably already tackling the new week's latest crimes.

"We're not talking something random here," scolded Meghan at our next informal gathering in the kitchen after Millicent's death. Baxter had just offered his commentary on the subject. He now remained silent.

However, Alan was sitting nearby, nursing his second cup of coffee and staring at a somewhat out-of-character lunch of two chocolate donuts.

"If you don't think it was a mugging, then who are you accusing of murder?" Even I was startled by his outburst. Fear had worn the edge off some of Alan's usual surface charm.

"I'm not accusing anyone of anything," replied Meghan. "But Millicent was too smart to have been in that awful lot at night by herself, and in the pouring rain. There must be a lot more to the story."

"Well, until we know, I'm keeping a lookout for criminals, and I'm not staying here after dark." Baxter spoke definitively before gathering the remains of his lunch wrappers and leaving.

"I guess we're all a little on edge," I commented. With that, I rose and left, deciding to spend a little time in the display room. Truthfully, it was a place to escape the tension and, in some way, I felt that somehow the displays might connect to Geraldine's discoveries. It wouldn't hurt to take another look before we met for coffee later on.

While I studied a series of letters in one of the display cases, the huge wooden door creaked open. I turned to see Ms. Tipton's formidable presence in the doorway. My gray-striped sweater suddenly became uncomfortably hot, despite the cool temperature in the room. I quickly broke out in a full-blown sweat.

"Emma," began Ms. Tipton. "I'm so glad you're enjoying our museum room."

Suddenly, I was at a loss for words. "It's...fas...fascinating."

"Those letters certainly are wonderful," she continued, walking in my direction and pointing at the pages securely placed under glass in the slanted case. "They're from some historic figures...Mayor Strong, Teddy Roosevelt when he was Police Commissioner..."

She waved a hand in the direction of the case. I'd been curious about the letter from Teddy Roosevelt, with its brief few lines of thanks written on the aging paper, one small corner worn off with time. I also spied a letter nearby from Lucretia Bauwers herself, but it had faded so badly as to be almost indecipherable. I'd love to see some of her other letters and keepsakes, now in storage.

"We have many more items in our rare collection, and we occasionally rotate them in and out of the displays. These documents are so valuable to our researchers. Our own Mr. Martin"—she gestured as if he stood nearby—"finds our holdings quite helpful with his research into the Roosevelts."

I assumed she was referring to Hedgehog. So that was his real name. *Why was Ms. Tipton here anyway? And why was she so anxious to keep talking with me? Did she think I knew something about Millicent?*

Despite my growing unease at being alone with Ms. Tipton, my interest in the collection was genuine. *Should I ask her about it?* Maybe this would make things feel normal.

Curiosity got the better of me. "Did the Bauwers family know all of these people?"

"Some," replied Ms. Tipton, fixing her usual intense gaze on me. *Or was it more than usual?* "Additional items were donated by other families when the archive came into being. The Bauwers family had a large social circle."

I remembered what Geraldine told me when we first met. There were a lot of people who were only too glad to dump their papers and miscellany at the archive. Some didn't realize, or care, what they had in their possession. *Just like Ralph.*

"This is one of our older letters." She indicated a page written by DeWitt Clinton, both mayor and governor long before the timeframe of most of this collection. "There are some fascinating ones in storage, too…Herman Melville, Philip Hone…Of course, these were before the era our archive focuses on. But historically, they're quite valuable."

Ms. Tipton continued her monologue about the archive's holdings while Geraldine's phone call from yesterday echoed in my mind. I shuddered with dread. If the archive really had come upon hard times and the sale of the property would yield a king's ransom of real estate money, then would Ms. Tipton be one of the beneficiaries? After all, her name was Tipton, and Geraldine said that both the Bauwers *and* Tipton families would inherit.

And could Ms. Tipton have killed Millicent so that her own share would be larger? But that was ridiculous because Millicent's husband was still alive. And what of Harlan Bauwers? From the little gossip I'd recently heard, his current stay in the hospital would be an extended one, and it seemed as if he might not return here. Suddenly an awful thought popped into my mind. It was true that Harlan Bauwers was quite elderly and frail. But what if someone did something to him to send him to the hospital? *What if someone tried to murder him, too?*

Ms. Tipton broke into my racing thoughts. "How is your own research going, Emma? Have you been able to determine the identities of those who owned the jewelry?"

This was uncomfortable. I still hadn't told anyone at the archive about the jewelry being fake and that now I was interested in the lives and careers of women writers and playwrights—and not those of thieves and crooks, unless they were part of a plotline.

"I'm working on it. There's so much information," I responded vaguely. "I think I've narrowed down some of the documents I need to re-read," I continued, grasping for a way to get out of this conversation without divulging anything. *Would it really matter if I did?*

The large door creaked open once again. Baxter. I held back a sigh of relief.

"Oh, I'm so sorry," he began, startled as always.

Baxter seemed like a frightened bird. His hand, predictably, went up to stroke his throat. "I didn't mean to interrupt. But Ms. Tipton, uh, a courier just delivered an envelope for you. I thought you'd want to know."

"Thank you, Baxter. I'll be right down to my office." Then she turned to me. "Emma, good luck with your treasure hunt. And please let me know what you find out. We're always interested in what our researchers discover." As she turned to leave, she added, "We're so proud of all of you."

Ms. Tipton then retreated from the room to turn her attention to yet another mysterious envelope. Was it similar to the one Baxter delivered during my first meeting with her?

When the door closed again, I finally breathed deeply. Ms. Tipton had been so pleasant. Maybe my imagination was just playing tricks on me. Surely there must be a logical explanation for all of this. Here I was suspecting Ms. Tipton of murder in order to claim a bigger portion of an inheritance. That didn't make any sense. And suppose Geraldine was wrong about the will? And suppose Ms. Tipton just coincidentally happened to have the same last name as a long-ago business associate of Prescott Bauwers? *And suppose Millicent really had been killed by a mugger? Suppose Harlan was truly ill and not the victim of attempted murder?* Maybe all of this was another of my wild fantasies like my jewelry which, in the end, turned out to be just a collection of theater props.

I again focused my attention on the museum room. At the moment, some peaceful time here would be nice before going back downstairs and then on to meet Geraldine for coffee.

First, I went to one of the high windows, carefully pulling back its sweeping red drape. It was quiet down on the street. What would the same scene have looked like a century ago? Surely that building across the street—the one with the haphazardly boarded up window—would have been elegant and well cared for. A shadow now fell on the sidewalk in front of it. A stooped man in a threadbare coat slowly shuffled up the street. A siren blared in the distance. I let the drape fall gently back into place.

Wandering over to a wall unit, I studied the shelf of attractive silver objects with its spoons, tankards, bowls. I had seen and admired them before. One pitcher in particular was my favorite. Its simple lines and fine engraving exuded an understated elegance.

Curious, though. A companion pitcher appeared to be out of alignment with the other items, as if it had been moved. The dust surrounding its original position clearly indicated a recent change. If some motion in the room jarred it, then why were all of the other pieces nearby still in place? Maybe it was taken out for repair and then replaced.

I glanced at the old clock on the wall. Only a little while remained before my meeting with Geraldine. I needed to gather my things in the research room now.

On my way down the stairs, I passed the Bauwers family portraits. Why wasn't Prescott's wife among them? Hadn't there been a portrait of her as well? I stopped abruptly in front of Elizabeth and studied her compassionate face. If only she could answer my many questions about this perplexing family and their equally perplexing archive and museum.

I immediately became aware of Ms. Tipton and

Alan Renleigh in the downstairs hallway, deep in what appeared to be a serious conversation. *What was this about?* Ms. Tipton moved into my view. She was clutching a catalog envelope close to her. *Was this the one just delivered by special courier? Were she and Alan discussing its contents?*

****

"Who do you trust there?"

Geraldine's question was bold and to the point. We sat at a pastry shop near the main New York Public Library building. Even though she had an evening meeting, Geraldine was anxious to get together now and share what she'd learned.

"Umm, Meghan, I guess," I said in response to her immediate question. "And Baxter, although he's so nervous I'm afraid he'd flip out with any more stress. Oh, and maybe Joe. Did I tell you that he and my friend Della have started to date?"

Geraldine's green eyes widened. "You didn't tell me your friend is doing research there."

"She's not. She came a little early to meet me one day and Joe sat and talked with her while she waited. I guess they hit it off and one thing led to another, and he asked her out."

"What did she say about the date?"

"Just that he's really nice. And they've been on a second date, too. I mean Joe seems like a regular guy, and he's not involved with any of the research stuff at the archive…"

"Which means absolutely nothing," chimed in Geraldine with her signature directness. *Did she suspect Joe? She'd already mentioned he was fairly new at the archive.*

"True. But Della is totally picky about men. She had an unpleasant divorce and, basically, the few dates she's been on have not worked out. Like I said, she's careful."

"Hmpf," snorted Geraldine. "Sometimes the ones who work out are the real con men."

"Jeez, Geraldine! Even my radar tells me Joe isn't a con man." *Still.*

"All I can say is I don't know Joe or Della, so I'm keeping an open mind."

I had to smile. Geraldine and Della would make an interesting pair. And as far as Joe was concerned, Geraldine would have to meet him to decide for herself.

"Look," I broke in, eager to get back to Geraldine's original question. "As far as the others are concerned, I really don't know them. There's Mr. Winthrop, who's just like an armed guard in the research room. And the other researchers? Well, there's Hedgehog and the Sherlock Lady. They're regulars, but I've basically done no more than say hello to them. And you know Alan Renleigh, always down in the stacks and driving me crazy with his whole Prince Charming routine. And there's one or two others who come on occasion, either upstairs or downstairs but, come to think of it, they haven't been there in a bit."

"Wait," interrupted Geraldine. "That's all? There aren't any more people?"

She was genuinely shocked.

"Yeah, that's about it, unless you count in Ms. Tipton, and we're not even going there in the trust department. And, oh, of course, there's Ashley, the college intern. But I doubt she's coming back. And I only met Harlan Bauwers once before he went to the hospital."

"Emma, when I visited to get information for my article, not even a year ago, there were more people doing research."

I was taken aback. True, it struck me on a number of occasions how the place was definitely underused but, now, seen through Geraldine's eyes, it seemed almost abandoned.

"I guess there's a cleaning crew that comes in at night? But they really aren't part of the archive." *Was there really even a cleaning crew?*

Geraldine raised a skeptical eyebrow at this.

"And Alan said that Harlan Bauwers had a companion of some sort who cooked and helped him, but she isn't there now."

"Then it supports what I found out."

"Please tell me, Geraldine," I pleaded. "This whole situation is getting to be way beyond upsetting." My fork was poised in mid-air for several minutes and now a small chunk of flaky chocolate croissant fell off its tines and into my lap.

"Eat, Emma." Geraldine smiled as she watched me remove the mess as subtly as I could. "Here's the story. I was able to read Lucretia's will, and it was a humdinger. She inherited money to spare as well as the house and property. This was originally the site of the Bauwers & Tipton headquarters. When they split, Prescott Bauwers moved his family in."

"Forever?" I asked. "That was the only place they lived?"

"Yep." Geraldine paused to point to her coffee cup, and our waitress acknowledged her signal. She waited for the refill before continuing.

"So, like I told you before, Lucretia was stuck at the turn of the century. Thought it was the golden age of everything, and she saved, collected, and received all kinds of stuff, crap included, and turned it into the privately run archive and museum display room."

"Noble, but expensive," I commented.

"Right. But if you have money, what the heck. Now, here's the deal. Looks like she planned the whole thing with a snazzy law firm that had a ton of partners. They handled the legal and financial stuff, or so it appears, and set it up in—what do they call it—perpetuity?"

"Yeah, but that was a long time ago, right?"

"Sort of, but here's the thing. Lucretia must have been sharp as a tack and had a will of iron to run the show for a long time. She died when she was ninety-five and that was in the mid-1970s."

I gave a low whistle. "Pretty far from the turn of the century, I'd say."

"Closer to the turn of the next one," said Geraldine, raising her blue coffee mug.

"So, you told me on the phone about a time limit or something," I prompted.

"Yes. Not just time, but a resources limit."

I gave her a quizzical look.

"Okay, here's what it appears to be. She arranged for the archive to be kept in business for the use of worthy private researchers for up to fifty years."

"That's a lot of funding. And," I continued, "fifty years still haven't quite passed."

"Yeah, well, there were stipulations. She also insisted the archive needed to seek outside grants and funds to ensure continuing operations on a practical basis well into the future. She took into account rising costs and inflation and had no intention of depleting the core of her estate in the process. And she stated that these outside funds would re-emphasize the worth of the whole enterprise over the course of time. And if not, well, then the archive would be in jeopardy and have to fold."

"She really was pretty sharp," I agreed, finishing the last of my pastry as I listened.

"Yeah. And she was probably trying to model the archive after some of the larger institutions in the city. That might have been her futuristic game plan. Anyway, it doesn't seem that this whole idea had legs, though, in the long run. Maybe the lawyers were busy elsewhere or the nature of what the researchers were working on didn't generate enough interest to attract funding in the percentages she mentioned."

"Then what?"

"If the outside funding and usage track record looked dismal before or near the time projection, and if Harlan moved or died, then the building and property were to be sold and the research contents donated to various earmarked institutions as the lawyers and remaining staff saw fit. Any monetary proceeds were to be divided among remaining heirs or, if no one was left, donated to charity."

"Hmm. That begs the question of how many remaining heirs there would be," I said. "And Harlan has a son. And now we have found out that Millicent was presumably his wife."

Geraldine smiled like the Cheshire Cat. "Right. But there's more, and I'm still digging into the heirs thing. Don't faint, though, when I tell you what I do know."

"This has got to be a whopper," I said, my eyes wide with anticipation.

Geraldine was thoroughly enjoying herself. "Let me keep you in suspense for a minute. It appears that the oldest living heir, although he is not doing well, is Harlan. He was Lucretia's *great*-nephew. Sort of all made me wonder, since Lucretia only had a sister."

"Elizabeth, whose portrait is on the wall. And whatever happened to her?"

"She died relatively young, compared to Lucretia anyway. Now, she never married nor, purportedly, did Lucretia."

"So where did a nephew, or great-nephew, come from?"

"Well, I'm digging further into the nitty-gritty details, but here's the capper. It's how Harlan—our current Harlan—was listed in the will." She paused for effect.

"Harlan Tipton Bauwers."

Chapter Twenty-Seven

The next day, I decided to move ahead with a plan. Geraldine asked who I trusted at the archive, and Meghan was at the top of the list. It was time we talked. I caught up with her halfway down the block after closing time.

"Do you have a few minutes for a cup of coffee?" I asked as the startled young woman turned to face me. Like the rest of us, she was probably on edge. Eerie shadows were beginning to lengthen on the quiet block. Autumn dusk would soon turn into night, and nighttime seemed to be what the mugger favored.

"Umm. Sure. Where do you want to go?"

I remembered the Café Alabaster where we had gone with Alan Renleigh. Why not? It was close by and quiet enough to give us a chance to talk. And there were two of us, hopefully not an appealing target for one mugger.

Meghan and I walked in semi-silence for the few blocks en route to the café. She had been particularly somber since Millicent's death.

"I wish the police would find who killed Millicent," I said. Our silence, only punctuated by our echoing footsteps, began to unnerve me. It might be best to bring Meghan out of her deep thoughts before we reached the café and rekindle that same upbeat person who first took me on a tour of the archive. *Had that only been a few weeks ago?* It felt like years.

"Emma. I know what we've both been thinking." Meghan stopped and looked at me directly. "Millicent's death was not random."

*Was it so obvious to everyone what I'd been thinking?*

"We both know this was murder," she continued.

I looked down at a crack in the sidewalk and nodded sadly. Meghan pulled her burgundy scarf closer against the sudden wind, or was it a sudden chill prompted by the mention of murder? She'd already been upfront about her suspicions in the past few days. And much as I tried to remain noncommittal, it was no use hiding my thoughts now.

We chose a small table in a windowed corner of the Café Alabaster. It was a bit disconcerting to sit near one of the café's signature sculptures—a giant alabaster ear mounted on the wall adjacent to the window. We did not need extra ears, real or otherwise, privy to our conversation, but this little niche was quiet and the sculpture didn't seem to register on Meghan. We ordered coffee and a small plate of homemade cookies and continued talking. "Okay, Meghan," I began. "Please tell me why you think Millicent was murdered, especially since the police still seem to be writing it off as another random crime."

Meghan sighed and looked down at the tablecloth for a minute. "Because I don't think the mugging before this was random either. Maybe the first one was, but not the second. And certainly not Millicent's."

"Why?"

"The first one was maybe random. We didn't know the person or the complete circumstances. And let's face it, muggings aren't exactly big news in a neighborhood like this. But the second one…I knew the woman. Sally. She was the last victim before Millicent, and one of our researchers. No one wants to talk about her. She wasn't at the archive for very long, only to finish some short-term research for a school paper. It was one of those deals where she went back to college after being away for years. She wanted to finally get her degree."

"Okay," I said, allowing Meghan to sip her coffee. I pushed the plate of cookies in her direction. "And what was Sally researching?"

"Oh, it was something pretty straightforward about contrasting the stories of two immigrant families with the stories of two rich families around the turn of the century. Of course, she was at the Bauwers to find out about the rich people." Meghan took a cookie and then continued thoughtfully. "She wanted a diary or some letters or something that could give her a real flavor of the people and the times. Then she planned to use another archive for the immigrant portion of her project. I suggested the Tenement Museum or the Five Points History Museum. I was a summer intern at both."

"That all seems reasonable. Why would anyone have a problem with Sally doing any of that?" I was genuinely confused how something so clear-cut could lead to foul play.

"That's just the thing," said Meghan, finishing her cookie and beginning to nervously twist her paper napkin. "It *was* reasonable, except that one day Sally noticed something weird."

I raised my eyebrows in question.

Meghan sipped her coffee. "She was in the research room and asked for a box of letters sent by some branch of the Astors to another prominent New York family. This was the second time she'd asked for it. Seems as if two of the letters were gone."

"Two letters she had seen before?"

"Yes. And you know how careful Mr. Winthrop insists we have to be. It seemed impossible that these were misplaced." Meghan bit into another cookie, and we paused while the waitress refilled our cups.

When she walked away, Meghan continued. "Sally was upset and for good reason. Obviously, the letters had information that was useful to her and she wanted to double check it. And, yes, she took really good notes, so she knew exactly which letters she was looking for. But she was also worried that Mr. Winthrop or Ms. Tipton would think she'd taken the letters, so she reported them missing immediately."

"Well, I can't imagine how anyone could take anything with Mr. Winthrop watching," I said, hoping for a little smile from Meghan. Who could resist an innocent joke about the ever-watchful Mr. Winthrop?

"What happened then?" I asked, catching the small look of amusement on her face.

"Nothing really. There was a big fuss for Baxter and me because they made us search through all recent items we brought back to the rare research storage, suggesting that one of us had misfiled it. It's possible, but we really try to be careful."

"How many people have access to those rare files?" I asked.

"Aside from Baxter and me, there's Mr. Winthrop and Ms. Tipton, of course. But once in a while Ashley went there and picked up files that had already been pulled. And Joe has access to do repairs and check on building maintenance there. And, of course, Harlan Bauwers could go anywhere." Meghan took a sip of coffee. "No one else has formal access, but there's no security guard or cameras or special locks, so a random researcher could slip in. But, as you've probably noticed, there's not a lot of people who use the place. I mean, it's not impossible that the letters were misplaced. But one way or another," she concluded, "they're just gone."

So much for narrowing down the list of possible culprits.

"That's weird." I thought for a minute. "Was there anything special in them that would have been of interest to someone other than a researcher?"

"That's what everyone asked Sally, but she really didn't think there was anything unusual. They were just about a special occasion sponsored by some organization or other, and they were signed by a member of the Astor family. It seems unlikely that anyone would have taken them. And for what good reason anyway?"

I shrugged. "And no one blamed Sally?"

"No. They probably figured that if she'd been guilty, she wouldn't have said anything in the first place. After all, the chance that someone else would request that exact same box or those exact same letters was pretty slim. No one would have found out."

We sipped our coffee in silence for a minute. Twilight settled in the outside sky, and the little candle on the table cast a strange glow on the alabaster ear.

"Okay, Meghan, but then why do you think her

mugging wasn't really a mugging?"

"That's just the thing. It wasn't the letters themselves that made me wonder, but it was what happened afterwards." Meghan twisted the coffee cup in her hands. "Sally stopped me in the hall one afternoon and said she had something she needed to tell me. She asked if we could meet somewhere offsite and talk. I had something to do that night so we agreed on breakfast the next morning before the archive opened."

I could feel my pulse quicken in anticipation. "What did she say when you met her?"

"She never made it to breakfast that morning. She was mugged after hours the night before—on the same day she came to me. And she was hurt." Meghan looked down at her hands. "I wish I had canceled my original plans and met her that night."

I shuddered as Meghan shook her head sadly as she continued. "I went to see her in the hospital. It seemed as if she was afraid to talk. That's what made me think it wasn't a random attack. I mean, if you've been mugged, you'd want to tell the whole story, right? Exactly how it happened. What the person did to you. Everything you remember. But she held back, and she had a hard time looking at me. I asked her what she'd wanted to tell me, but she said she forgot."

There were tears in Meghan's eyes when she looked up. "Emma, I know she didn't forget. Maybe I'm wrong, but I have a feeling that it had something to do with those missing letters and maybe more than that. She was scared of something and never came back to the archive. I tried calling her to see how she was doing when she got home from the hospital, but she never answered my calls. There was something more going on. I know it."

"What about the police?" I asked. "What did they say?"

"The usual. It's a questionable area. Higher crime than elsewhere. Please be careful and don't stay after dark. And it seems probable that Sally didn't tell them anything either. And why was she on the street after dark anyway? It doesn't make sense."

Meghan stopped for a breath.

I was at a loss to figure out these new details. "I'm so sorry."

"Me, too," she replied sadly.

"What about Millicent? It seems as if her situation was entirely different," I commented. "Especially now that we know she was part of the Bauwers family by marriage, at least."

"That was something I didn't know, and it makes me feel a little bad because, well, maybe we would have considered her a little more seriously. You know what I mean."

"Yeah, I do," I agreed. "And now I'm wondering if she wanted to conceal her identity for some reason and that maybe that whole plain and drab look was some sort of camouflage."

"That occurred to me, too. But why? And evidently Ms. Tipton knew who she was."

"Did she? I mean before the police let that bit of information drop?"

A shadow crept across the wall. But it was only the waitress re-lighting a candle that had gone out at an empty table.

"I just assumed so because she told me that Millicent was Harlan's daughter-in-law. But, then again, maybe that was after she found out from the police." Meghan took another sip of coffee and stared woefully at the flickering candle.

"Do you remember the day you introduced me to Millicent? Her handshake and the ring that made such an impression on my palm?"

"Yes." She looked up and offered a half-smile. "She had quite some firm grip and those stones really dug in. It looked like they hurt."

"They did." I smiled, too. "But here's the thing. That ring looked awfully similar to the one that Elizabeth Bauwers was wearing in her portrait. Could it be the same one?"

"Possibly," replied Meghan. "If Millicent was a Bauwers by marriage, that makes sense."

"The part that doesn't make sense," I said, "was the person who killed her didn't take the ring."

"Didn't you tell me the cops said a mugger might have been frightened off?"

"True, and fair enough," I agreed. "But it's still strange. And why did she always keep the stones facing toward her palm in the first place. Hiding them. She said they slipped around, but she didn't try to adjust them. And why wear the ring to the archive at all?"

"I wish I knew," replied Meghan. "And there's another thing I wish I knew."

*There was more?*

"I heard Millicent tell Ms. Tipton she needed to sit down with her soon and talk at length about something. I'm sorry I didn't hear what it was. Maybe I would have had more information to give to the police."

"Could it have had something to do with the photographs?"

"I have no idea."

We sat in silence for a couple of moments. There was a soft murmur of conversation from a lone couple sitting across the room. Otherwise, the place was empty. The alabaster sculptures went from feeling eerie to downright sinister.

"Emma, why do *you* think she was murdered?"

"Well, in the little contact I had with Millicent, it struck me that there was a lot more to her than met the eye, and there was probably a lot more to her research, too. Plus, something just didn't feel right about her getting into a position where she'd be vulnerable after dark in the vacant lot. She was smarter than that. There must have been a good reason she was there."

Meghan ran her finger over the handle of the coffee cup as she spoke. "Both Sally and Millicent knew something. And maybe they were tricked into staying after dark."

"Agreed," I said. "And now I need to tell you something else I just found out. You may or may not already know this, but I know I can trust you, and this could shed some light on everything else." *Could I trust Meghan? I was in too deep at this point not to trust her.*

"I trust you, too, Emma."

Nodding, I told Meghan about Lucretia's will and its stipulations. Meghan's eyes widened at the news.

"That explains a lot of things," she said ruefully.

"Like what?"

"Like why there've been so few new researchers lately. It's as if things have been getting ready to shut down. There's not the same energy to the place. And aside from being included in that article a while back, the archive hasn't been actively trying to get new business. Oh, Ms. Tipton was quite pleased when you came. And now with what you just told me about the will, I'm wondering if she thought you might make some large discovery and attract some funders."

"Sort of a last-ditch effort? Ha! And I'm just one person researching a family thing. And that's a whole other story at this point." I still hadn't told Meghan how my own project had changed. Maybe this was going to be the time.

"And there've been a whole lot of mysterious envelopes delivered by courier, from some law firm I think, especially after Mr. Bauwers went into the hospital. It's got to be connected."

*So Meghan was curious about the envelopes, too.*

Now was the time to deliver my most surprising detail. "Did you know that Harlan Bauwers' middle name is Tipton?"

"*What*?"

"There's more, Meghan, and I'm not sure how to connect all the dots in this."

I then told Meghan everything—how my personal research had been a dead end or, rather, a fake jewelry end. Then I filled her in about Louise and everything she told me and how, subsequently, I'd been reading newspapers online about my own ancestor and had come up with the details about Prescott Bauwers and Morgan Tipton quite by accident.

"Whoa!" exclaimed Meghan, sitting up ramrod straight and looking at me directly. "That is totally bizarre. And given what you just told me, this doesn't exactly put Ms. Tipton in a good light."

"True," I agreed. "But we need more information about the two families. I'm looking into it and so is a researcher friend of mine."

"I can do something, too." Suddenly, some of Meghan's old spark came back into her eyes. "Emma. We have diaries and letters from the Bauwers family along with all of the other research things. Oh, sure, they're in the rare documents storage rooms but I could read some while I'm up there pulling files. And I'm wondering if there's some way for you to request some of it as part of your research. This could give us a lot more of what we need."

"And I think I have an idea that might actually double our efforts."

Meghan looked at me quizzically. I smiled. A totally crazy plan was starting to form and it was, in Geraldine's words, a humdinger.

Chapter Twenty-Eight

"And how do you know you can trust Geraldine? Or Meghan?" Della spoke frankly after I'd spilled everything about my conversations with them. Trust was a hot topic these days.

"I'm going with my gut feeling. I know it's been wrong in the past, but what am I supposed to do?" I hesitated and then asked Della my burning question.

"And Joe? Umm, do you feel you can trust him with information? And in general?" There. It was out. I asked it. Della had gone on her second dinner date with him, and I wanted everything to be okay for her, and I wanted to be able to trust Joe, too. It's just that as a newer member of the archive staff, it raised questions about the timing of his arrival.

"Totally! Why would you even ask such a thing?"

Della's voice was emphatic and her face looked stunned and hurt. I felt wretched.

"Okay, okay, look," I began. "I like Joe, but I just want everything to go well for you."

Della's expression softened, but only a little. "I know you do. But Joe's a great guy. He really cares about his grandkids and spends a lot of time with them. And he's nice to me, Emma. I mean, we've just gone out to dinner twice, but we've really hit it off."

I took a deep breath and then burst out with my latest thought. "Hey, I have a great idea. Why don't you bring Joe to Ralph's Halloween party? I know it'll be fine with Ralph as long as I bring enough pumpkin cookies."

Finally, something resembling a tiny smile broke out on Della's face. "That sounds really good. I'll ask Joe on Sunday. We're spending the day together. You know, meet all of the grandkids, take a drive…"

"Gee, Dell. This sounds serious. Umm, I don't suppose you guys talk about the archive or anything like that." I left my question hanging.

"You wouldn't be pumping me for information now, would you?"

"No…yes…well, I mean if Joe just happened to say anything." *I could hope, couldn't I?* Any morsel would help.

"Look. He's only there a couple of months. I don't know how much you know about Joe, but he's a retired police officer and worked in security for a while."

I was surprised. *And he's doing maintenance for an archive? And then there was Geraldine's comment about con men.* A trickle of suspicion crept into my throat. "I mean that's sort of, umm, different. It's not exactly in his field."

"Emma. There's more to the story, I think, but I know he'll tell me in time. I mean, we just started dating. And it's maintenance combined with a little security."

Images of corruption and of being let go from former jobs raced through my mind. "But what if…"

Della didn't let me finish. "It's okay, Emma. Really."

I decided not to pursue it further now, but I was worried. *Suppose Joe was…*I couldn't even think it. My instinct told me he couldn't possibly have committed any crime, no less murder. After all, he was the one who ran to Millicent first to see if she was still breathing. But that didn't necessarily mean anything, did it? On the other hand, what motive could he possibly have? I couldn't begin to unravel the story, not to mention my own thoughts.

"I can see the wheels working in your head," continued Della. "It's okay. Believe me. Now tell me about this wild plan of yours."

"All right, but it's top secret."

"Agreed," said Della.

Taking another deep breath, I told her everything about my latest plan to gather information.

Della was surprised. "Wait a minute. You're going to ask Geraldine to go back to the archive and say she's researching a follow-up to her original article? And have her request Lucretia's diaries and letters as background? Won't that be a little obvious there's a fishing expedition going on?"

"Not as obvious as Meghan trying to read letters and diaries on the sly and getting caught red-handed, or me asking for some of the same Bauwers documents for a made-up but pretty transparent reason," I responded.

"On the surface, it's logical. In reality, this is nuts! Have you run this by Geraldine yet? Or Meghan?"

"Well, not exactly. I was hoping you'd tell me what you think first."

"Oh, jeez! I don't want to say yay or nay and be responsible if things mess up."

"But you just said it's logical, right?" I asked hopefully.

"In theory. In the working out, I'm not so sure."

"How about this? I'll get everyone together—you, Geraldine, Meghan, and me—and we can all discuss it in person."

"What? Emma, what do I have to do with it?"

"You're my best friend and you've been in on the whole story since the beginning. And you're dating Joe, and he works at the archive. Don't you want to be doubly sure he's not in any danger?" This was my most persuasive argument and a better way of putting it than asking if she wanted to be sure he wasn't guilty of something.

Della looked at me wryly. "Okay. Okay. Now here's another question for you. I will keep it top secret because you asked me to. But think about this for a moment: wouldn't it also be helpful to bring Joe in on the plan?"

I winced. "Okay, but let's work out the details of Phase One first."

Della brushed her green-streaked bangs away from her face and looked at me directly. "I'm just saying, it could be a good idea."

"And it could. But let's have this meeting together first with the four of us."

"All right, Emma. I hope I can help."

"I know you can."

I knew that Della was a bit disappointed that I didn't include Joe in the meeting, but I had to think through the whole thing first. *And come to grips with any trust issues I had about Joe. But should I also be having trust issues with Geraldine and Meghan?*

As soon as Della left, I texted Meghan to tell her I wanted to get together to discuss a sort of crazy plan. I'd call her soon with the details.

But, of course, I needed to run my crazy plan by Geraldine before really forging ahead. I dialed her number. *Here goes.*

"Great minds work alike. I was going to call you tonight," she answered. "What's up?"

I filled her in on the latest developments since we'd met for coffee. A lot had happened in the past twenty-four hours. I then outlined my plan about the four of us getting together, and why. Finally, I announced that I had a major role in mind for her and, after all, it could yield a good story or stories. However, I was pretty sure she hadn't counted on being quite so integral a part of things. And besides, she did have her own busy freelance career to attend to, so she might not even have the time to get involved. I took a deep breath and launched into my idea.

"Quite diabolical," commented Geraldine when I finished. There was a moment of silence during which I thought I had gone way too far out on a limb and figured she might tell me to jump in the lake—or something more colorful to that effect.

"I like it! This could be a great story, especially if the archive is going to fold. It'll have history, human interest, intrigue. And I'll feel like a genuine undercover spy, too."

*Good grief! Why had I been worried? And what had I just started?*

I was relieved. "I'm so glad. We can talk about it more when we all get together."

Geraldine agreed to the meeting date, and it looked as if the plan was already in the works.

"By the way, you said you were about to call me. Anything new?"

"I thought you'd never ask," said Geraldine. "I have this friend who can get me some genealogical information fast. You won't believe this one."

"Uh-oh."

"You know how we wondered what branch of the family Harlan came from and how he got the name he did? Well, here's what I found out. Despite the fact that Prescott Bauwers and Morgan Tipton had a falling out, their kids were engaged."

"What?"

"But it appears to have been broken after the business split." Geraldine paused dramatically. "However, it seems as if Lucretia Bauwers and Morgan Tipton, Jr., stayed in close touch. Very close touch. I can't find any evidence that they ever married but it looks like they had an *affaire du coeur* at the very least. Now for the capper. It seems that Lucretia had a son."

"Wow."

"Now, remember, that's what it appears to be, but you know how sketchy old records and certificates can be. *If* it's true, she might have given birth on one of those long trips abroad that were so popular in those days. That's just a guess, and I'd have to check the details carefully and put a little more two and two together."

"Yeah, but how do you know the father was Morgan Tipton, Jr.?"

"I don't," said Geraldine. "It's an educated guess. But there was a clipping with an engagement notice in the genealogical files, although no record of marriage. They could have eloped, though, I suppose. The dates for all of this have generally matched so far. At any rate, the family could have said they took in a distant relative and were raising him and, eventually, just said he was a nephew. I'd suspect that Tipton Junior may have had no idea of any of this at the time. And hence, the kid's last name was Bauwers."

"*Our* Harlan's father?" I ventured a guess.

"Could be. The dates would match. I still have some digging to do to verify all of this. That would make our current-day Harlan a great-nephew for public purposes. On the other hand, he could be Lucretia's grandson. But what's in a name?"

"If that's the case, then *our* Harlan might have gotten his middle name of Tipton because of the family connection. Although it does make you wonder how this happened if his lineage was so secret and the animosity so great," I continued, thinking out loud. "And where did Morgan Tipton, Jr., figure in? Did he ever know?"

"Well, now, that's another mystery to be solved, isn't it? And remember, none of this is gospel until I can verify it. Some is logical speculation on my part." But Geraldine was certainly scrupulous about getting her facts correct.

"So that raises another question. How does Ms. Tipton figure in all this? And does this put her on the top or bottom of the suspect list?" I asked.

"Patience, Emma. I'm working on it. We're all working on it. And maybe some of these historical details could shed some light on everything that's happening now."

"You mean on who killed Millicent?"

"Yes, although you realize this could just be old family soap opera and have nothing to do with anything. And the cops could be right about the random angle." Geraldine paused. "But still, Emma, please don't take any chances. There's a strong possibility there's something that someone doesn't want known. We really don't have any idea of what it could be until we look into it more. Sometimes too much information can be a dangerous thing."

"Well, there's safety in numbers," I said. "And there'll be four of us looking for that information. Less danger, right?"

"Hopefully," responded Geraldine. "All right! Can't wait till our Fabulous Foursome gets together."

Chapter Twenty-Nine

"What are these called?" Meghan peered at the amber liquid in her glass.

"Stormy Hurricanes," I said, now a staunch fan of this tasty cocktail.

Della studied the menu etched on the wall. "Is the chili good?"

"I've never tried…" I began.

"I have," chimed in Geraldine. "Trust me. It's the best."

"Could you please pass the spicy pretzels?" Della was eager to try these special snacks.

"Sure. Where did you get those earrings?" Meghan looked inquisitively at Della's feathered creations.

"I made them."

"Awesome! I'd love a pair like that."

Thom, the bartender, raised his eyebrows in amusement as he mixed a second batch of Stormy Hurricanes and listened—couldn't help listening—to the buoyant chatter from our table. The sleuthing team had gathered for a Big City Café dinner. Our first time as a group. All seemed to be going well and everyone blended together genially.

"How did you even find this place?" asked Meghan.

"It was cold outside and I just walked in." Geraldine was her usual direct self.

And so, the getting acquainted conversation continued. After the first round of Stormy Hurricanes, everyone was chatting like old friends.

"You're an artist?"

"Taking the train was easier."

"I haven't seen Christmas lights like that since I was a kid."

"Those are cool mocha suede boots."

Soon, the second round was on its way along with an eclectic mix of dinner selections. It was time to talk about our sleuthing plan, especially since everyone had been brought up to speed at this point. The question was: what to do with this random information?

Meghan dug into a decadent bowl of bacon mac 'n cheese. "Look, I work at the archive so if anyone *needs* to stick their neck out in this whole thing, it should be me. The rest of you don't *have* to put yourselves in danger."

"Hmpf!" retorted Geraldine, crunching down on another spicy pretzel for emphasis before tackling her dinner. "Getting into a little bit of danger is the only way for me to get a good story. And I smell a few good stories here."

Meghan grinned. "You're totally right. And I smell a good chili burger in front of you."

"Smells almost as good as one of those stories," said Geraldine with a laugh.

"Since I'm dating Joe, I want to be sure he's safe. I'm not worried about danger." Della placed her Stormy Hurricane on the table near the small candle. Her green bangs reflected in the amber liquid. She continued while cutting a piece of spicy catfish, a tough choice between this and the chili. "As a matter of fact, I feel bad I'm not in the trenches with the rest of you. Online research at home isn't exactly risking life and limb."

"But it's important," I added quickly, pointing a gigantic sweet potato fry for emphasis and then addressing everyone in the group. "Speaking for myself, I want to help find Millicent's killer. I really can't explain it. It's just something I have to do."

"The archive's become a part of all of our lives, hasn't it? In one way or another," added Meghan thoughtfully. "Dangerous or not."

"Hear, hear," toasted Geraldine with her Stormy Hurricane. But her green eyes were solemn as she continued. "Seriously, though. Meghan's right. Everything else aside, there could be some danger here." She turned to Della. "Even for you, Della. I can vouch for the fact that internet research can sometimes lead to more danger than you realize." She grabbed a paper napkin and wiped her hands. "We should keep open to all possibilities, from muggings to murders to the unexplainable. Just be careful." She took another long gulp of Stormy Hurricane. "Okay everyone. Now let's eat!"

Chapter Thirty

"I need to tell you a story. About Prescott Bauwers."

It was a different kind of dinner on a different evening. Yellow leaves swirled by the windowpanes next to our table at Bella Notte, our favorite Italian restaurant. It was an all-too-rare night out for Steve and me. We stared at the town center brought to vivid life by waves of autumn wind mixing with glimmering streetlights. Dusk already gave way to pre-winter darkness.

"Okay, Emma." Steve reluctantly turned his attention from the window. As much as he tried to be his old genial self, I still caught him looking into space frequently. Reaching out and touching the sleeve of his jacket, I made a clumsy attempt to get him to focus on my words.

"It might give you something to think about while you're working things through with Hank." I paused. "Look, Steve. I'm going to be at the archive. I like it, and I want to be there. So we might as well talk about it."

He tried for a smile. "Okay, Emma. Prescott Bauwers is the guy in the portrait, right?"

"Right. The one with the severe look on his face," I confirmed.

Steve was not thrilled about my insistence on

remaining at the archive to do my research. He'd also been skeptical after learning that our new foursome met for dinner the other night. I emphasized that our goal was to *discuss* the archive's history to see how it might shed some light on current events. I avoided referring to our group as sleuths.

"While you're researching one thing," I commented evasively while telling him about some of our findings, "information about something else is bound to come up. You know."

Our glasses of chianti sparkled in the light of the table's small, globed candle. Steve took a sip of wine before speaking.

"Okay, Emma. Why don't you tell me about Prescott Bauwers. You said I might find him interesting."

Obviously, Steve was trying to keep our dinner conversation pleasant and not revive the well-worn debate about my continuing presence at the archive, a place we both knew I had no intention of abandoning. I relaxed when he returned to the subject of Prescott Bauwers.

"Geraldine found out some interesting details about him," I responded.

A delicious aroma interrupted with the arrival of our dinners. For me, tender, thinly sliced eggplant, breaded and piled high. For Steve, a veal dish with mushrooms and olives in wine sauce. Side dishes of pasta came next. We ate in companionable silence for a few minutes.

"So, Geraldine's been reading some of the Bauwers family diaries." I picked up where I left off before taking the first forkful of eggplant.

"At the archive?" Steve's eyebrows shot up in surprise. "Didn't you tell me the four of you were just *discussing* archive history…over dinner…at a restaurant? Now Geraldine is suddenly at the archive and reading family diaries? Won't this be the same as waving a banner saying you're looking into Millicent's connection to the Bauwers family?"

Steve put down his fork and looked up at me intently.

I grabbed a piece of warm, crusty bread from the basket and dipped it into some olive oil before responding.

"Yes, well, true, but we have a plan. A cover story."

"Cover story?" repeated Steve.

*Oops!* Bad choice of words.

Steve's incredulous reaction made me question if our master plan might not be as clever as we'd originally thought.

"Eat," I said to him. He reluctantly picked up his fork.

I cut another small piece of eggplant and soldiered on. "Since Geraldine already included the archive as part of an article she wrote about small and unusual libraries and museums in the city, she told them she wants to do a follow-up story on the history of some of the more intriguing places." I paused for a minute. "It seemed like a good idea when I…we…dreamed it up." Then I quickly added, "After all, it's just looking into history."

"Suppose," Steve began as he speared a piece of veal with a little more force than necessary, "they ask if she's doing this for the same publication? And maybe they want to see the finished article? What's she going to say?"

Actually, we hadn't worked out that part yet. "First, the process of publishing takes a while. So, there wouldn't be anything to show for a couple of months anyway. And knowing Geraldine," I said with as much confidence as I could muster, "she'll come up with a really good answer for all of this." *At least I hoped so.*

"Emma, this is starting to sound dangerous. You said you and your friends got together to discuss history, not to do detective work, which this is beginning to sound like." Steve took a deep breath. "I think you should leave that to the police."

"Who said anything about detective work? We're just doing historical research. And we're touching on current events at the archive, too."

"I know you, Emma. You're turning this into an investigation of Millicent's death, and you think it was a murder."

*Ah, so it seemed that Steve didn't totally buy the mugging theory either. Why did I tell him as much as I had about the whole situation?*

"Except," I jumped in defiantly, "the police think it was just another random crime."

"But you don't, do you?" Steve was reluctant to let it drop. "Emma, I was worried enough as it was. But if that poor woman was murdered, the last thing you need is to dig into it. Either way, you shouldn't be going to the archive at all."

"It's a part of me, Steve," I said, tearing off another piece of crusty bread with frustrated vigor. "I have to stay there until I'm ready to leave."

"And you've gotten Della involved, too. Aren't

you worried about your best friend?"

"Sure I am. But she's worried about Joe who, if you remember, works there. And besides, she's not doing any research on the premises."

"And you're sure that Joe isn't a mugger or a murderer?"

*Oh, boy, even Steve was sounding suspicious of Joe now.*

"Oh, come on, Steve. That's ludicrous."

A moment of silence followed. We were at an impasse.

I broke in suddenly. "I'm just doing historical research, Steve. It's what people do at an archive. If anything weird comes up while I'm there, then I'll go directly to the police. Quit worrying. You have enough on your mind anyway," I continued, quite eager to change the subject. "Umm, how's it going with Hank?"

Steve grimaced, conceding his position in the battle for the moment. "Not well. At first, he seemed resigned to the break-up of the partnership. But now he wants me to reconsider."

"You're not…"

"No, Emma. Truthfully, I'm stunned that he even asked."

I broke in. "So am I. He has no right!" I angrily tore off another piece of bread as Steve continued.

"Hank's feeling like a trapped animal now. Despite his inference that I'm being unreasonable, he and I both know that dissolving the partnership is necessary. We're both dealing with a lot of resentment now and for different reasons. It doesn't help."

It was my turn to worry about Steve. "I'm so sorry."

Silence fell over the table once more.

Steve wrinkled his forehead skeptically. "Okay. We're supposed to be having a relaxing dinner." He tried for a smile. "So back to what Geraldine found out about Prescott Bauwers."

"Okay. There's a whole story there. Remember Elizabeth Bauwers? That kind-looking woman in one of the portraits? One of Prescott's two daughters? Well, Geraldine has been reading some of her diaries. Fascinating stuff. Elizabeth did some sort of social work and was quite a humanitarian. Anyway, she was upset about the split between Prescott and his business partner, Morgan Tipton."

"As in Ms. Tipton."

"Right. But I'll get into that more later," I said, intent on the main part of my tale.

"So, originally, Prescott and Morgan were in business together. It's a bit hazy what they were involved in, but it seems to have been some sort of finance and real estate enterprise. Anyway, they had a terrible falling out."

"Who did what to whom?" Steve was understandably interested.

"From what Elizabeth alluded to in the diary, Morgan Tipton used company funds to purchase and develop property without Prescott Bauwers' knowledge or consent. Prescott felt that Morgan was going behind his back, which he was, and was trying to do it for some sort of personal gain, rather than allowing the partnership to reap the benefits. It seems possible that Morgan did it to help get his son started in some sort of business. But, in any event, it wasn't the right way to go about it."

Caryl Janis

"Story old as time, with a few variations," mused Steve, twisting the corner of the linen napkin in his hand.

"Yeah, well, that's true. But this one got even more complicated. First, there was the business part. But Prescott's other daughter, Lucretia, and Morgan's son were engaged. And it looked as if parental forces broke them apart after the business split. Lucretia went on one of those tours abroad to possibly get over the break-up, and Morgan's son vanished."

"That *is* sad," said Steve.

I paused as the waitress arrived to clear our dinner plates and glanced enviously across the room at a young couple holding hands. They were totally engrossed in each other's company. "Sad" was obviously not part of their conversation.

It would have been impossible to eat dessert after the large and delicious dinner. So we ordered coffees before getting back to the Bauwers and Tipton family saga.

"But where did Elizabeth fit into all of this?" Steve brought my attention back from the young couple.

"As I said, she seemed like a good soul. She felt that Prescott should forgive Morgan for the shady business deal. There had been a lot of animosity over it, and the business split certainly had a terrible ripple effect on their children's lives. Elizabeth believed that all of that bitterness would only lead to more sorrow."

"Noble, but what did she do about it?"

"She begged her father to sit down with Morgan, to find out why he did what he did in detail. At first, of course, he refused. She evidently went to some of his other trusted friends and even their family clergyman for support. Elizabeth emphasized that the anger between them had caused enough heartbreak for their children."

Steve looked up. "A tenacious woman."

*If I was as tenacious as Elizabeth, could I at least deflate the anger that Steve and Hank now felt toward each other? Then Steve could forge ahead with the business on his own. And we could go on with our lives.*

"True," I agreed. "And Elizabeth was not only tenacious, but she was successful. She eventually got the two men to talk in person. No one knew the exact gist of their meeting but, afterwards, they agreed to shake hands and bury the past. Geraldine is still looking for more details." I paused, smiling at Geraldine's single-minded determination.

"No matter," I continued. "She did find out that Morgan donated the money he made on his private deal to a charitable cause. Prescott was fine with this. It wasn't about money for him. It was about honor. But Elizabeth knew that the anger had to stop before the pain it caused kept growing."

"Did they ever go back into business together?" asked Steve.

"No, that wouldn't have worked."

Steve was quiet for a moment. Our coffees arrived, and he stirred his milk in carefully, staring at the hot mixture while deep in thought.

"Of course, you're thinking about my situation with Hank."

I looked up at him. "Maybe Prescott's story is sort of about not letting hurt and anger dig so deep that it causes lifelong harm."

"And without Elizabeth, he never would have

realized this?"

"Maybe not. But she did something really good. Unfortunately, it didn't happen in time to ease her sister's heartbreak."

"That part is truly sad." Steve took a sip of his coffee. "And I have a feeling you're taking a page from Elizabeth's book and trying to help mend some fences in my situation. Lessen some of the negative feelings."

I smiled. "I'm just telling you a research story. I thought you'd be interested. It's just historical research."

Steve smiled, too. "I *am* interested." He sighed and looked out the window for a brief moment. "You said there's more to the story."

"There is. But I'll tell you later. Maybe you just want to think about this part for now."

We both smiled and then sat for a quiet moment, gazing out the window at the autumn night, lost in our separate worlds.

****

Dinner out had been a welcome change, but Steve and I arrived home somewhat drained from our conversation about the archive, the Bauwers family, and Hank. He sank into an armchair with the newspaper, and I decided it was a good time to call Ralph.

"You saw Louise? Without me?"

"I said I *called* Louise. I had some questions about Antonia Emmaline's books and papers. And some of her answers pointed me in an even better direction with my research. Relax, Ralph. Next time I plan to visit her in person, I'll call you. She said to give you her best. I know you enjoyed seeing Louise *and* eating those sugar cookies."

"You're a riot, Em."

"Speaking of cookies, the reason I called was to ask if Steve and I can bring the pumpkin cookies to your place on Friday night when we drop off the extra folding chairs and tables you wanted. We figured this would be easier, especially since we're taking Della and Joe with us to your party on Sunday. Then we won't have to worry about any of it. We have a lot of containers, and I want them to arrive safely. I don't want to risk breaking any of the cookies."

"That *would* be tragic," said Ralph immediately. "I was going to call you anyway. While you're here, maybe you and Steve could also give us a hand setting up those chairs and putting up a couple of decorations here and there."

"Sure, Ralph. We'll be happy to help. Oh, and I need your solemn promise not to take even one cookie before the party on Sunday."

"You can rely on me."

"I certainly hope so. Maybe I'll mention something to Sheila."

He ignored this. "See you Friday night then."

We hadn't signed off for more than a minute when the *quack-quack* of my cell phone sounded once more.

"What is it Ralph?"

"You'll put faces on the pumpkin cookies, right? I always liked faces on the cookies."

"Yes, they will all have nice pumpkin faces, Ralph. Don't worry."

After hanging up with Ralph, I was aware of the mild autumn breeze catching some stray leaves and the sound of Chester barking—continually.

Just before it was time for bed, Mrs. Ryan called.

"I hate to bother you so late."

"It's okay, Mrs. Ryan," I assured her. "Is everything all right?"

"I guess so, but I thought you'd like to know that Chester has been looking out the window and barking off and on for a while. He does that sometimes, you know, but I thought I'd check and see what was bothering him. I can't swear to it because it's dark, but it looked like someone was walking in your backyard near the window. It might have been a shadow, but I couldn't go to sleep until I let you know. Just in case. Whatever it was isn't there now."

I shuddered. "Thanks for letting me know, Mrs. Ryan. It's good that Chester was barking. But I'm sure it was only a shadow, or maybe the leaves."

Even though Steve and I turned on the outside lights, we didn't see anyone in our yard. And with the autumn leaves and the dark night, it could have been anything that Mrs. Ryan saw.

"It was probably just a shadow," said Steve. "And you know how Chester is."

"Right. I guess so."

But I stayed up for a long while afterward, listening. Convinced that Chester hadn't been upset by a mere shadow—and thankful for his small, but vocal presence.

Chapter Thirty-One

"We are delighted you'll be doing a follow-up piece on the archive."

I froze. Ms. Tipton's voice sounded outside in the hallway. She must have cornered Geraldine the moment she walked in the front door this morning for yet another chat. I slid back into the research room and headed straight for the card catalog alcove, burying my nose in the first drawer I could grab as if my life depended on it.

"Can I help you with something?" whispered Baxter.

Startled, I almost jumped off the ground. "No, oh, thanks. I didn't see you there."

"Sorry, sorry. I just came around the corner and you looked perplexed. I thought you couldn't find something you needed."

Even though we both spoke in hushed whispers, I could see Mr. Winthrop across the room. He raised his eyes an additional fraction of an inch above his glasses. His red bow tie seemed to positively glower.

"Thank you, but I was just thinking." My voice was almost inaudible.

Baxter nodded and moved down to another row of drawers.

A few minutes later, Geraldine entered the research room. Concluding that she had managed to quickly wrap up her conversation with Ms. Tipton, I closed the catalog drawer and walked past her. We exchanged an almost imperceptible glance, having agreed before any of this officially got started that it was better not to acknowledge that we knew each other.

Each person in our little sleuthing society had a role in this private investigation. Geraldine was reading the historic diaries, purportedly as research for her follow-up article but, in reality, as a means of unraveling the mystery of the Bauwers-Tipton family intricacies—specifically, their fortune. Meghan planned on grabbing random family documents whenever possible and checking those for additional information. Della promised to pay careful attention to anything Joe might say that could shed light on things and, also, do some internet searching for other helpful items.

My job was to remain observant, noticing anything odd that only an outsider spending substantial time here might pick up. Della joked that my addiction to crossword puzzles made me especially attentive to details. Part of my mission was to carefully study everything in the display room, with an eye to little details that might pinpoint something useful.

With this in mind, I headed there now while pondering the entire situation. Could Ms. Tipton really have committed a murder? How did she fit into the whole historical picture? And was she even in line to inherit anything? There were others who would also inherit, including Millicent's husband. Would she kill him, too? It didn't make sense.

Who else possibly had anything to gain? Certainly not Mr. Winthrop, Baxter, or Alan. Or even Hedgehog or Sherlock Lady. Unless one of them, like Millicent, wasn't who they appeared to be on the surface. But suspecting everyone like this was crazy.

And the troubling part was that the murderer had also gone after Sally, that poor researcher who never returned to the archive. Was there more to those missing letters or was there something else she'd found? Had she discovered a plot to kill Millicent that was somehow connected to the Bauwers-Tipton inheritance? That seemed crazy, though.

Then there was Harlan Bauwers. He was elderly and ill and might not live much longer. Had someone tried to kill him, too? But that was also preposterous. The archive and property would certainly have to be sold when he died. What if he rallied and lived for many years? Alan Renleigh's worries over the fate of the archive after Harlan was hospitalized seemed out of proportion. Did he have a reason for this other than liking to spend time at the place? Was he a long-lost Bauwers relative? And then there was Geraldine's surprise at the dwindling number of researchers.

Nothing added up.

I reached the display room and within a mere five minutes, a second voice that morning made me jump.

"Emma, where *have* you been?" It was Alan Renleigh.

"Alan, you startled me." My sharp intake of breath was audible. I was on edge and less than happy to see Alan. I wanted some time alone to scrutinize the exhibits. Plus, I promised to meet Meghan here in a few minutes so we could update each other on any new findings.

"Where have I been? I'm usually hiding out in the research room," I replied, trying to get into the conversation with a breezy tone, although it came out wooden and uneasy.

"So you are. And how is your research going?"

"Great, great!" By now, I was feeling sort of manic, just wishing he would leave.

I continued, picking up the pace of my chatter. "And here I thought you spent all of your time hiding away in the book stacks. What brings *you* here?"

"Curiosity," Alan answered slyly. "And what brings *you* here, Emma?"

I wasn't ready for a game of cat-and-mouse, so I decided to improvise.

"I wanted to take another look at some of those letters and cards," I said, making a sweeping gesture in the direction of one of the display cases. "You know, compare the handwriting on them to the handwriting in the diary from my family's memorabilia."

It was the first thing I could think of, and I was already standing near a display case.

I glanced quickly at the case to reinforce my statement. Strange. Hadn't some sort of letter or card from Teddy Roosevelt been there last time? Maybe it was somewhere else. But I could swear I'd seen it right here in this case. Then again, the last time I was here, Ms. Tipton was in the room and I was feeling under a lot of stress. Maybe my mind was playing tricks on me. Only an ornate invitation card to some sort of event occupied the place where I thought the Roosevelt note had been displayed.

But I had bigger things to worry about now, including how to get rid of Alan before Meghan arrived. We needed at least a few minutes to talk in private without Alan engaging in his usual round of pointless and flirtatious conversation.

"Emma, we really *do* need to get together—just the two of us this time—and exchange notes on our research." He'd purposely put aside his recently failed attempt to convince me that my family's "diary" was linked to some sort of historical girl gang. The last thing I wanted now was another pointless theory of Alan's.

And much to my relief, Meghan later told me that her knowledge of gangs came from one of her several internships at city museums, not from personal experience. She learned about the subject while helping out with a special exhibit.

Now I felt desperate. "Sure. Great idea. Soon. And what's happening with your research?" Back went the conversational ball.

"Wonderful. I came here to look at a program on display from one of the most important organizations I'm studying. It's not here anymore, though. It must have just been on rotation."

*Of course! Hadn't Meghan or Ms. Tipton mentioned the archive's rotating display system? Silly of me to forget. This explained the missing Teddy Roosevelt letter. It had no doubt been put back in storage and replaced with the event card. But why this particular item?*

"Well, then Mr. Winthrop's your man. He can let you look at it in the research room. And we'll see each other there." Now I talked as fast as a TV game show host. *If only Alan would just leave. And yet…he always seemed to point out interesting information.*

"Emma, that will be the bright spot of my week," he assured me. He then took my hand, giving it a suggestive squeeze. "Till then." And with a smile and a wink, he left the room.

I waited until he closed the door securely behind him. Then I breathed a sigh of relief so deep that it took a couple of minutes to collect myself.

The moment I turned to look at the display case once more, Meghan entered.

"Alan's been here," she announced. I noted that she'd stopped referring to him as "Mr. Renleigh". Maybe his faux pas in girl gang scholarship had diminished his personal appeal.

"Met him on the stairs?" I asked.

"No. But I can smell his cologne a mile away. He once told me it's called something like He-Man. But I think of it as Eau de Flirt."

I burst out laughing. "Good grief, I thought he'd never leave."

"I know. He's like that sometimes, although he's not up here too often."

"He said he was trying to find some program in one of the display cases from an organization he's studying. Since it wasn't here, I told him to see Mr. Winthrop."

"It's probably on rotating exhibit. Mr. Winthrop's definitely the one," said Meghan. She shifted from one foot to the other, obviously in a hurry. "Look I only have a couple of minutes, but I wanted to tell you something that I found in a letter to Lucretia from Morgan Tipton, Jr."

"What? From Lucretia's fiancé?"

"Seems so. And most likely written after their engagement was broken. I wish I could have copied it, but I didn't dare. Anyway, he asked her to wait for him and said he'd be back after making his fortune and proving himself worthy in her father's eyes. And then, let me remember this exactly." Meghan scrunched up her face. "Then they could be together always and do something wonderful for the cultural life of the city they both loved."

"Maybe a museum and archive?" I conjectured.

"Maybe," said Meghan. "But it seems he never came back."

"Nothing about what happened to him?"

"Not that I've found. I'm still looking."

"So is Geraldine. Please be careful."

"Trust me, I am." Meghan moved toward the door. "Look, I need to get going. Mr. Winthrop will have a fit if I don't get some files downstairs soon." She spread her hands, palms upward, with a shrug. "Can you believe they're on nineteenth-century horticulture?"

"Sherlock Lady?"

"You got it."

"Strange! Anyway, maybe we can talk more later or sometime tomorrow."

Meghan gave a small wave and flew back through the door, anxious not to anger Mr. Winthrop or delay Sherlock Lady's horticultural pursuits.

*What could have happened to Lucretia and Morgan, Jr.'s plans?*

Chapter Thirty-Two

*—Call when u can.—*

Della texted me two hours earlier but my cell phone was off, buried deep in my bag in one of the research room cubbyholes set aside for items not permitted at the tables. Although cell phones were allowed for taking photos of research materials, I preferred to jot down notes with pencil and paper instead. It forced me to concentrate on smaller details that I might otherwise overlook.

Now, though, on my way to the lunchroom, I checked the phone and read Della's text. I quickly ducked into the hallway bathroom and dialed her number. The sounds of Joy and Julie wafted in the background before Della even said hello.

"What's happening?" I asked in hushed tones, my hand cupped around my mouth to further keep my words private.

"Where are you? You sound like you're in hiding."

"Sort of. I'm in the bathroom. It's the only place I can talk for just a few minutes. Is everything okay?"

"Everything's fine," said Della. "But I thought you'd want to know about something I discovered on the internet this morning. I'll make it quick so there won't be a line forming outside the bathroom door."

"Ha! Thanks!"

"I found Morgan Tipton, Jr.'s death notice. It

wasn't even a real obituary. And believe me, I found it totally by accident. Anyway, he died in a shipwreck on the Great Lakes in 1906. All it said was that he was a businessman born to a prominent New York family."

"That's so sad," I whispered. "And it might also explain a few things."

"Yeah. If we compare it to some other dates, it could help in piecing together the whole story," said Della.

The background noise on Della's end grew louder, accompanied by the familiar theme song from *Animal Circus*. "Uh-oh. Show's over. Butterflies are restless. I'll keep digging."

"Thanks, Dell."

I was tempted to text Geraldine but I didn't want to stay in the bathroom too long. It would either seem suspicious or make people think I was sick.

Time for lunch. I joined Meghan and Baxter at one of the tables in the kitchen.

"Where were you?" began Baxter by way of greeting. "You missed the excitement."

"In the bathroom," I blurted out. "What excitement?"

"Detective Reynolds dropped by to tell Ms. Tipton they arrested someone in an attempted mugging two nights ago, just a block from here. The guy could be connected to Millicent's death. He said if anyone remembers any more details to please call him."

"Millicent is still not officially a mugging until they completely check out the guy." Obviously, Meghan didn't buy this latest development. "It's a sure bet there's more than one mugger around here."

"Well, they *are* the cops. They must have some

241

basis for thinking there's a connection," responded Baxter. "And I hope there is," he continued. "I don't want to walk around in continual fear. And I'm sure both of you feel the same way."

"I want the truth first." Meghan stared into the depths of her coffee mug.

There was a moment of silence.

Finally, Baxter crumpled his sandwich wrapper in frustration. "I have to get back to work. Mr. Winthrop wants me to check a collection for some specialty group or other. I'd better get started." He rose from the table glumly and left.

"Meghan, I have to tell you some…" I began as Hedgehog arrived, sending my sentence in another direction. "…thing. That sandwich smells wonderful. What is it?"

"Chicken salad with a blend of spices that I found in my neighborhood store." Meghan didn't skip a beat, catching the apparent reason for my ridiculous question.

"Funny," said Hedgehog, sniffing the air near our table. "I don't smell anything."

*Maybe your whiskers are in the way?*

"I have a very keen sense of smell," I said, watching him frown in perplexity.

"Oh, Emma." Meghan rummaged in her bag for a pen. Grabbing a paper napkin from our table, she began writing. "I'll write down the name of the blend for you."

"I'll leave you ladies to your spicy discussion," said Hedgehog, downing a cup of water and leaving.

Ms. Tipton walked by as Meghan pushed the paper napkin in my direction with a knowing look.

"Hello, Emma," greeted Ms. Tipton. "Excuse me,

Meghan, but if you're finished, I need you to handle a request from a small historical society."

"Be right there," she answered cheerfully.

I rose, casually glancing at the napkin's message before stuffing it into my own voluminous bag. *More info. Alabaster after closing today?*

"See you, Meghan," I called as she headed to the doorway, following Ms. Tipton to her office. Meghan turned in my direction for a split second, just as I nodded.

When they were gone, I grabbed my cell and quickly texted Geraldine.

*—Later? Alabaster Café right after 5:00?—*

It was time to analyze some details. Unfortunately, Della wouldn't be finished babysitting the Butterflies until around 5:00, and then it would take her a while to get to the city. I texted her my best alternative.

*—Skype today after 5:00 with group?—*

Now I headed for the stacks. As Alan commented recently, I hadn't spent a lot of time there in a while.

**** 

*"Women Playwrights at the Turn of the Century?"*

It was hard to hide my frustration with Alan as he glanced at the title of the book I had just placed on the study desk. It was almost as if he'd been waiting to pounce the moment I came down to the stacks.

"But, Emma, I thought you were researching jewels and thieves and such."

"Well, I saw something interesting about playwrights and, out of curiosity, just wanted to look it up." Aside from Meghan, I hadn't revealed anything to anyone about the fake jewels and the whole change in my research. "You know how it goes with research,

Alan. One thing gets you curious about another and there you go…off on a tangent." I tried for a lighthearted laugh. *I am not a good liar.*

"You wouldn't be holding out on me, would you Emma? Some juicy bit of research you've found? Maybe a woman playwright was your jewel thief?"

*Antonia Emmaline would have enjoyed that plotline!*

"Heavens, no! When would she have had the time?" I laughed again, just as Baxter rounded the corner and headed for a shelf near Alan.

"Busy here today," commented Baxter.

"I think Emma's come upon some fabulous details about her jewel thief, but she's being mysterious," said Alan, tossing a sly glance in my direction.

Baxter turned to me. "Have you had those jewels appraised yet?" he asked. "I'm still curious about the history of that horseshoe stick pin."

"Horseshoe stick pin?" chimed in Alan.

"I'm working on it," I countered evasively.

"Baxter? A moment, please." It was Sherlock Lady.

"A moment is all I have," he answered, pulling a massive tome off a nearby shelf. "I have to grab this volume and then get back to a project for Mr. Winthrop."

*Was everyone down in the stacks today?*

"Excuse me," I interrupted, picking up my book and taking advantage of the perfect opportunity to exit. "I'll let all of you get back to your research." Alan opened his mouth to continue the conversation, but I'd already made a beeline for the stairs. I didn't stop for air until I reached the main floor, hoping to escape to the Victorian parlor and read for a while. Maybe I could find some peace and seclusion there.

Few books were available about women who were writers and playwrights in Antonia Emmaline's era—a time that, at first glance, hadn't seemed filled with opportunities for them. Yet, they were inspired by a growing city filled with divergent people and events, changing social boundaries, and widening cultural horizons. The book from the stacks that I held just now, although written many years ago, promised to open another window on their world. I looked forward to reading it.

Now would be my first time back in the parlor since being interviewed there by Detective Reynolds. I tried my best to shake off the unhappy memories of that awful day. Hugging the book close, I settled into the antique sofa, taking a deep breath and glancing around the space for a moment. The room seemed unusually cool.

Then I noticed something on the floor by the window. A couple of pieces of broken glass shimmered against the richly designed rug. I walked over and drew back the long curtain. Sure enough, one of the large bottom windowpanes was broken, almost as if someone had thrown something at it. No wonder the room was cold.

So much for peace and quiet. I hurried down the hall to report this to Ms. Tipton. Luckily, I first spied Joe in the lunchroom, finishing up his sandwich.

"No rest for the weary," I joked. "After lunch, you'll probably want to take a look at the parlor. Appears like someone broke a window there."

He looked up in surprise. "Jeez. It's always

something these days with the building."

The floorboards creaked noisily under our feet as we walked down the hallway together. Joe began pondering out loud. "That sure would have taken some effort. Those windows are pretty high above ground level, and the fence is a deterrent. This was a perseverant criminal, if you ask me. Or else one with a pretty good pitching arm."

"There's only a little bit of glass there," I explained, pointing to the pieces on the floor. "But enough of the windowpane is sure gone."

Joe knelt down and examined the glass. "I'll be right back, Emma. I'm going to take a look around outside."

I watched from the companion window as Joe walked around the front of the building. He knelt down to check the ground there, too.

When he returned, he looked even more perplexed. "This is unusual, Emma. There's more glass on the ground outside than in here. If someone tossed something from outside, more glass would be on the rug along with the object that was thrown." He sighed. "But it looks like someone broke the window from the inside."

"Why would anyone do that?" I asked. "It makes no sense."

Joe's face settled into a hard line. "A lot of things don't make sense here these days."

Ms. Tipton seemed to appear out of thin air in the doorway.

"The window is broken." I felt the need to explain immediately, uncomfortable under her impenetrable gaze. She nodded silently.

"Thanks for pointing this out, Emma," said Joe.

Then he looked up at Ms. Tipton. "I'd better get to work and repair this now. We do not want any open windows here."

Not waiting to hear the rest of their conversation, I grabbed my book and retreated to a far corner of the research room to try and read. But my concentration was gone.

*Something was definitely wrong.*

## Chapter Thirty-Three

"What is that thing?" Geraldine wedged into what was becoming a familiar secluded corner of Café Alabaster.

"It's an ear," I explained.

"Just what we don't need."

"As long as that mouth across the room isn't attached to it," I observed, indicating another disturbingly large wall sculpture.

"Okay, guys," Meghan broke in, motioning as she set up a skype session on her laptop. Soon, Della appeared onscreen, ready to join us, almost as if she was there.

"Sorry," I said. "The only thing you're missing is the special Alabaster Latte."

"And experiencing the décor in person," chimed in Geraldine, rolling her eyes.

We toasted Della with our lattes while she shared her latest news about Morgan Tipton, Jr.'s death notice. We all spoke in hushed tones, even Della. We needn't have worried. The place was empty except for our little group and the waitress.

"So, let's piece together what we have," said Geraldine after Della finished. She pulled a notebook and pen from her green tote bag and began writing on a blank page as she spoke. "Going back in time, there's business partners Prescott Bauwers and Morgan Tipton,

Sr. They split when Morgan did a shady deal behind Prescott's back."

Della chimed in next from the computer screen. "And their children, Lucretia Bauwers and Morgan Tipton, Jr., officially broke their engagement soon afterwards."

Geraldine scribbled furiously in her notebook. "What comes next is sort of hazy. Lucretia and Junior didn't really part. They only broke off their official engagement. Junior promised to come back after he made his fortune, or something like that."

"Something like that." Meghan smiled. "And then they planned to work together to enhance the cultural life of the city they loved. Possibly start the archive? Or maybe a huge historical society and museum. Who knows?"

"So, they were just biding time," I added. "And meanwhile, Elizabeth Bauwers somehow got her father and Morgan Tipton, Sr., to at least shake hands…"

"…maybe thinking this would lead to Lucretia and Junior officially getting back together," broke in Geraldine.

The waitress interrupted with our next round of lattes.

"Sorry, Dell. We promise to bring you here soon," I told my friend. "You'll have to give one of these a try."

"I'll hold you to that promise. They look good." Della nodded, her feathery earrings swaying with her.

"They probably melted down one of their wall sculptures to make them," joked Geraldine, taking a sip and frowning once more at the oversized ear.

It was Meghan who brought us back on track.

"Judging by some letters I found this week from Elizabeth Bauwers, it seems that Lucretia and Junior had a child together. This supports some of the genealogical details you found, Geraldine."

"And it would explain the long trip to Europe," concluded Geraldine.

"Now, the question is: did Junior know about this?" I asked.

"Here's a possible scenario." Geraldine was enjoying every moment of the speculation involved. "Junior went off to seek his fortune, oblivious to the fact that Lucretia was having his baby. Lucretia returned to New York from a tour abroad, and the family concocted some story about taking in the child of a distant relative who died. The sisters, and I guess Prescott, raised the child with the last name of Bauwers."

"And Junior," said Della, "died in that shipwreck and never had a chance to make his fortune, come home, and discover he had a son."

"So far, it makes sense," said Meghan. "Of course, at some point, the child must have learned of his heritage. His name was just plain old Harlan Bauwers," she added. "Harlan was a family name from poor Mrs. Bauwers, Prescott's wife, who died young. And that would explain why there's no portrait of her."

"It gets confusing when everyone is named after everyone else," I commented.

"Until," interrupted Geraldine, "the original Harlan married and had a son himself. And that son would be *our* Harlan. And because of the family circumstances—which, most likely, were revealed at some point in time—he got the middle name of Tipton."

"Fine," said Della. "But it still leaves us with the mystery of solving Millicent's murder."

Our group contemplated this for a couple of minutes while staring at the alabaster sculptures in the light of flickering candles on the tables. We had become so wrapped up in the history of the Bauwers and Tipton families that we almost lost sight of the present day murder.

"The archive property will be sold, and the Bauwers and Tipton heirs will inherit. But there aren't a lot of them and it would seem that the sale will bring a lot of money." Meghan spoke as if she was thinking out loud.

"Harlan may not live much longer. His son, the lawyer, is doing well financially and doesn't seem interested in the archive. We don't even know for sure if Millicent was going to get anything beyond that ring because she wasn't a blood relative." Geraldine sighed. "And depending on how, or if, Ms. Tipton is related, she could either get a big chunk of cash or nothing."

"Then who would gain the most from murdering Millicent?" Meghan asked. "I mean maybe it's not about money. Maybe for Ms. Tipton, it's about settling some old scores, like the identity of Lucretia and Junior's child as a Tipton being shrouded in secrecy for so many years."

"But why would she care?" asked Della. "That was so long ago, and we haven't been able to figure out how she was related to them anyway. And why Millicent?"

We pondered this for a moment.

"Suppose there's someone else who's connected to the family?" continued Della.

"You mean at the archive? Someone like Millicent

whose name isn't the same but is related somehow?" asked Meghan. "Then it could be anyone."

Suddenly, Geraldine shook her head and looked up. "And suppose there's something else we haven't figured out? Suppose there's another reason entirely for Millicent's murder?"

Total silence descended on our group after this last question.

Finally, I spoke. "Then all of us could be in danger."

## Chapter Thirty-Four

"Just how many batches of these cookies are you planning to make?" Della cast a quizzical look at the generous stack of rectangular containers lining my kitchen countertop.

"A lot." I grinned. "Ralph said there'd be over two dozen people at the party."

"Really?" said Della. "But isn't the party just for Ralph's immediate neighbors and us?"

"Yeah, but you know Ralph. There's always a few extras. He likes to party, and it adds up." I pointed to the pile of cookie containers with a shrug.

It was pumpkin cookie baking night. Since Ralph's party was in three days, Della and I decided to team up and make sure there would be plenty of cookies for everyone. Our own little group of costumed partygoers had grown. Steve and I would be joined by Della and Joe. And Louise was more than thrilled to be going, too. It all added up to a lot of cookies. Of course, that was provided people had room to eat them after diving into the appetizers, six-foot heroes, salads, chips, and whatever other dessert confections there would be. I also bought little Halloween bags in case people wanted to bring some cookies home with them.

"By the way, I'm planning an extra special batch for the Butterflies."

"Thanks, Emma. They'll love them! But you

realize," she cautioned, "that once the girls taste these cookies, they'll want you to teach them how to bake some."

"We can do that. There's still a little time left before Halloween."

"Butterflies in the kitchen baking? You have no idea what you're in for." Della burst out laughing.

I rolled my eyes but couldn't resist laughing, too. The Butterflies were a handful.

"Okay, Dell. I guess we better get this first batch going. Why don't you mix the sugar and butter in that big bowl over there, and I'll do the pumpkin and eggs... Or, wait. Maybe I got it wrong. I better check the recipe and be sure. It's been a long time since I've made these cookies." I grabbed the worn recipe card.

Della grabbed a sturdy yellow bowl. She clutched it to her full-length apron, emblazoned with a whimsical design and the words "Cooks like it hot."

I checked the recipe card, made a couple of adjustments, and the two of us began.

Despite my annoyance with Ralph's continual reminders about the pumpkin cookies, I really did enjoy baking them and was pleased he'd asked me to contribute some to party night. It was going to be fun— everyone in costume, decorations a la Ralph, and plenty of food.

"So, we're still nowhere closer to finding our murderer, are we?" asked Della with a shake of her pale blue feathery earrings.

"I don't know." I grabbed a couple of eggs. "When the four of us put together all of the facts, it seemed even more confusing." I made a face, waving my bakery whisk at the same time and splashing pumpkin batter all over myself.

"Are you wanting to become a pumpkin cookie, Emma?" asked Della, handing me a paper towel to wipe the mess off my sweatshirt.

"Very funny." I dabbed at my shirt and continued with my speculations about the murder. "This still begs the question of who had the most to gain by Millicent's death. Nothing adds up. And what was Millicent researching anyway?"

"I don't know, but I have a feeling Geraldine was right. We might all be looking at the wrong motive." Della stopped mixing and looked at me.

"Yeah, I know. No matter how you scramble the possibilities, it still doesn't make sense," I concluded. "Who and why?"

"Emma, I sort of hate to say this, but did you ever think that the cops just might have been right? After all, the neighborhood is pretty desolate and it's obviously in transition. Besides, you'll have to admit that Ms. Tipton doesn't seem the type to knock off someone in the style of a petty criminal. She strikes me as more of a poison or pearl-handled derringer type. You know, something a little more refined. Maybe it really was a random crime, and maybe we're all cooking up this conspiracy theory and just spinning our wheels. And it could be coincidental that it happened just when the archive could possibly fold. After all, it doesn't seem as if they're turning away crowds at the door."

I plunged my whisk into the bowl in frustration. "I know. You're right. It's just that my instinct tells me there's more to it than that."

*Quack-quack.* Guess who?

I wiped my hands on my already stained sweatshirt

and answered my cell phone.

"Hi, Ralph." Who else? "I'm putting you on speaker phone. Della's here, and we're making the pumpkin cookies."

"Excellent!"

"Hi, Ralph," chimed in Della.

"Hey, Della. It'll be good to see you. Can't wait to meet this new guy of yours."

"You'll love him," said Della enthusiastically. "And he'll be there in full costume."

"What's doing, Ralph?" I asked. "And don't worry. Steve and I will drop off enough folding chairs and small tables tomorrow night. And remember, no stealing any of the pumpkin cookies before Sunday."

"I'm shocked you'd even think I'd do that," said Ralph in mock horror. "Anyway, I just wanted to check in and ask if all of you want to come over a little earlier on Sunday, maybe around 3:00 or so, before the neighbors arrive and the party really gets going. Then you can get the latest grand tour of the whole property, and we can spend some time getting to know Joe. Louise insisted on taking her car service over. I invited her driver to join us and come in costume, too."

"Sounds good, Ralph. Della? Okay for you and Joe?"

"I'm sure that'll be just fine."

"Great!" Ralph was childlike in his excitement. "And don't tell me what costumes you've planned. I want it to be a surprise."

"Trust me, there'll be lots of surprises! Bye, Ralph."

Della and I went back to our cookie project after Ralph signed off.

"This will really be fun," said Della. "Joe's going to enjoy it a lot, too."

"It's really going well, isn't it?"

Della looked at me, her face lighting up. "Yeah, it is. And I can't thank you enough for being the one to introduce us."

"I'm so glad it's working out." I flashed my brightest smile. *For Della's sake, please let Joe really be as honest and nice as he seems.*

Steve poked his head in the kitchen. "Pumpkin cookies, right?"

"Yes, and no pilfering is allowed!"

I seemed to be delivering this speech pretty frequently tonight.

Steve was, no doubt, delighted that Della and I were busy with pumpkin cookies here and not digging up clues to murder. I let him believe that baking was our sole preoccupation now.

I continued scanning the ingredients and directions for making the cookies. It had been quite a while since the last time and I'd forgotten some of it, despite the fact that Ralph referred to them as "Emma's famous pumpkin cookies."

"Uh-oh," I said, holding up a small bag. "It looks like I should have bought more candy corn for the faces. I think I picked up lots of bags of chocolate morsels by accident instead." The pumpkin cookies needed a little frosting and happy faces. And Ralph specifically asked for cookies with faces.

"Look," suggested Della. "Why don't we just use the candy corn faces for the cookies you're giving to the Butterflies. Then we'll use all of those chocolate morsels for the party batches. You sure bought a lot of them. It's just a little substitution, and no one will really know that chocolate morsels aren't in the original recipe."

"Good idea," I agreed.

"Unless," asked Della, "will Ralph know?"

"As long as he gets cookies with faces, he'll be happy."

A few hours later, the cookies were done, packaged, and ready for party day.

"Thanks so much, Dell," I said, giving her a hug along with a big container of the cookies with the candy corn faces. "And please tell the Butterflies that we'll show them how to make these any time they want."

"Will do. I guarantee they'll take you up on that offer. See you Sunday!"

I spent a few minutes putting away a couple of things but then decided it was time to sleep. Tomorrow would be a full day at the archive. Later on, Steve and I would deliver the cookies, chairs, and little folding tables to Ralph and Sheila, and we'd help decorate a bit. I'd save Saturday for finishing up my costume. Then all would be set for the party on Sunday.

Steve was asleep. I climbed into bed, but just couldn't settle down. I kept running things over in my mind—the archive, Millicent, Ms. Tipton, cookies, Joe, costumes, Baxter, Alan, decorations, Meghan, Halloween, Butterflies…Soon, they all blended into a pleasant haze, and I started drifting off to sleep. It was like a crossword puzzle filled with silly clues.

Della's suggestion of substituting chocolate morsels for the candy corn in the original recipe was the last thing that floated through my mind. What a funny idea. I was almost drifting off…relaxed. Substituting chocolate morsels for candy corn. Just a little substitution for the pumpkin faces. We'd laughed. And wasn't it humorous to fool everyone with some chocolate morsels? Even Ralph probably wouldn't notice. No one else would certainly ever know they weren't in the original recipe. Almost asleep now…pumpkins seemed to be in the air…even they were getting sleepy…and then the chocolate morsels turned into sheets of paper floating…taking the place of candy corn…just like…

With a sudden jolt, I bolted wide awake. What had been lurking somewhere at the edges of my mind became startlingly clear, all because of the role of chocolate morsels substituting for the real ingredient in the recipe. How strange. But now I knew everyone had been looking at everything wrong. Even the cops. This was no random mugging. And it had nothing to do with an inheritance or the Bauwers family history. The killer had an altogether different reason than any of us had imagined. It was coming into focus now. I was almost sure I knew the motive. And the killer.

Chapter Thirty-Five

I tossed and turned for hours, mulling over every detail of my theory. *This had to be the explanation for everything.* Finally, I dropped into a fitful, exhausted sleep.

The facts hit me all over again like a crashing wave in the groggy morning light.

One quick look at the clock confirmed I'd overslept. Not surprising. Sleep eluded me until around 3:00 a.m. Now that I was awake, I needed to hash out my theory with someone from our sleuthing team to see if it was totally ridiculous—perhaps just an awful figment of my overactive imagination. Maybe the cops were right and poor Millicent was a random victim. *Or maybe I didn't want to face what I believed had really happened.*

The covers on Steve's side of the bed were pulled back long ago. He must have gotten up at the crack of dawn and gone to the office, still knee deep in paperwork and meetings to straighten out the mess with Hank. Anyway, running my theory by him would have been a mistake. Aghast at my continued sleuthing, he would have urged me to go to the cops immediately with my suspicions, for whatever good that would do.

Hastily grabbing my bathrobe and slippers, I headed to the kitchen to brew some coffee. Then I half-heartedly took a bite of a corn muffin. I needed to get to the archive, late or not.

I started texting Della but remembered midway that she was bringing the Butterflies to a birthday party at the local museum. She'd also promised to help out and, given this added responsibility, her cell phone would be out of commission for a few hours, or there'd be so much pandemonium that she wouldn't have the opportunity to check it.

Geraldine was next. She answered my text quickly, saying that she'd get back to me later. Already in some conference room or other, it was two minutes before the kick-off of an interview meeting for a lucrative new project.

Once I got to the archive, I'd pull Meghan away for a few minutes. Now I sent her a text, saying it was crucial for us to talk now. But she didn't respond at all, no doubt already at work, her phone stashed in her purse downstairs in her office while she was upstairs pulling files for Mr. Winthrop.

Coffee. I took a few welcome gulps. Yes, this would clear my head and set things straight. I dressed quickly, grabbed my purse and tote bag, and ran out the door.

The bright sunshine jolted me into reality. Everything seemed so logical while I was drifting off to sleep last night. Now, in the bright light of an autumn day, I started to have doubts. *What if my theory was wrong?*

I was so completely lost in thought that by the time I dashed down the block to the archive, I almost knocked over Mr. Winthrop as he rounded the corner. *Mr. Winthrop—late?*

"Good heavens. We certainly are in a hurry this

morning," he began by way of greeting.

I gasped. "Oh, I'm so sorry. I didn't mean to startle you. It's a very busy day for me."

"Busy is a good way to be," he commented in a crisply authoritarian voice with what appeared to be a disapproving frown. This was the last of any conversation. We navigated the remaining quarter-block of our journey in silence. It felt like a quarter-mile as I nervously plunged my left hand into my coat pocket and crumpled the tissue there into a tiny ball.

*Why was he late? Who was minding the research desk? And why was today's choice of bow tie—bright green with a tiny, indecipherable design—looking so askew?*

The moment we were inside, I tossed my jacket in the closet and ran down the hall to find Meghan. Baxter was in the office, absorbed in a large pile of paperwork.

"Didn't mean to disturb you, Baxter," I said clumsily. "Is Meghan here?"

He looked at me blankly. "Oh. Emma. Yes, well, Meghan said she had an appointment this morning. She'll be in later. Can I help you with something?"

"No, no thanks." I was at a momentary loss to come up with a reasonable explanation for my eagerness to find his office mate, not that I really was obligated. "Uh, I just had a quick question for her about an art class she mentioned...For a friend of mine...I'll catch her this afternoon..." Flustered by my own ludicrous words, I quickly returned to the hallway.

There I spied Joe hanging up his coat in the hall closet. I waved and headed for the research room, catching sight of Ms. Tipton retreating into her office. Had she filled in for the tardy Mr. Winthrop who was now in his usual place? *What was going on this morning?*

Mr. Winthrop, efficient as always, immediately produced the materials I requested yesterday. Stashing my purse and tote bag in one of the storage cubby holes by the door, I took a seat at a table, carefully placing my pencil and blank paper nearby. Soon, I pretended to read the century-old periodicals spread out in front of me.

I felt totally adrift from our little group of sleuths and desperately wanted to talk to at least one of them. But everyone was off the grid. I now felt so sure that we'd been on the wrong track, thinking that the murder—and, yes, Millicent must have been murdered—had anything to do with any kind of inheritance or century-old Bauwers-Tipton intrigue. There was a far more clear-cut and logical motive and a far more logical killer. *This had to be true, didn't it?*

An unexpected chill ran through me. Did I have the right motive but the wrong person? Maybe it wasn't as simple as it seemed. *Could someone else have had a similar reason to kill?*

The most preposterous part of my whole theory was that I had arrived at it based on Della's joke that no one would ever know if we substituted chocolate morsels for candy corn in the original pumpkin cookie recipe. *How ridiculous was that?* But it was the parallel premise—substitution—that was reasonable. And I was sure about it…*almost.*

I felt Mr. Winthrop's eyes on me as I gazed off into space. His bright green bow tie seemed to have grown in size. It was horribly disconcerting, and I tried not to focus my eyes on it. My nerves were getting the better of me.

Heaving a long sigh as if in deep contemplation over something I had just read, I turned back to the pages in front of me. *Where the heck was Meghan? And why did both Della and Geraldine have to be occupied for so long on this particular day? Why hadn't I tried to talk to any of them last night? But it had been after midnight, and they would have thought I was crazy. Chocolate morsels substituting for candy corn as my "aha" moment? And I still wasn't certain.*

A loud sneeze somewhere behind me interrupted my jumbled thoughts. I jumped. But it was just Hedgehog, the only other person in the research room now, aside from Mr. Winthrop and me. The dust from a Teddy Roosevelt file must have gotten to him.

My stomach was now growling so loud that I swore it echoed off the high ceilings. It was long after lunchtime and I'd forgotten to bring a sandwich or even a candy bar. Maybe just stretching my legs would make me forget about my hunger. Motioning to Mr. Winthrop that I'd return, I walked out of the research room and spied Alan Renleigh at the end of the hallway. He was just coming upstairs from the book stacks. A look of anticipation spread across his face.

*Not now.* I smiled broadly, gave a friendly wave, and then quickly ducked into the tiny hallway bathroom, securely closing the door. I was not in the mood to deal with Alan. I let out a sigh of relief, which soon turned to chagrin. This would have been the perfect time and place to try texting one or all of my friends again, but my purse and tote bag, with my cell phone neatly tucked away with them, sat in a research room cubby hole. At least I had a few moments to collect myself and avoid Alan. But suppose he was standing outside? Maybe he had to go to the bathroom. Or maybe he was eager to tell me about another arcane organization from 1902, like a jewel thieves singing society or the pickpockets' annual banquet.

I stayed for as long as seemed reasonable and then opened the door. The hallway was empty. Had Meghan finally arrived? A quick check of the office provided the answer. Baxter was still there alone, looking as if he hadn't moved from his chair. I did a quick about face and headed for the kitchen. Maybe she was there.

Again, no luck. Joe stood at the countertop, looking through his toolkit. A rusty and convoluted piece of pipe was on the floor next to him. Plumbing, heating, something else?

"Hey, Joe," I said, trying to sound lighthearted. "All set with your costume for Sunday?"

"Almost," he smiled. "Della's meeting me in the city for dinner tonight, and we're going to pick up the last pieces of our outfits. I'm really looking forward to the party."

*Had Della told me about tonight's dinner when we were baking the pumpkin cookies? Or hadn't I been listening?*

Joe sighed. "I need to run out now and order a replacement for this pipe." He pointed to the grungy object on the floor. "I put in a temporary but there needs to be something new next week." He looked at his watch. "I'd better get things in motion before the supply place closes."

"Good luck with it," I offered, not wanting to get into a discussion of what had gone wrong with the pipe and the mechanics of how it needed to be fixed. "Well,

I just wanted to say hi. I won't keep you."

"Thanks, Emma." He gave a quick wave as I headed for the door. I waved back as he reached for the pipe on the floor.

*What had Della meant about there being more to Joe's story?*

I now looked at the staircase leading up to the museum room. Maybe I could just run up for a couple of minutes. Just to be sure my mind wasn't playing tricks on me. Just to be sure I wasn't crazy after all. Where had the time gone? It was getting late. It was best to do this now before retrieving my things from the reference room cubby hole.

Hurrying up the stairs past the portraits of the Bauwers family, I pushed open the heavy door to the museum display room. What a relief. No one was there.

The musty smell of old objects, even in their glass cases, seemed more obvious today. Did I imagine it or was the faint aroma of Alan's cologne in the air? Perhaps still lingering in the dust after his visit the other day.

I circled the cases, studying each one in turn. Yes, there were the same inconsistencies I remembered. I looked at the letter from DeWitt Clinton. It wouldn't have been part of a rotating exhibit since it was much older than the usual objects on display and quite rare. But the contours of the real letter's frayed edges were faintly visible in the background. And there was something a little different about the handwriting, too. Almost imperceptible, but still different. I was getting good with old handwriting after all of my research.

Then I looked in the silver display cabinet. The piece I'd recently noticed out of order with the others was shinier, thinner. Not quite the same quality as its companions. A fake.

Other things weren't right. The program Alan had been searching for might have been rotated to make room for something else to be exhibited in its place for a while. But the item there now was of little interest. I was willing to bet that the program was valuable—and gone.

The same was true of the letter from Theodore Roosevelt, the one with the worn-off corner. Something of less value replaced it.

Sally must have known all along. She'd reported those two Astor letters missing. They had most likely been lifted, someone thinking they'd never be requested again after Sally completed her research. But she wanted to see them one more time. Misfiled? No. Just gone. They might have contained something of special value to a collector.

It all amounted to theft. Subtle theft. Some things that were filed for years were probably just gone. They might never have been missed. Also, because of the museum's policy of rotating parts of the exhibit, it was easy to assume that there was nothing wrong if something wasn't on display anymore, like Alan's program. It was logical to believe it had been replaced with another item to be put on view. Just a little substitution.

But what of those pieces on permanent display? Some were also replaced, but by reasonably well-crafted fakes. So it appeared as if the original was still there. Would anyone really scrutinize a long-displayed object closely, or would it just be assumed that all was well with it, that it was the original? Would anyone really be looking for a forged letter? A fake piece of silver? Perhaps not. It was just as Della said—no one would realize that substituting chocolate morsels for candy corn wasn't part of the original recipe unless they were really looking for a deviation or knew the original exceptionally well. It was just a little substitution. But in the case of the display room, a substitution was not such a little thing.

And I was positive I knew why. And almost positive about who had done it.

*What if I was wrong?*

It was getting near closing time now. I stayed far longer in the display room than I intended. I pulled back one of the drapes a couple of inches. Dusk was already setting in on the street. It was time to head home. I realized that Steve and I needed to quickly run over to Ralph's place and deliver those chairs, tables, and cookies, and then help for a little while with the decorations. If I didn't hurry, someone might turn off all the lights, not realizing I was still here. I needed to grab my coat and gather my purse and tote from the research room. I'd have to wait to get in touch with my team of friends until I was outside. The archive would be locked up soon. *And who was locking up tonight anyway?* Not Joe, since he'd gone to order that replacement pipe and would then be off to meet Della. *Why had I lingered here so long?* But I needed to check the museum display room one more time, just to be sure.

A sudden creaking sound startled me. I whirled around toward the main door. It was closed. I stood still for what felt like a long moment.

The sound came from another door, the one

between two wall unit displays—a door I hadn't paid much attention to. It was the door for the small elevator. There was one on every floor, meant for people who didn't want to take the stairs. Meghan pointed it out on my first day at the archive. Harlan Bauwers had used it.

Now the door opened almost fully. I gasped.

"Hello, Emma."

Chapter Thirty-Six

My throat went dry. "*You*...have...a gun?"

I never expected a gun. Not inside the archive.

"Don't look so surprised, Emma. There are guns all over the city."

I suddenly felt lightheaded, but I was too frozen with fear to reach out and steady myself.

"You had to pry into things that didn't concern you."

I swallowed hard. "Don't be ridiculous. I don't know anything."

The gun trembled slightly, its worn surface holding the promise of terror.

"You're the one being ridiculous. All of those innocent questions. Visits to these displays. Bringing in your friend for research."

"I thought *you* were my friend." I was stunned at my own outburst.

Silence followed my words, only to be broken a minute later by a faintly muffled noise. *Did someone come to help me?* I carefully shifted my eyes toward the main door. It was still closed. No movement there.

"You can't shoot me. They'll hear you downstairs. There'll be too much evidence."

"It's after closing, Emma."

My glance moved beyond the heavy red draperies and musty display cases. Up to the old wooden clock on the wall. "But it's not even 5:00 yet."

There was an impatient sigh. "Emma. It's long after 5:00. I turned the clock back. I had a feeling you'd come here. Oh, and I removed your coat and bags from downstairs. Everyone's gone. They assumed you went home, too."

*Home. Would I ever see home? Steve was right to be worried, wasn't he?*

The muted overhead light reflected off a silver tray exhibited nearby. I focused on its eerie glint while trying to figure out what to do. My words now tumbled out in a panic. "The cops will trace your gun. With your fingerprints."

"Save it, Emma. It's too late."

There was that muffled sound again. Then nothing. Just the ticking of the old clock on the wall.

"I didn't mean for Millicent to die, you know." There was a faint hint of pleading in this statement.

"I don't believe you. And I trusted you." It slipped out before I could stop myself. Beads of sweat pooled under my hairline and cascaded down my face. Fear was coming in spasms.

"And what about Sally?" I continued. "You mean you didn't try to kill her either?"

"I only meant to scare her, to make her forget about the archive and those letters."

"Then why did she need to go to the hospital?"

"It had to seem like a mugging, nothing to do with the archive. I grabbed her purse. But then she hit me. I didn't expect that, and I was afraid she'd see through my disguise. I hit her back hard and ran. It all happened so fast."

"What about Millicent? Why did you kill her?" My

voice had risen about an octave now out of fright. It quavered badly. I was biding time, hoping someone would burst through the door. But, then again, that might mean two people dead.

The gun trembled. *It looked so strange. Nothing like in the movies. But I knew nothing about guns.*

"I didn't mean it. You've got to believe me, Emma." There was that pleading again.

"I'm supposed to believe you while you're holding a gun on me?"

I swallowed hard. Sweat continued to pour down my neck, my back. But my hands were cold, and I pressed them hard into my sides to hide how much they were trembling. I couldn't stop myself from talking now, babbling really.

"You stole things from this room. Valuable things. At first, it must have been easy to pretend they were on rotating display, so you just took them and put other things in their place. And you probably took rare items from the storage rooms, too. You thought no one would ever request them or even miss them. But then Sally came along and everything changed when she reported those letters gone. You had to stop her from talking about her suspicions."

*Keep talking, Emma.*

It was hard to hide the trembling in my voice, in my body, but I kept going.

"And then you got more sophisticated and figured out you could substitute a credible fake for an original, here in the displays. After all, who was going to scrutinize anything that carefully anyway? Everyone was too busy." I paused. "It was the substitution part, the minor variations from the original, that really made me think. And you must be good at forgery, a real artist, or else had to have found someone to help you."

"Very clever, Emma."

I let out a heavy sigh. *I was still alive*.

"And you must be selling them to private buyers," I continued. "You couldn't possibly have gone to any reputable dealer without getting caught."

"Yes, I cultivated some quite lucrative private financial sources. There *is* a market for everything."

We both stopped talking for a moment, aware of that sound again. It was less muffled than before. I looked toward the draperied windows. But there was no movement there.

My captor was getting more agitated now, pacing a few steps to the side and then back again. Not a good sign. And the gun was still aimed in my direction.

"Why? Why would you do this?" My shirt was now dripping with sweat, and I gripped my hands so tightly to my sides that it was painful.

"Because why should I struggle so much?" Now the voice was charged with anger. "Would anyone in the Bauwers family miss the letters? The silver? The artifacts? Who's left? Harlan's almost dead. His son is rich, and he doesn't care. What was I going to do? Spend my life in poverty while a bunch of crazy eccentrics passed their days thumbing through musty old files, here or wherever the collection will go when the archive closes?" There was a telling pause. "Did you *have* to dig into this? Why couldn't you have just minded your own business?"

"Because someone got hurt and someone got killed." For a moment, my own anger made me ignore my fear. "If you hadn't killed Millicent, I never would have realized something was wrong. It's your fault that I started to look into things."

The gun trembled again. But it was still locked in place.

"I told you. I didn't mean to kill her."

There was that muffled sound once more. I was now sure it was coming from the elevator. A moan? Maybe the sound was in my head.

"She knew too much. She knew where I hid things. And about the distractions."

"Distractions?"

"Like those broken pipes and leaks behind the walls and bookcases."

"You did that on purpose?"

"Grow up, Emma. Of course. And a lot of other things. I needed to keep Joe occupied so he wouldn't be in my way checking on something at the wrong time."

"The broken window in the parlor?"

"I needed to get rid of something quickly and pick it up outside later on. Thank goodness no one was nearby. I muffled the sound with some cloth."

*So Joe was innocent. I felt terrible for doubting him.*

My captor shuffled several steps one way and then back again with each new revelation. My fear had grown to such a peak that I could feel the room start to spin slowly. I was afraid I might faint.

The voice was matter-of-fact now. "Millicent confronted me. I told her to meet me later that night— that I'd explain everything. She wanted to meet outside. Maybe she thought it was safer, even though it was starting to rain by then. We drifted into the vacant lot. I offered her a cut of the profits if she'd only keep quiet.

I didn't find out until later that her married name was Bauwers, and money was not her motive. She called me a fool. I got angry. And I pushed her."

The pleading tone returned. "Her foot caught in the mud, and she lost her balance. She fell back and hit her head on that broken cement bench in the lot." A look of pain preceded the next words. "It was an accident. Just a push. But when she fell, she hit that cement bench hard."

I was speechless as I contemplated the scene.

"She fell at such an odd angle and then landed face first in the mud. I panicked and ran."

I was in shock. "You could have called for help. You just left her? Overnight? Hurt, and in the mud and the rain? Maybe you could have saved her."

"Please understand." This was a full plea now. "I would have lost everything."

"But Millicent lost her life."

A pause. Then the arrogance returned.

"You don't get it, do you? I almost had enough money. Enough to get away. Away from this trap. From this job. From the ridiculous expectations everyone had about my future."

The moan returned, too loud to ignore now. Then I watched in horror as a cramped figure half rolled into view on the elevator floor. Shame washed over me. To think I had once suspected Ms. Tipton of Millicent's murder. Now there was her familiar solid figure, bound and gagged. Stung with pity, I fought back a wave of nausea.

"She knew, too, didn't she?" I asked, nodding in Ms. Tipton's direction. "You would have done anything to anyone for the money, wouldn't you? When we all talked about winning big money in the lottery that day at lunch, you were the only person who really sounded serious about ditching everything for money. You threw me off for a long time with your whole timid act. And that's all it was, wasn't it? An act. Who would have thought you were capable of stealing and killing. But you're the only one it could have been, Baxter."

Chapter Thirty-Seven

There was a flicker of anxiety in Baxter's eyes as he stroked his throat with his free hand.

"It was an accident," he repeated feverishly, slightly gesturing with the gun. "I didn't mean for Millicent to die. I *didn't* murder her!"

*Keep him talking, Emma.*

"Okay. Okay. But what about now? You have your whole life ahead of you. You can get through this with professional help. But are you going to risk everything by intentionally committing murder? By killing both of us?" I looked at poor Ms. Tipton.

My question hung in the air for a moment. The gun trembled. *Was he considering putting it down?*

"Does it matter? I'm in deep enough already. And by the time anyone finds the two of you, I'll be on my way out of the country."

I shuddered.

"You'll be living life on the run."

"I'll be living life...period. And with a new identity."

My stomach lurched. *He was going to kill us and escape before we were found.*

There was another moan from Ms. Tipton. Baxter pivoted a bit toward the elevator, still pointing the gun in my direction.

"We're wasting time, Emma. Get in the elevator

and face the wall."

I hesitated a moment. Baxter's face suddenly flushed with anger.

"Do it, and don't try anything! Or I'll shoot her right now and it will be your fault."

Tears stung my eyes. If I was alone, maybe I could do something—create a distraction, scream, anything. But I couldn't let him kill Ms. Tipton. I moved into the elevator.

"Hands in front of you on the wall, Emma. Where I can see them."

I had no choice. Two lives hung in the balance now.

The space was claustrophobic. Baxter stood behind me and pushed the gun into my back. "Don't do anything you'll regret," he cautioned.

*What could I try? One or both of us would immediately get shot. I couldn't risk it. Keep talking, Emma. Keep stalling for time.*

Quickly closing the squeaking door, he set the elevator in motion.

"My friend Della will know something's wrong because I didn't get back to her." This was true, although I wasn't sure what good this information would do in my current situation.

"Emma," said Baxter as if talking to a child. "I already took care of that."

"What do you mean?" *Had he done something awful to Della?*

"You really should have gotten a password for your cell phone."

"You took my cell phone?"

"I told you. I removed your bags from the research

room downstairs. I have your cell phone and wallet right here in my pocket." His mirthless laugh filled the space. "You made it so easy for me. Yes, Della texted you. And I texted back, pretending I was you. I told her you'd be home late and would call her tomorrow. I even said to say hello to the grandchildren."

*The grandchildren?* Della would know in a minute that something was totally off. I never called the Butterflies "grandchildren." Della was seeing Joe tonight. Would she have gotten the text? Would she tell him about it? I'd asked her to keep everything secret from Joe but now I desperately wanted her to break that promise. *Why had I insisted? Why didn't I want her to tell Joe about our investigation? Why had I doubted him?*

And what about Steve? He would worry when I didn't come home right away. We were supposed to go to Ralph's tonight. But he might not realize something was wrong until it was too late.

Suddenly a new thought made me recoil in horror. "What about Meghan? Where is she?"

In my anxiety, I started to turn around. Baxter shoved the gun deeper into my ribs.

"She needed to call out of work today."

"What did you do to her?"

"Nothing really harmful. She's just cleaning up some water damage at home. Did you ever see where Meghan lives?"

"No," I managed to choke out through my fear.

"It's one of those basement apartments in a brownstone. A few crumpled papers and other materials thrown strategically by her outside door, followed by a match, can cause a lot of flames and smoke. Not to mention fire department action."

"You did that? They're probably looking for you right now. There are security cameras all over these days."

*All except where they're needed most. Like in this neighborhood, near the archive, and in the abandoned lot.*

"But I won't be on any of them. A few dollars of encouragement given to a local street person with a flexible approach to legalities was all that was necessary."

The elevator reached the ground floor. Baxter pulled open the door with his free hand. A hallway stretched out in front of us, one I had never seen.

"Where are we?" I asked, frightened.

"Another part of the archive, not open to researchers," said Baxter. "There are many entrances here."

I shuddered.

"After you," he said, pushing the gun even closer into my ribs than I thought possible.

I stepped into the hallway with Baxter close behind.

*If he was going to kill us, why hadn't he done it by now?*

"My esteemed employer will remain here in the elevator. Given its age, the vents are probably at least partially blocked. I'm going to lock it now. No one will be here till morning."

*Suffocation? That was cruel.*

"But, Emma. I have other plans for you."

I started to partially turn in shock. "Don't make me shoot you here." Baxter's voice had a chilling edge. His anger was rising to the surface more visibly now—the same anger that had led him to hit Sally, push Millicent, and incapacitate Ms. Tipton. I had to hang on or get shot.

We inched forward toward a door near the rear of the archive. Was this the entrance used by Harlan's caregiver? No wonder I'd never seen her.

"Open the door, Emma. Carefully. Don't even think of trying anything."

By now, my ribs were totally bruised. The gun still pushed hard into them.

The door slowly swung open, revealing the dark night sky. It led to a short walkway on the side of the archive, right next to the empty lot, one of several places where the separating fence had been removed by vagrants. Right near where Millicent was found.

"Walk slowly forward." Baxter spoke carefully as he removed the gun from my aching ribs. "Turn around and face me. Slowly. Remember, this gun is still pointing at you."

I did as he asked. We were both outside now. Facing each other in the empty lot. It seemed darker than usual. The street even quieter. Was the area really this devoid of streetlights?

"You're going to make my final exchange for me." He patted his left coat pocket. "My biggest. No more letters from society matrons or political documents or silver medallions. I've done that long enough to build a substantial bank account abroad. This time I'm dealing with a very high-end connoisseur. It will complete my plan."

"What are you talking about?"

"I have Lucretia Bauwers' heirloom necklace. The

one in her portrait. You know, the portrait I saw you studying so carefully. The necklace was in safekeeping here at the archive, unlike so many of the other jewels that went to Harlan's family."

"Like Elizabeth's ring? The one that Millicent wore?"

"Yes, but the necklace has a history, a pedigree that goes back to before the French Revolution. It could be worth a fortune on the open market, but it's worth a bigger one off the record to my premiere collector who isn't interested in the specifics of how it was obtained."

Who was this awful buyer who valued a necklace more than anything? Who would trade a life to become its owner? And what kind of a monster was Baxter who would make it happen?

"Given all that's gone on recently, I'd rather not show my face," continued Baxter. "However, you will deliver this on my behalf and accept the final payment in cash from the buyer's emissary. And it won't do any good to ask him for help. He's a willing part of the plan. Besides, we'll be in a remote location. Of course, I will be close by. And I still have the gun."

"Then what?"

"Once he delivers the necklace, he will probably vanish, at his employer's discretion. And, regrettably, Emma, so will you."

*Oh, God!*

"Why should I go along with your plan? Why don't you just shoot me now, Baxter? You're going to do it anyway."

An abrupt noise interrupted our exchange. A vagrant entered the street side of the lot, perhaps the same man I'd seen from the museum room window the other day. He was intent on picking through some garbage on the ground. He moved slowly, probably old and not in good health. His gaze was lowered, fixed upon something in the rubble.

Baxter frowned. "Don't pay attention. Those people are always out there. We'll wait until he goes away."

The figure lumbered slowly and painfully for a few paces, head down and shoulders slumped, the shredded ends of his coat hanging loosely. He picked up a small object and examined it, oblivious to our presence.

Baxter was wound as tightly as a steel coil ready to break apart with devastating force. He stole a glance at his watch. The time for the clandestine exchange must be coming soon. Perhaps things were not as well planned as he thought. The vagrant, however, remained intent on his foraging expedition. Even though Baxter most probably didn't want to make noise and draw unwanted attention, I was still worried that he was unhinged enough to shoot the guy.

The moon, moving an imperceptible distance on its nightly course, illuminated only an additional inch or two of our surroundings. Yet it more clearly defined the gun in Baxter's right hand. He watched me carefully, stealing an occasional sideways glance at the vagrant on his agonizingly slow quest for small treasures.

*Was there no way to escape?*

The air was so still. Almost as if the rest of the city had disappeared. The motor of a bus hummed softly in the far distance. I heard my own breath coming in a quick, shallow rhythm.

Then…a loud, jarring noise pierced the silence.

*Quack-quack.* My cell phone—in Baxter's pocket.

He veered in surprise, the gun lurching away from me and toward the back of the lot. On sheer instinct, I leaped forward and pushed Baxter with every ounce of force I had. He staggered and fell backward, the gun dropping by his side. I lost my balance and toppled half on top of him and half into the rubbly mess.

Instantly, the vagrant sprang to life and ran toward us.

Baxter pushed me away, but I rolled back and punched him. He groaned as he reached out for the gun. At that instant, a sturdy suede boot heel emerged from the shadows and stomped onto Baxter's outstretched hand. His cry of pain tore through the night air.

By this time, the vagrant stood with his own gun trained on Baxter while nimbly removing the other one from the ground.

"Don't move," he commanded Baxter. "The police are on the way."

Then he addressed us amiably. "Looks like you ladies almost didn't need me. That was some take-down."

"We always need you, Joe," replied Della who removed her boot heel from Baxter's hand and helped me scramble up from the ground. I clung to her tightly in gratitude and relief.

*Quack-quack.* My cell phone sounded again, still in Baxter's pocket.

"For once," said Della, "your brother timed it perfectly."

Chapter Thirty-Eight

"The moment I saw the word *grandchildren*, I knew something was wrong." Della finished a handful of tortilla chips and removed several crumbs from the feathers of her parrot costume.

"Something was wrong for a while," added Joe, his pirate attire a nice complement to Della's outfit. "I only wish I could have *proven* it sooner. Maybe Millicent would still be here."

"There was no way you could have prevented that, Joe," I told him with conviction. "No one had any idea that Millicent was going to confront Baxter, and even he hadn't planned on murder."

Light poured in through the generous windows in Ralph and Sheila's sunroom. It was just two days after the archive incident, and our little group more than welcomed this festive Halloween get-together. Ralph insisted that Meghan and Geraldine also join us after hearing of Friday's misadventures.

"So, what exactly did happen?" asked Ralph, eager to hear the story from start to finish. And he was immensely proud of the critical part that he and his cell phone call had played in the action.

Joe began. "It looked like certain things were missing from the collections for a while, but there was no real evidence. The staff was small and overworked, so it was always possible that the items were misplaced.

And if theft really was involved, it was tough to pinpoint the most likely suspect. It seemed as if anyone could have been the culprit. When the old maintenance guy retired, it was the perfect time to start checking into things, though. Ms. Tipton hired me to investigate undercover." *Ah, so that was Joe's real profession after retiring from the police force.* "Everything appeared so normal that I began to think there might not have been any thefts at all. But then things started to feel off."

"Baxter must have been quite a clever thief," commented Louise, smartly dressed as a 1920s flapper.

"He had quite a scheme going," Meghan began. "He was selling items from the archive to private collectors and building a nice overseas bank account. The necklace was going to be his biggest, and final, deal before vanishing."

"The collectors must have known this was illegal," concluded Louise.

"Right," said Joe. "But some people just don't care. They don't show off their collections and they don't identify their source."

"How did he meet them?" asked Ralph. His comfortable furry bear suit came without a mask, making it easier for him to munch on party treats.

"He broke down and spilled everything the other night, probably to throw some of the spotlight off himself and implicate his major buyer," said Joe. "It's amazing how he built contacts through contributors to exhibits and academic causes as well as through random conversations with high-end antiques dealers. It took a while, but it eventually paid off. Baxter was subtle and planned every detail, all to avoid getting caught. He even created some diversions at the archive to be sure he could quietly replace a particular item or make away with an original piece during a busy time."

"Such as breaking a pipe so you'd be kept occupied with repairs," added Meghan. "And then there was my apartment!"

The sun began to set, casting a serene glow over the room. Little foil pumpkins hung suspended from the ceiling. Sheila turned on some soft music in the background. This was the most relaxed I'd felt in weeks. Steve, too. The aftermath of Friday night left him devastated. I assured him that it had been solely my choice to remain at the archive and that none of it was his fault.

"What about Millicent?" he now asked, aware that her fate could well have been mine.

Meghan was quick to offer the details. "Millicent loved historic photographs and by coincidence had seen several at a small exhibit that looked strangely familiar from the Bauwers private collection. One of Baxter's contacts must have inadvertently let them out of his or her hands. So, Millicent posed as a researcher—a very plain and undistinguished one at that—to check out the photographic holdings and see what might be missing. Harlan knew she was there but then he took ill and went to the hospital. And until she died, the only clue to her identity was her ring. It had belonged to Elizabeth Bauwers, the one she wore in the portrait, and Millicent cherished it. Never took it off. It was a wedding gift from her husband." She turned to me. "Emma made the connection about the ring first."

Joe finished off a mini hot dog and picked up the story from there. "Millicent found a number of discrepancies, and since Baxter pulled many of the photographic files, she questioned him. When his answers were vague, she became suspicious, and it all went bad from there."

"What about Ms. Tipton?" Ralph was immersed in this tale of intrigue, almost as much as in the deviled eggs he kept sampling.

"That's a whole story in itself," chimed in Geraldine who, along with Meghan, had come dressed as candy corn. Della pulled the outfits together for them last night after we all pitched in to help clean up the water damage in Meghan's apartment. "Poor Ms. Tipton. We suspected the worst when all along her heart was in the right place. She's descended from Junior's brother's family. Actually, everyone mended their differences way back in the day, and the Tiptons were treated as equals, no revenge or anything like that. She's a born researcher and just loves the archive and is desperate to keep it intact. But that's another story I'll get to in a minute. Joe, it's yours from here."

"You came along, Emma, and started putting two and two together, just like Sally and Millicent. And you were friendly with everyone at the archive, including Baxter. He was interested in your jewelry memorabilia, too. Remember your neighbor's dog barking at something in your yard? He actually checked your house to see if it was possible to break in at some point."

"Good old Chester," I said. "Must have frightened him away."

Joe continued. "Then you gathered your band of super sleuths and Baxter actually followed you when you got together one time. He realized he was in danger of being discovered and started losing his grip. He was worried that the four of you were on to him, especially as his biggest coup was getting closer."

"And, as it was, we were all going down the wrong road, suspecting everything and everyone else until the very end," I commented.

"So he waited until Friday to take the necklace?" asked Steve, obviously stunned by the unfolding story. "And after he'd already set up the switch for money?"

"Not exactly," answered Joe. "The deal had been in the works for a while, but he only took the necklace a week before. He kept it safe at the archive in his secret hiding spot, a small inset in a remote wall. Problem was that Ms. Tipton agreed to loan some items to a historic exhibit in a desperate attempt to attract supporters for the archive. The necklace was going to be the centerpiece. Then she discovered it was missing."

"But didn't Baxter replace the originals with fakes?" I asked.

"In many cases he did. But this one was too involved and expensive. It had already been on rotation in the display room the previous year. If it hadn't been for the loan request, the necklace would have remained stored and no one might have discovered it missing for years. Baxter would have gotten away with it." Joe sighed and shook his head.

"But how did Ms. Tipton know it was Baxter?" I asked.

"She didn't at first," Joe said. "Then the exhibit people called her after she missed the delivery date of the items, all because she never knew when the date was supposed to be. She never got their letters since Baxter intercepted them. Baxter was the one to sort and deliver the mail, and he always looked so eager to make sure everyone got their letters and envelopes."

Joe grabbed another mini-hot dog and then continued. "Since Ms. Tipton never received the delivery date letter, she thought the exhibit might have been postponed and she put off preparing the items. She was stunned when she got their call. She immediately sent Mr. Winthrop to personally pull everything from rare storage and deliver it that Friday morning. That's when they discovered the necklace, the centerpiece of the exhibit, was missing. She made some excuse to the exhibit administrators and promised to bring it to them first thing on Monday morning. Then she confronted Baxter."

Everyone was so mesmerized by the story that they stopped eating treats for a moment. The little foil pumpkins even seemed to stop twirling.

"Why Baxter, though?" asked Ralph. "Did she suspect him all along?"

Joe was quick to answer. "Ms. Tipton and I had been putting together details that could have possibly implicated Baxter in some of the thefts, but he was certainly deft about it. We needed more solid proof. She never had a chance to tell me about the exhibit disaster that Friday since Baxter messed with the plumbing again. I was doing the repair and had to run out to order the new pipe. Then Ms. Tipton totally acted on her own in confronting Baxter."

"And," added Meghan, "Baxter was sure the last person anyone would have figured for a murderer."

Ralph waved a furry bear paw, sending pieces of deviled egg flying to the carpet. "Okay, but what happened when Ms. Tipton confronted Baxter about the necklace?"

Joe continued. "Baxter couldn't believe his bad luck. He was scheduled to make his move that night. Ms. Tipton accused him of theft. Desperate, Baxter took her up to Harlan Bauwers' apartment where he said he'd give her the necklace. He suggested using the elevator to avoid their being noticed. Of course, once they were in the elevator, he knocked her out and tied her up. By this time, he was really improvising. Emma, he thought you'd overheard them earlier, since you were one of the few people left in the building. And everyone knows what happened from then on."

"Wait, wait!" Ralph waved a furry bear paw in the air once more. "What happened to Ms. Tipton and Mr. Winthrop? And Baxter?"

"And what about the archive?" chimed in Louise.

Everyone started asking questions all at once. By now, though, our team of sleuths already knew some of the answers.

"Okay," said Joe. "Baxter is obviously in custody. It's going to be a long process with a slew of charges filed against him."

"Guess he won't be using that overseas bank account anytime soon," commented Ralph.

"But what about Ms. Tipton?"

Meghan adjusted the hem of her candy corn outfit and smiled. "Ms. Tipton is fine, just badly shaken and bruised. Mr. Winthrop was totally crushed when he found out what had happened. They're having lunch together today and discussing the future of the archive."

"It'll do them both good to get out," commented Geraldine with a laugh.

Meghan sighed. "Sorry to say, the property will be sold. It's been going in that direction for quite a while.

It's too expensive and impractical to keep. Harlan Bauwers won't be able to return to his apartment because of ill health." She took a deep breath before continuing. "But the contents will be donated by category to three larger collections and in this way, they'll be assured of being well cared for and used by a much wider group of people."

"And hopefully, no one will be filching papers and artifacts from any collection anymore," added Della.

"Where will the funds come from for this?" asked Louise.

"That's one of the nice parts," said Meghan. "Millicent's husband will work with the archive's legal team to set up funds from the sale of the property to help the collections. There's still plenty there for Harlan to be properly cared for and the heirs will all benefit just fine. But everyone's anxious for the collection to continue in some form. And here's more good news. They're working it out so that Ms. Tipton, Mr. Winthrop, and I will help in the transition, and we'll probably be kept on with jobs. So some of our remaining researchers—or resident eccentrics—can still delve into their special interests with us. It'll just be at another locale."

I smiled, thinking of Alan Renleigh, Hedgehog, and Sherlock Lady.

"What about the rest of you?" asked Louise.

Geraldine's words spilled out in a rush. "I'm searching out new contacts for high-paying articles about the life of stolen artifacts, historic jewelry, the stories behind famous portraits, and curating private collections—for starters. And I'm going to make a proposal to the three accepting institutions and offer my services to write the story of the Bauwers' archive *and* to seek out additional grants for the upkeep of the collections in their new homes."

Geraldine's green eyes flashed with keen excitement as she continued. "This will be a whole new world for Emma and for me."

I burst out laughing. "Now I'll be able to fully research those women playwrights and writers from the turn of the century, especially Antonia Emmaline."

"Tell them about your other plans, Emma," coaxed Geraldine.

"I want to write about all of them."

Louise was beaming.

"A book," interrupted Geraldine.

"Yes, a book. And, also, maybe give some talks about the women so their contributions won't be forgotten. And Della has agreed to handle the marketing for all of this." I smiled at my best friend and watched as Joe squeezed her hand.

A round of cheers and applause broke out.

"And now," said Ralph, raising a furry bear paw, "let's party!"

## A word about the author...

Caryl Janis has been a fan of mysteries since childhood and is now writing her own, beginning with an urban cozy titled *To Sketch a Killer*. She is also a freelance musician and nonfiction author who enjoys theater, museums, and spending time with family and friends. https://www.caryljanis.com/

Thank you for purchasing
this publication of The Wild Rose Press, Inc.

For questions or more information
contact us at
info@thewildrosepress.com.

The Wild Rose Press, Inc.
www.thewildrosepress.com

Milton Keynes UK
Ingram Content Group UK Ltd.
UKHW020910220424
441551UK00017B/1100